THE UNWILLING SPY

ONE MAN'S RELUCTANT JOURNEY INTO SPYHOOD

THE UNWILLING SPY

One Man's Reluctant Journey Into Spyhood

Sue CHAMBLIN Frederick

Copyright © 2012 by Sue CHAMBLIN Frederick

ISBN: 978-0-9852104-1-0

Word Jewels Publishing

ACKNOWLEDGMENTS

To my five brothers and sisters who thought my wild imagination was dangerous – see, you guys, I've channeled that imagination into a terrific novel! To my young Chopin, Lawrence Jacinto, thank you for your expert guidance in the piano scenes – you're amazing. Thank you, Teresa Kennedy, Village Green Press, for your superb editing – what a great gal you are! My special thanks to Brenda Osborne Cochrane, proofer extraordinaire. To Robert (Rob) L. Bacon of "The Perfect Write" who tirelessly contributes his wisdom of the writing world to both published and unpublished authors. You're the smartest guy I know!

VISIT THE AUTHOR AT: www.suechamblinfrederick.com

PART I

PROLOGUE

Chopin's *Piano Sonata No. 2* filled the small cottage, the notes scattering in the air like a wish made on a spent dandelion. Garcia Quinones hunched over his piano, his nose mere inches from the warm keys. He played with a lilting tenderness, his delicate fingers choosing the notes as though guided by a far-away voice, an angel perhaps. From one end to the other, he moved smoothly across the ivory of his treasured Bösendorfer piano, unaware that deep within his brilliant hands, dormant and undisturbed, was an ability to kill.

Though quite famous across Europe, the Spaniard's name had never surfaced in the thousands of World War II espionage cases being worked at Whitehall, near London, where the British Secret Intelligence Service had no idea the tall, thin Catalonian even existed...until their agent in Barcelona sent a coded message: *the farmer is on holiday.*

The Gestapo was also unaware of Garcia Quinones. If they had been, perhaps they would have made note of his unlikely link to Heinrich Himmler, Reichsfuhrer of Nazi Germany. The connection was remote, but significant, for throughout Berlin and Paris, Himmler flaunted a mistress, a woman the pianist had known some ten years earlier, merely an acquaintance, coupled with an occasional greeting. It was an unremarkable alliance, yet it would catapult him out of the serenity of life in a remote village in northern Spain and into the dark world of espionage.

Now, in his modest house on the outskirts of the village of Brasalia, Garcia sounded the last notes of the sonata, oblivious to the burgeoning scrutiny of His Majesty's Secret Service as well as that of the feared Gestapo. Both searched for him desperately – but for altogether different reasons.

Chapter One

The *Apartamentos Magníficos del Puerto de Barcelona* stood on *Avenida de Madrid*, only four blocks west of the busy port where ships from across the world anchored in the azure waters of the Mediterranean. It was early evening, blustery, as it often is near the sea. Juan Castillo studied the grand facade of the opulent apartments, an imposing structure that rose high into the Barcelona skyline. Manicured gardens, lush with purple lilacs, grew beneath the tall, thin poplars surrounding the grounds, where his eyes searched the avenue across the tree-lined landscape leading to the square. The city crawled with Gestapo; he could spot them in an instant, but none mingled with the Spaniards leisurely walking along the avenue.

From the shadow cast by a high stone fence, he watched the building for signs of anything out of the ordinary. The entrance doors shone with a soft gold patina, the outer edges trimmed in an iridescent blue, the same color as the sea. A cool wind whipped down the avenue, battering his worn fedora. Suddenly chilled, he remembered a night in Paris when his boots had frozen to the pavement while he waited in the snow for a late night rendezvous. Only a hard tap from the butt of his gun had loosened the ice and allowed him to move. The memory angered him. He had been inexperienced then; a young spy who wanted desperately to stay alive as the Germans made plans to conquer Europe.

The Service hailed him as a battle-hardened, covert warrior. His lessons in tradecraft had been learned well; of course, they had. The bullet entrance and exit hole in his shoulder branded him as an evader of death. Had he not plunged from a bridge in the middle of the night in a city named Berlin, he would have ended up in the cemetery of the unknown. He carried no identification when he hit the water at roughly three meters per second. The blood he lost in the half-kilometer swim to safety was significant enough that immediately upon reaching the shore, he became unconscious.

Juan's hand shook with cold as he struck a match to another cigarette. He smoked only a few minutes, then left the shadows to walk across the cobblestone street and up the five steps to the portico. One last look down the street before he knocked softly on the door.

He stiffened as he heard a woman's high heels clicking across the foyer. When the door opened, the woman stepped forward and looked at him rather coldly, her eyes large and black as ripe olives. "Yes?" she said, through lovely but unsmiling lips.

Juan observed her. Large turquoise earrings dangled almost to her shoulders where a thin white gauze blouse, plumped with shoulder pads, draped across her chest. The sleeves were capped with a split that folded loosely together, revealing her slim arms. The lace camisole she wore beneath her blouse was faintly visible, tantalizing to a man who appreciated beautiful women.

The woman lifted her chin, her expression haughty. She watched him for a long moment, examining him carefully. "You need a bath," she said, turning from the doorway and into the house.

Juan followed her dutifully through the elegant entrance hall, up the carpeted stairway and across a stone landing where they entered her private chambers, rooms that smelled of French perfumes and fresh-cut lilies. Her slim hips swayed slightly as she continued across the great room and entered her boudoir. Candles flickered everywhere, casting soft shadows that promised a fleeting moment of tranquility. Unhurried, she laid out towels and soaps. Her lovely hands turned the faucets of the tub and the sound of running water filled the room.

Silently, she moved toward him and deftly removed his worn jacket and unbuttoned his shirt. In one swift movement, she unbuttoned the fly on his trousers and in moments he was naked. She ignored his arousal and motioned him into the large ornate tub. Again, he obeyed.

The warm water embraced him like thousands of white pearls, pulling him down into its depths like the warm hands of a spirit. He rested his head on a small pillow and smelled soap made by Arabian handmaidens, infused with secret elixirs that promised more than sensual pleasure. With half-closed eyes, he reached out for the glass of whiskey she had poured and held it to his lips. Above him, the beautiful señorita unbuttoned her blouse and slid her skirt from her hips, watching him all the while. She pulled the thin straps of her camisole to her waist, revealing exquisite breasts with nipples like perfect pink flowers awaiting the morning sun.

Across the room, wide mirrors mounted in ornate gold frames reflected her nakedness and gave the illusion that there was more than one of her in the room. Juan's eyes traveled from one reflection to the other, and then to the woman who stepped lithely into the tub with him. He was afraid to speak; he knew she was angry.

Iliana Lanzarote picked up her own whiskey glass and tipped it toward him. "Your timing amazes me. I have been waiting for you for days."

Juan sipped and nodded slowly. "My line of work is not conducive to a precise schedule. My heartfelt apologies."

Still, the black eyes were angry. "I have had a belly full of your apologies. It is only my love for you that keeps me from forgetting you forever."

He smiled at her, a sad smile that sent a message of regret. "It is my love for you that keeps me coming back, despite my unacceptably unreliable schedule." He saw her face soften slightly, the lips part to reveal the whiteness of her teeth and the pink of her tongue. "Come," he said and reached out his hand.

She obeyed and moved her body toward him. The wet of her skin and the damp tendrils of hair on her neck again aroused him. He pulled her on top of him and kissed her whiskey lips. Her hair smelled of the wild lilacs that bloomed along the edge of the mountains. "Wash me," he whispered.

At last, a smile. "You are like a baby."

From a large porcelain bowl, she lifted a bar of ivory-colored soap scented with almonds and lathered a cloth. Gently, she washed his neck and ears. He watched as her breasts swayed back and forth in sensual rhythm only inches from his face. Closing his eyes, he breathed deeply and fell into a dream-like trance while the filth of war and the smell of death were washed away by a beautiful woman whose hands were like an angel's kiss.

The bed sheets were as soft as the skin of the woman beside him. He carefully dried her hair and placed a pillow underneath her head. In the yellow candlelight, he kissed her, his lips moving from her mouth to her neck, to her breasts. He felt her hips rise, begging him to hurry.

Early morning light swept Iliana's bedroom as she lifted her head and reached out to touch him. "How long can you stay?"

"Not long." He lit a cigarette and pulled her into his arms.

"Back to London?"

"Not yet," he answered vaguely.

"Where?"

"Not sure."

"Alone?" She raised her eyebrows.

"No."

"Who?" she asked, not knowing if he would answer.

He paused and looked away. "I think I shall take Felipe with me."

"Felipe?" she asked with surprise. "Why ever Felipe?"

"Your brother is a powerful man and I need him."

"Does he know?"

"Not yet." Juan smoothed hair away from her face and kissed the smooth skin of her cheek. He could see she was flushed.

"He's due back in court today, around ten o'clock. He'll be here for lunch, though."

Juan fumbled for his watch. "That's four hours from now. Can you have him come sooner?"

"Perhaps. Sometimes, it is difficult when his court is in session. But I'll try."

"Call now. It's important."

"Does he know you're here?"

"Here in Barcelona or with you?"

Iliana laughed. "How ridiculous. He knows very well that if you are in Barcelona, you will be with me."

"No, he doesn't know. Go now. Make the call."

Iliana slid off the bed and picked up the telephone. Juan's eyes followed the long shapely legs and her lovely backside.

When the connection was made, Iliana handed him the telephone.

"I'm leaving for Brasalia tonight," he said quietly.

"What about the farmer?"

Juan lowered his voice. "We'll talk. Can you come for an early lunch?"

The spy returned the telephone to Iliana, then slowly lifted his head and captured the nipple of her right breast.

Chapter Two

The tall, thin Spaniard lived in a three-room stone cottage in the foothills of the Pyrenees, some twenty-five kilometers northwest of Barcelona. Today was Tuesday and he was in a hurry. The early mist hid the soaring peaks as he hiked along the rugged ridges, herding his few goats to the small clutches of brush that sprigged the mountainside. He left his goats and scurried back down the mountain, eating a piece of bread while his long legs maneuvered the brush and rocks. Every Tuesday at nine o'clock he was expected at Señora Lanzarote's house where he would spend one hour teaching her the piano. He knew better than to keep her waiting.

At precisely eight-thirty, he pulled his thrice-repaired bicycle from the barn near his cottage and traveled the narrow road toward the señora's house, which paralleled the town square. His strong legs pushed the pedals in quiet rhythm, the patched tires bumping across small stones as he picked up speed on the downhill and steered around a bend precariously close to a sheer drop-off to the valley below. The tires of his bicycle skidded close to the edge and sent pebbles bouncing down the mountain. He slowed considerably, his heart thudding, and admonished himself for his carelessness. He was quite aware he had never learned to fly.

Ahead of him, near the edge of a deep gully and leading a scrawny burro, Señor Pablo Zaragosa, a nearby goat farmer, waved to him from the roadside. "Garcia," he shouted, "Come." There was urgency in his gruff voice as he called again. "Hurry."

Garcia slowed to a stop in front of the old man and readied himself for a conversation about goats. "*Buenos dias*, Señor Zaragosa."

Today, however, Pablo reached inside his shirt and pulled out a tattered newspaper. He slapped the paper on his leg and opened it, pointing to the headlines: NAZI GERMANY DESTROYS TWO U. S. ARMY BATTALIONS IN CISTERNA AS ALLIES INVADE ITALY.

"Garcia, my friend," he said, with a tremble of excitement. "This is the latest news of the war." His weathered hand shook as he tapped his thin brown finger on the large print headline and looked up at Garcia. It amused Garcia how much Señor Zaragosa resembled his goats, a triangular-shaped face with a wispy gray goatee. Tufts of white hair ran across his wide scalp and rested on his large ears. His eyes, the irises as dark as the pupils, were large and questioning. Garcia expected him to bleat any moment.

He looked from Pablo to the date of the newspaper: February 15, 1944. "What is it that excites you, Señor Zaragosa?"

"Excites me? Ha, it is the thought that the Nazis may cross the mountains into Spain! Only that doesn't excite me – it angers me." The old man pulled on his straggly goatee. "I do not wish to see their tanks rolling over the mountains, do you?" The withering Spaniard had had enough of the Germans in 'seventeen. His nose twitched, sniffing for Germans.

Garcia glanced up at the peaks of the Pyrenees and wondered if, indeed, the Germans would push their troops from France into Spain. He looked back at Pablo.

"Señor, you must milk your goats and forget the war. Germany is not interested in Spain."

"Forget the war?" Señor Zaragosa spat into the roadway, barely missing his burro. "What is in your feeble brain, Garcia? You sit in your cottage conversing with your piano as if the war were some… some fantasy. It is real, my friend, and ignoring it will not make it go away. I suggest you pay close attention to what is happening all around you." The farmer narrowed his eyes. "How funny it would be if a German tank turned its turret toward your cottage and blasted you into the heavens."

With that, Señor Zaragosa swatted the air in frustration and pulled his burro down the roadway, away from Brasalia and away from a

perplexed Garcia Quinones. Garcia watched the road long after the
image of Señor Zaragosa faded, along with his spiteful words.

It was true he was indifferent to the war. He realized Europe was
crumbling under Hitler's massive armies when he left Paris. German
troops had already invaded Poland, crossed into Belgium and were
heading for France. Yet his reasons for leaving his beloved Paris had
nothing to do with the war, but rather the collapse of his soul and the
shattering of his heart. His beloved wife had died the same night he
performed at the Theatre du Chatelet, his last grand performance for
the French. After her death, he used what little sanity remained to ship
his treasured Bösendorfer piano to Spain and board a train at the Gare
de Lyon which would take him south, across the Pyrenees.

A thoughtful and brooding Garcia pushed his bicycle a few meters
down the mountain. The war did not concern him. He was a Spanish
citizen, neutral and uninvolved in the makings of war across the
mountains.

He pedaled slowly past the towering beech trees and purple lilacs
that lined the village road, their branches swaying in the breezes that
blew from the green seas of the Mediterranean. Purple lilacs, his
favorite flower, flowers he had used to cover his mother's casket. He
had traveled only a few meters when he slowed his bicycle to watch a
hawk circling in the wind. He tilted his head back farther, looking
north toward the higher elevations, when his eye caught a cloud-like
movement high in the sky. "I do believe that is a parachute."

He watched as the white cloud danced a Viennese waltz, skirting
the peaks and becoming smaller as it soared away. Its plumes of white
silk, a harness dangling its passenger like a spider in a giant web,
glided to a landing some three-quarters of a kilometer away, and
seemed to disappear.

Puzzled, Garcia continued staring at the sky and wondering if he
had seen it at all. Perhaps it was an apparition, like a mirage on a
desert. Yet, somehow he knew he had not seen the last of the parachute
and was certain the gods had decreed they would meet again.

Chapter Three

Señora Lanzarote's house was without a doubt the grandest in the village, perhaps in all of Catalonia. Made of stones bleached yellow and gold by the Spanish sun, it lay hidden behind shadowed courtyard walls, obscure and uninviting, surrounded by tall trees that shaded its red tile roof. Its rooms harbored a woman whose wealth was known throughout northern Spain; a woman who wore priceless jewels, jewels that were meant to placate her as she watched the road from Barcelona, waiting for the return of her unfaithful husband.

Garcia leaned his bicycle against the wall of the nearby police station and walked across the square to the señora's house. He greeted the old caretaker who meticulously swept the courtyard grounds, using his broom to keep the chickens out of her flowers.

"Ah, Señor Quinones, I see it is Tuesday."

Garcia winced, his ears rebelling at the sound of Tomas' gravelly voice. His delicate hearing seemed like a curse at times, though he admitted it was this sensitivity that hailed him as a prodigy when he was only six years old and playing concerts in Andalusia in the south.

"*Sí*, another Tuesday. You are well?"

"I am old. What else can I say, señor?"

Garcia watched as the old man's long, gnarled fingers placed a thin cigarillo between his lips. "You may be old, Tomas, but you did indeed see the sunrise this morning. Eh?"

Tomas grunted in reply just as the heavy wooden door of the house swung open. Señora Rosina Lanzarote stood without speaking. The two men exchanged anguished looks, Tomas' wiry body shrinking back into the shadows of the tall trees that leaned over the house.

A shiver ran across the back of Garcia's neck as he looked into her dark eyes. "Señora Lanzarote," he said, acknowledging her presence with a solemn nod, waiting for her permission to enter her home. She nodded slightly, turned away and walked stiffly down the stone hallway that led to the music room. Garcia glanced at Tomas and smiled wanly, shrugging his shoulders.

Garcia entered and carefully wiped his feet on the rug that had been placed there for him by the señora's housemaid, a silly little girl who groveled at the señora's every word.

"*Gracias, gracias*," she murmured, as he scraped his shoes, careful to remove every tiny bit of dirt lest her mistress chastise him.

The señora positioned herself at the piano, her back unyielding. Her hands lay in her lap as she waited for her instruction. Sunlight filtered through the tall windows behind her and framed her silhouette, a sight he found curiously pleasing. He considered her a very lovely woman, though quite pensive, a sadness etched in her eyes.

It had been two years since Señora Lanzarote asked him to teach her to play. Except for holidays, at which time she left for the beaches of Spain's shoreline, Garcia had faithfully pedaled to the señora's house each and every Tuesday. Promptly at nine o'clock, he arrived at the dark wooden door and presented himself.

Without fail, she met him in the same manner, unsmiling, and only a stiff nod to direct him to the red brocade chair while she seated herself at the piano bench.

Garcia glanced at the chair. It sat to the side of the piano bench like a vise, waiting to capture him, bracing him for the moment the señora first touched the keys of her grand piano.

He moved to his ordained place and removed his hat, placing it on the floor. He cleared his throat. "Señora Lanzarote, you may begin."

She placed her hands on the keys and began to play. Her fingers, slender and quite delicate, were lifeless, as if they belonged to a clay mannequin forgotten somewhere in a dark, desolate place. The notes reached Garcia's ears as he closed his eyes and felt only sadness for the woman.

When the music ended, Garcia opened his eyes, though hesitantly, and looked at his pupil. He noticed her hands, limp and waiting. "Very nice, Señora. I see you have practiced well." He saw her chin quiver ever so slightly and then a quiet intake of her chest as she breathed a shallow breath.

"What makes you say that?" she asked, without looking at him.

The question startled him. "Say what?"

"What makes you say I practiced well?" Her hands moved into the folds of her skirt as she looked away.

Garcia stuttered. "I…I…the notes were lovely," he lied.

She turned toward him and unleashed a quiet anger.

"Señor Quinones, you have been teaching me to play the piano for two years." She rose in frustration, then turned to face him. "Never have you said anything but 'Very nice. You have practiced well.'"

She returned to the piano bench and stared at Garcia with such anger that he began to shake in his chair like a tambourine.

"Is there nothing else that comes to mind when I play for you?"

The deliberate coldness of her words chilled him. Wide-eyed, he simply stared at her. At last, he found his voice. "Please play again."

Señora Lanzarote held his gaze for a long moment as though his command had been arrogant, her compliance questionable. At last, she turned and placed her fingers near the middle C, their whiteness blending with the whiteness of the blouse she wore, the sleeves of which fell at the very edge of her wrists, a tiny fringe of lace sprinkling across the smooth clear skin. Stiff cuffs, long and tightly buttoned to her forearms, were lined with silk-covered buttons that shimmered as they moved.

How cold, he thought. He looked up and saw her dark eyes watching him.

Slowly, as if in a dream, Garcia saw his hands move from where they gripped the arms of the red brocade chair and float toward her as if they were detached from his body.

He lifted her hand and pulled it gently away from the piano keys toward him, turning it over and leaning toward it until his lips hovered above the icy skin. The heat of his breath touched her until he knew the skin had warmed. It was then that his lips fell to her palm and rested there, where he found the taste of her skin as fresh and sweet as the juice of a ripe pomegranate.

His lips moved to her fingertips that had, moments before, played Liszt without the slightest warmth. He breathed on each one and tenderly kissed them. One by one, he folded her fingers into her hand and slowly placed it in her lap. He then reached across for her other hand.

Again, Garcia held the palm of the señora's hand upward and kissed it softly, eventually moving to each of her fingertips, where he felt a slight tremble.

When he sat upright, he found the black eyes of Señora Lanzarote watching him.

"Señora," he said, his voice a rough whisper.

With the most remarkable grace, she extended her hand to him and whispered, "More."

A command with unequivocal authority, it was quite comprehensible to Garcia Quinones. He hesitated only a moment before he reached out to unbutton the tiny silk buttons that held the cuff of her blouse tightly to her arm.

The same hands that played at the Brussels Conservatory, had written compositions for French pianist, Selva, and had held the French Grand Cross of the Legion d'honneur for his piano performances, gently massaged the señora's slender forearms.

"Loosening these muscles will help you endure the long technical challenges of the music you play," he said in his teacher's voice, low and soothing. He looked up and smiled at her. "We must keep your fingers flying over the keyboard without rest. You do not want your forearms to cramp while you are playing, eh?"

He continued until he felt her muscles relax, then pulled her sleeves to the end of her wrists.

"Ah, at last, the final button," he said as he straightened the tight cuffs and placed the señora's hands back onto her lap. He breathed deeply while something stirred within him, remnants of his old self, the virtuoso, whose performances had left Europe breathless, had cautiously emerged. Timid at first, he'd felt a flicker of something or someone waiting.

Garcia leaned over and retrieved his hat from the floor.

"Good day, Señora Lanzarote. I shall see you next week at the same time." He bowed slightly and walked away, the heels of his boots tapping an E note on the rough stone floor of the music room. He smiled when he saw a spring breeze lift the draperies and billow them upwards as if orchestrated by the maestro of a symphony. Everything he saw, everything he heard, reminded him of music.

Chapter Four

In the courtyard Tomas leaned against the trunk of an olive tree and whittled a piece of wood, the chips scattering at his feet, the chickens wondering if it was food. He did not look at Garcia; he merely laughed, a chuckle that rumbled in his chest.

"Señor Quinones, you have survived yet another Tuesday."

"Ah, Tomas. You have no idea." Garcia bowed his head and shook it slowly back and forth. Tomas laughed again.

"And what is so funny to you, Tomas?"

Hard and calculating, the old man's eyes lingered on Garcia. "It is funny that one day soon the Judge will see you and know how handsome and virile you are. Then, my friend, he will kill you."

"Preposterous, Tomas! You speak of ridiculous things."

"Maybe. Maybe not, señor. After all, you spend much time with the señora while the Judge is away." Tomas turned the wood in his hand, pushing the knife in deliberate movements across a shape that resembled an owl.

Garcia glanced back at the door of the great stone house and thought of the woman inside. He heard a soft note from the piano, a C. He had never met the Judge; it seemed the prominent solicitor was always in his courtroom in Barcelona.

Garcia stepped closer, hesitating. "You must not say these things. I am a mere servant to the señora." Annoyed, Garcia left the courtyard only to have Tomas call out to him.

"Garcia, I ask you. Do you own a pistol?"

"A pistol?" Curious, Garcia turned and walked back toward Tomas. The old man was small, hardly taller than the señora's young housemaid. Yet, he plied much mischief from that brain of his, like a young trickster whose only purpose in life was to provoke others.

Again, that mysterious laughter. "You are definitely a dead man if you do not own a pistol, my friend. Do not be foolish."

Garcia watched the knife as it struck the wood in Tomas' hand. He asked himself what an old man knew of lovers and beautiful women. Perhaps Tomas' memories of his youth and trysts in a stack of fresh hay remained vivid, the thought of them teasing him into conversations of desire between a man and a woman, no matter how frivolous. "My only desire is to teach the señora how to play the piano. Why should that earn me a bullet in the head?"

Tomas pointed his bony finger in the direction of the village cemetery. It lay on a gentle slope north of Brasalia, its tombstones visible from the village below.

"My friend, take a walk to the cemetery and ask those who are buried there."

Garcia turned his gaze to the hillside, feeling perspiration along his brow and a coldness in his chest.

His black eyes narrowed and shifted back to Tomas. "I cannot feel threatened by the Judge just because I teach the señora the piano." Garcia tapped his index finger on his chest, emphasizing the word I. "*I* am a piano teacher – that is all." Against his will, his eyes traveled again to the cemetery.

"As I said, Señor Quinones, visit the cemetery. Many men are there who have loved a beautiful woman." He looked toward the closed door of the house. "She is beautiful, eh? Lonely, too." Another titter. "Too bad you are so handsome."

Garcia stepped closer to Tomas and raised his hands. "Why do you gossip like an old woman? I find your words insulting."

Tomas' brown, broken teeth protruded as he grinned at Garcia. "You are a strange man, Garcia. You hide in your own world and your lover is a piano."

Garcia said nothing as he watched Tomas light a cigarette and blow smoke into the air, dismissing their conversation. He turned his old, watery eyes to Garcia and lowered his voice. "Do you know of the parachute? And the spy?"

"Parachute? Spy?" He stared at Tomas and his questioning eyes. He would say nothing of the white cloud he had seen floating over the mountains, nor of the man he thought dangled from its ropes. He turned toward the village. "Gossip," he muttered as he walked away.

Tomas' haunting laughter followed him through the courtyard as Garcia left the house of Señora Lanzarote and headed toward the town square. Señora Blanka Albeniz squatted in a shady corner outside the police station, waiting for someone to buy her fresh-made empanadas. Early that morning before the mountain mist had evaporated, the señora had placed them in her basket and hobbled down the mountainside to sell them in the square. The savory meat and peppers were seasoned with spices so hot that one did not buy the old woman's savory delights unless they had a cool *cerveza* nearby.

"*Buenos dias*, Señora Albeniz," he called while taking monedas from his pocket. "One, please."

"Just one?" the old woman asked in her thick voice. "You are whip-thin, Garcia Quinones. You need meat on those bones of yours." She clucked her tongue and handed him a warm empanada.

"Ah, but my stomach can only survive one of your pies, Señora Albeniz. I will have to pedal quickly to arrive home before my body is ravaged by your fiery spices." Garcia laughed and unwrapped the peppery meat pie.

"What is this meat, Señora Blanka?"

"One of your goats, señor." A peal of laughter spewed out as she threw her head back and exposed her toothless gums.

Garcia chewed heartily, then stopped and sent a sly look to the old woman. "I shall count my goats when I return home."

"Señor Quinones," she said, a grin stretching her withered mouth, her eyes pleading. "Before this old woman dies, I must have some scallops from the sea. I am too old to travel to Barcelona, but you are a young, strong man. Surely, you would not deprive me of my dying wish."

"Scallops? You would have me travel the road to the sea just to buy you scallops?"

"What do you mean *just* to buy scallops for me?" she asked, her voice rising. "This is my dying wish, Señor Quinones. Yet, you give it a flick of your hand as if an old woman does not matter and does not deserve to be happy before she dies." The señora pulled herself closer into the shade and swatted at the flies.

"So, you think you are dying?" Garcia finished his empanada and moved into the shade with the squatting señora. He wondered if the old woman even had legs underneath the long dirty skirts she wore. He could not recall ever seeing her standing.

"Of course, I am dying, you foolish man! It is obvious to me that I am not long for this world."

"Not long for this world?" Garcia studied the old woman's face. What did that mean? Hours? Days? Weeks?

"That is correct, Señor Quinones. Not long for this world." She closed her eyes and did not speak again.

Garcia watched the flies buzz around her face yet she remained still. Her short wiry lashes fluttered ever so slightly as her head fell forward onto her chest.

"Señora Albeniz?" Garcia whispered. He reached out and gently shook her shoulder. She did not respond.

Squatting down beside her, Garcia watched the señora's chest rise and fall, like a low ebb tide on the seashore. "Señora Albeniz, I will get your scallops," he said gently.

A small twitch of her cheek revealed her awareness of him. All at once, she was wide-eyed.

"Bless you, Garcia."

Garcia stood and took a deep breath. Barcelona? Scallops? It was almost thirty kilometers to the sea, an all-day trip across mountain roads. What had he done? Going to Barcelona was like traveling to the moon.

He recanted. "Señora Albeniz, I...my bicycle will never travel to Barcelona."

Saliva glistened on bare gums as the señora grinned.

"I did not expect you to ride your bicycle all the way to the sea, Señor Quinones," she said with slight admonishment in her voice. "I shall give you Pedro, my prized donkey, to carry you. You will have no trouble returning with my scallops if you ride my strong Pedro. He is a small donkey but he will serve you well."

"Pedro?" Garcia looked around and saw no donkey. "I've never seen you with a donkey, Señora Albeniz," he said.

Blanka clucked her tongue. "Ah, Señor Quinones, Pedro is in his stall eating lots of fresh hay and grain and waiting for me to come home to brush his beautiful coat. That is the truth."

"I see," Garcia said, shaking his head. If she said she told him the truth, would it be true? "I will come Thursday. Early, before the sunrise." He turned and walked away, only to have her call to him.

"Señor Quinones, come." She waved her hand, a look of excitement on her face.

Reluctantly, he returned to her little spot on the square.

Her voice lowered in a conspiratorial whisper. "I have seen the parachute."

Garcia stood still and watched the old woman's excited face. First Tomas. Now Blanka.

He responded irritably. "How could eyes as old as yours see a parachute in the sky, Señora Albeniz?"

Immediately, Garcia regretted his reference to her failing eyesight. Before he could rescind his question, she spat, missing him by mere inches.

"I may be old, but my eyes can see that you are an ignorant man. I should pour scalding water on you and throw you down a well."

Humiliated, Garcia offered a slight bow. "My deepest apology, Señora Albeniz. I did not mean to offend you." He paused, choosing his words with care. "I feel I do not wish to discuss the parachute. It is mere gossip."

Addled, Garcia moved backward before turning around and leaving the old woman squatting in the square, an uneasy feeling in his stomach. Whether it was the empanada or the old woman's threat was uncertain, but it was clear he could no longer ignore the *paracaidas fantasma* –the ghost parachute. Or the alleged spy who had landed in the foothills.

The war was coming closer. It seemed he could no longer close his eyes. Just as Pablo had said – the war was not a fantasy but very real. His sighting of the parachute had been an omen, one he must reluctantly acknowledge.

Bewildered, Garcia retrieved his bicycle and looked cross the square. He saw Tomas watching him and was reminded of his prediction. He bristled at the thought. Not once in the two years he visited the señora had he touched her. Why, today, when he had not only touched her, but gently kissed her hands, had Tomas mentioned the Judge and the pistol? Surely, the Judge was not a jealous man. But, then, there was the cemetery.

Annoyed, he pulled his bicycle from the stone wall of the police station and pedaled through the countryside to his cottage nestled on a high ridge under a small stand of trees. He decided he would rest before his next lesson, scheduled for three o'clock with Señorita Jordana Rios, the most beautiful girl in all of Catalonia.

As he turned on the lane, he looked up toward the high peaks of the Pyrenees. Clouds, the color of brushed charcoal, gathered in the west and moved across the mountains to the sea. Unbeknownst to him, a pair of binoculars held him in its scope, resting on his face, studying his profile, making note of his dark intelligent eyes, and then moving to his hands, hands that would perhaps end the War.

Chapter Five

Garcia leaned his bicycle against the wall of the cottage and lingered in the sun. A hawk sailed above him and sent its piercing cries toward the heavens. The downslope of the mountain range that separated Spain from France extended as far as his eyes could see. *Exquisite*, he said to himself as he sat in a wooden chair in the shade of an olive tree. *The peaks are like the scale of a piano from low to high, from flat to sharp, rising and falling as if a concerto.*

He leaned back and closed his eyes while the warmth of the sun lulled him into a drowsy melancholy, a result of nights spent in perpetual restlessness, a restlessness that had begun in what he called his '*no hay esperanza*' days. *There is no hope.*

Garcia felt his existence was a simple one, one that required only the beating of his heart and the intake of his breath. A daily piece of fruit or one of Señora Albeniz' empanadas. And, of course, his beloved Bösendorfer piano. It wasn't an ordinary piano – no, Ferruccio Busoni had carressed its keys, breathed on the ivory with his genius breath when he played Liszt' *Reminiscences d'appree Don Juan* at *Concertgebouw* in the *Grote Zaal*. The great concert hall was no longer standing, German bombs in '40.

He pulled his straw hat over his face. In the distance, he heard the hawk again, calling to its mate. As always, he dreamed of Maria. Six years had passed since he had married his beautiful wife, a fellow student at the Brussels Conservatory.

Two years into their lives as husband and wife, Maria became distant, retreating into her own private world. She stopped playing the piano and began to spend her days sleeping or staring into the sky. Diagnosed with schizophrenia, she would not eat and died one year later, leaving Garcia to mourn to such an extent that he left their home and his music in Paris to seek sanctuary in the remote mountains.

He awakened with a start. He wasn't sure how long he'd been asleep, but the sun had moved farther across the sky to the west of the cottage and behind the mountains where it would be setting soon.

He pulled his bicycle away from the wall of the cottage and pushed it down the lane toward Brasalia. Once again on the main road, he pedaled until he came to the bridge that crossed a small winding stream that flowed from the mountains. From there, he took the left fork in the narrow road that led to Señorita Jordana's house, which lay in the recesses of the foothills.

When he arrived, he found Jordana waiting for him in the shade of the olive trees that filled the courtyard. As he leaned his bicycle against the pillar of the entrance gate, he looked her way and felt there was something different about the señorita.

"Señorita," he said, studying her with discerning eyes. He thought he saw evidence of dried tears on her cheeks and an unusually deep sadness in her eyes. Wisps of dark hair blew around her face. He wanted to reach out and slip the run-away hair behind her delicate ear, but he felt his touch might linger and thought better of it. Instead, he glanced away and momentarily watched ants scurrying back and forth across the bottom of a window sill.

Finally, almost shyly, he looked at her. "Ah, there is nothing like spring, señorita. It is difficult to stay indoors." He laughed softly. "We do not have to have a piano lesson today." He spoke casually. "You know…if you'd rather not."

Jordana turned her eyes away and scanned the courtyard as if looking for something that wasn't really there.

Garcia studied her profile and for the hundredth time was reminded of her loveliness, a Spanish princess who possessed not only exquisite beauty, but a quiet sweetness that had appealed to him from their first meeting. Her beauty reminded him of his mother, a lovely woman who had placed her only son's hands on the keys of a piano when he was only three. Garcia waited quietly by her side, leaning against the tree that was providing them shade, noticing the gentle throb in her neck where the blood rushed through. He was startled when she finally spoke.

"Señor Quinones, I am sad to tell you I am leaving Brasalia."

Garcia raised his eyebrows. "Why is that?" he asked, his dark eyes questioning.

Jordana faltered. "I...my...mother is sending me to Madrid to live with her sister."

"Oh?" was all Garcia could say.

Jordana turned her lovely face and looked at him. "My mother says there is no opportunity in Brasalia for me to find a husband." She hung her head, pinkness pooling in her soft cheeks. "I really...don't...want a husband."

Garcia laughed softly. "Eh. No husband?"

"Sí. No husband. All I have is my music and now it seems that my only happiness is being taken from me."

She struggled with the words, a slight tremble in her voice. "I have to thank you for giving me so much joy. It has been the piano that has kept me from going insane." Her eyes swept his face and then looked away.

Garcia asked, "When are you leaving?"

"Saturday," she said, her words a weak whisper. She picked at a thread that hung on the cuff of her sleeve, then jumped sharply when she heard her mother calling her.

"Jordana! You must come inside!" The woman's voice was as shrill as the call of the hawks that circled above.

Jordana reached out and touched Garcia's cheek. "I shall never forget you," she said. "You have lifted my sadness these past few years. I shall always be grateful."

The señorita rushed away, leaving Garcia standing alone in the quiet of the courtyard. For a long moment, he looked at the closed door through which his young student had passed. He would miss her; she had a passion for music which delighted him. As he watched the closed door, he knew he would miss something else about the señorita. Something that had to do with his heart.

With a sad shake of his head, he guided his bicycle through the gate and toward Brasalia where he knew a cold *cerveza* waited for him.

Chapter Six

The setting sun left long shadows on the streets as Garcia pedaled toward the small *taberna* at the end of a dusty street near the Church of the Holy Father. He looked across the street to see if Father Eduardo was in his small garden at the rear of the church. The Father was a gentle man, lovingly caring for his small flock of villagers who found solace in his Church, a peace that shielded them from the war that hovered only seventy kilometers to the north.

Garcia found himself brooding over what could have been. Though his teaching had softened his lingering emptiness, he missed his intoxicating days at the conservatory, the fervor of rehearsing for a performance, the thrill of resounding applause. The piano he'd brought from Paris lay under a woolen blanket in a corner of his small cottage, a link to his past, to his dead wife. Feeling unusually melancholy, he decided he would play DeBussy late into the night, play until he was so exhausted he would sleep without dreams.

As he rounded the corner of Señora Lanzarote's house, he heard the words Tomas had spoken earlier in the day, warning him of the Judge, encouraging him to obtain a pistol. The very idea of owning a pistol for protection was almost comical. He was a simple pianist whose life was his music, not of pistols or wild love affairs with beautiful women. The old man's proclivity to exaggerate frustrated him. Apparently, his reputation as the town gossip was well-earned. A pistol, indeed.

Garcia leaned his bicycle on the trunk of a malalucca tree whose large branches shaded the small tavern and provided a comforting dark place that promised nothing but an empty few hours of time. He stepped away from his bicycle and saw Luis Neruda's white mule turn and give him a cursory look. Tied to a small post outside the tavern, the mule lifted her long and dirty tail to swat flies, then stomped a rear hoof. Garcia knew before the night was over, Luis, plied with whiskey, would climb on the back of his faithful mule, which would then take the sleeping man home through the foothills and deposit him onto the floor of his barn. Some thought the mule was smarter than Luis.

Inside the small, dark structure, cigarette smoke hung thick in the stale air. Garcia covered his mouth and coughed. Across the room, he saw Lope Espinosa and Jorge Carreras leaning across the table between them, their mouths moving in rapt conversation. They spied Garcia and waved.

"Ah, Señor Quinones, you are early today." Lope's voice boomed. Behind the bar, Miguel reached for a tall glass.

Garcia hesitated, his expression unreadable. Only his eyes held the message of his blatant contempt for Espinosa and his companion; a contempt that summoned up memories he'd rather forget. He turned toward the bar, ignoring them. He watched their reflections in the glass, their movements, the lifting of their glasses. Even a reflection showed their malice. He did not care to sit at their table and listen to their views of the war. The men were members of the Blue Legion; Spanish volunteers who fought alongside German soldiers on the Eastern front. What a travesty; in their minds, the guns they carried and the Russians they killed made them heroes.

They wore a soldier's uniform, a red beret, red for blood, perhaps, Khaki pants and a blue shirt. Garcia's contempt was well-founded. Convinced by whiskey, the two men held a fierce, fervent belief that they were the saviors of Spain's future and that an alignment with the Third Reich was the true path to power.

"Come, Garcia. Sit with us." Jorge, also a zealous follower of Hitler, waved at Garcia.

Garcia barely acknowledged them as he turned his back and leaned into the bar. "I see the two are again together in drink." He lifted his glass and swallowed.

Miguel glanced across the room. "Eh, they perceive themselves as Spain's last hope for heroes. They must be watched carefully."

Miguel lowered his voice. "Eh, General Franco must declare Spain's alliance with the Allies instead of this abhorrent man Hitler. And he must do it soon."

"Do you think he will?"

"Who knows? Every Spaniard knows Franco is indebted to Hitler."

Garcia nodded. "No way could the General have won the Civil War had Hitler not come to his aid."

"True. And look what he's done now – Spanish volunteers are fighting alongside Germans against the Russians. The Allies cannot like that too much."

In the corner by himself, Luis Neruda sipped his whiskey, eyeing Garcia with interest. He was an intense man, with a stoic stare, which proclaimed him unapproachable. It could be his mule was his only friend.

"Garcia, did you hear there is a spy hiding in the mountains?" Lope's loud voice traveled across the room.

Miguel refilled Garcia's glass. "Spy?" Garcia asked, without turning around.

"*Sí*. A spy. His parachute was seen in the early morning."

"How did you hear this news, Lope?"

Lope's laugh was menacing. "I have my sources, Señor Quinones."

Garcia turned to Lope with a penetrating stare. "And, what kind of spy is this?"

"Kind of spy?"

Garcia smiled slightly. "Yes. Is it a Nazi spy, an Allied spy? And on whom is he spying?"

"I see, señor, you are not privy to the inner workings of the war." Lope said, his tone condescending. "A spy is someone who spies on an enemy. How can it be a Nazi spy when Spain is not Germany's enemy?" Lope leaned back in his chair and crossed his arms.

"Ah, well spoken," Garcia said. "So, we are Germany's ally? How can Spain be Germany's ally if Franco has yet to commit to Germany?"

Lope jumped from the table, overturning his chair, and walked toward Garcia, his face grim, and stopped inches away. Garcia's eyes fell to the large, brutish arms that hung like pine logs from his enormous frame.

"My friend, rest assured Spain is Germany's ally. It is just a matter of time." Garcia felt Lope's breath settle on him like a pungent fog. He saw black grit in the crevices of his skin, the dark eyebrows, meeting each other like trains on a track, and beneath his mouth, a deep cleft, unmistakably made by a knife.

Finally, Garcia replied. "Then, it seems to me, Lope, since you believe Germany is an ally of Spain and spies only spy on their enemies, that the spy hiding in the mountains must work for the Allies."

Garcia leaned closer. "That being the case, it would behoove you, as a friend of the Germans, to watch your back."

Lope flinched and drew a sharp breath. "Your intelligence amazes me, Señor Quinones. All at once, you have become an expert." His eyes widened and Garcia saw the reflection of the bottles of whiskey behind them.

Lope walked away; bulging veins ran the length of his powerful neck. At the doorway, he clicked his heels together and extended his right arm from his body. "*Heil*, Hitler!"

The tavern remained quiet for only a moment before Miguel slammed his fist on the bar. "That man is drunk! He has no idea what he is saying!"

Garcia continued to stare at the empty doorway. "He may be drunk, but he is also evil. If a spy is hiding in the mountains, those two will find him and kill him."

Chapter Seven

A three-quarter moon hung in the sky as Garcia pedaled home in the quiet of the night. Across the foothills far below him, the treetops trembled as the ghost winds of the mountains touched their branches. Above him, the light of the moon swept the rocks into distorted formations that seemed to move with him as he continued toward his cottage.

His encounter with Lope was troubling. Yet, why should it be? Garcia considered himself a citizen of Spain with no political ties, no animosity toward those who thought differently than he did. But, it was there. A gnawing at his soul as if he wasn't who he thought he was; as though there was an unraveling of his tidy life, thread by thread, exposing him to more than matters of the heart or his beloved music.

He thought of his father, who had believed in freedom and democracy. He loathed oppression and had he been alive, he would have been appalled with the rise of the Reich. Ironically, his father had been murdered by a German bullet, while tuning a piano of all things.

Garcia steered his bicycle around a small curve in the road and turned onto the lane that led to his cottage. To his dismay, he saw his goats pressed up against the door of the barn, waiting to be let in for the night. They bleated noisily when they saw him, their little tails twitching. He opened the barn door and let them in and swore not to neglect them again.

Inside his cottage, he lit a candle and sat down, too fatigued to eat his bread and cheese. He leaned back his head and closed his eyes. *I am a simple man. All I want is to play my piano and tend my goats. That is what I want.* He opened his eyes and stared at the blanket-covered piano in the dark corner of the cottage. His thoughts were too troubled to touch the keys.

Late into the night he slept and dreamed of the parachute, its whiteness smothering him until he awoke gasping for breath.

Morning came quickly. Garcia felt like he had just lain down when the sun came over the mountain and light streamed into the room. He dressed and left to tend to his hungry goats. At the barn, they waited for him, bleating loudly.

"Yes, yes. I will take you to some wonderful brush." He cut an apple and fed the small pieces to each of his goats, careful not to feed one twice. He looked at his little Tia who carried a kid or maybe even two and gave her an extra piece.

He led the goats to the mountainside to the north of his cottage and left them there. As he walked back down the mountain, he heard their bells tinkling in the key of G. He smiled to himself. There was music everywhere.

Garcia pulled out his bicycle and pedaled past Brasalia to where an eleven-year-old student named Eugenio lived. Eugenio, intelligent and curious, chattered about everything but his music. And, today was no exception.

"Eugenio," Garcia called as he leaned his bicycle against a fence. "Are you prepared for your lesson?"

"Hello, Señor Garcia!" The boy ran toward Garcia with unbounded energy, his dog, Pio, scurrying behind him. "I've been waiting for you!" Eugenio's cheeks were flushed and perspiration curled the dark hair around his face.

"Ah, Eugenio, it excites me that you are so enthusiastic about your music."

Eugenio hung his head. "I cannot lie to you, Señor Garcia. My music is not what excites me today."

Garcia studied the boy. "I am glad you are honest with me. Ah, it is important to be honest. No? Now, tell me what excites you today."

Eugenio lifted his eyes and spoke in a hushed whisper. "Señor Garcia, there is a spy."

"A spy?" How can this innocent boy become entwined in the gossip that ravages the mountainside?

Garcia was stern. "Eugenio, I think it is mere gossip; gossip a young boy should not be listening to."

Eugenio shook his head back and forth. "No, no, Señor Garcia. It is true!"

"How do you know it is true?" Garcia asked with mounting exasperation.

Eugenio leaned into the piano teacher, his words barely audible. "Señor Garcia, I have found his parachute."

"Parachute? You have found a parachute?" Garcia looked around the farmyard. His stomach churned, just like it had the day before.

"Yes! Right over the hill!" The boy pointed to the hills behind the farmyard.

Garcia placed his hand on Eugenio's shoulder. "Please shush. You must not let anyone else hear."

Again, Garcia's eyes scanned the farmyard. "Show me." Eugenio nodded, turned and raced away.

Garcia followed him to the barn and into the hillside, the dog running in front of them. "How did you find this parachute?"

The boy jumped from a small boulder in front of Garcia. "Oh, Pio found it. I saw him digging in the earth and then I saw the white of the parachute. When I pulled at it, out came the cords and fabric. In my books, there are pictures. And here, before my eyes, was a real one!"

They'd walked only three-quarters of a kilometer before they came to a small clearing. Garcia studied the hole where the parachute had been, the yards of fabric piled up beside a boulder, looking rather strange on the side of a mountain.

"Señor Garcia, I believe the spy's plane crashed somewhere but the spy parachuted to save himself."

Garcia deliberated. He knew nothing of spies and parachutes. He, along with the boy, was so callow that anything out of the ordinary in his life was to be treated with uncertainty. "That could be true, Eugenio. But, perhaps, there is no spy. What if something was in the parachute other than a man? What if something of value was dropped out of a plane and landed near your farm? Whoever was looking for it, got it and left the parachute. You know, a sort of rendezvous. He never dreamed your smart little dog, Pio, would find it. True?"

The boy listened attentively as they walked down the mountain. "Maybe."

"Eugenio, we must not tell anyone. It must be our secret. Eh?"

Eugenio skipped along beside him. "Señor Garcia, I have practiced well for you today. You will be proud of my performance."

"Yes. Yes, I am sure you will please me, Eugenio. But, remember, you and I have a secret. No?"

"Well, you mean you, me and Pio have a secret."

Garcia laughed. "Yes, the three of us will tell no one."

They arrived at the house where Garcia wiped his boots and followed Eugenio into the parlor to the piano. He sat while the boy placed his fingers on the keys and began to play a practice piece by Beethoven. As he played, Garcia closed his eyes. He thought of a time when he was Eugenio's age and practiced day and night the music of Gevaert and Brassin until his hands could play no more. Time had brought him to this moment; a moment where all he had to give was his knowledge of music. He was a simple piano teacher.

Chapter Eight

After Garcia left Eugenio, he headed to the village marketplace, his thoughts confused. Was the man in the parachute really a spy? What kind of spy? An Allied spy? Generalissimo Franco may not have entered Spain in the war, but there was no doubt where his sympathies lay. His Nationalist troops would pounce upon an Allied spy without hesitation in order to pry as much covert intelligence as possible from him and turn it over to the Germans.

The web of politics and the war had suddenly become inescapable. It was as though seeing the parachute had pulled him in, as if the universe had decreed him a pawn in some clandestine plot that had yet to be revealed. He shuddered and did something he rarely did – he cursed. "*Condenacio!*"

At the market, he bought fruit and pedaled toward Señora Albeniz' where he knew a hot empanada waited for him. Had he not wished for the delicious meat, he would not have stopped at her tiny corner by the police station. Their confrontation from the previous day had left a vision of her spittle flying through the air.

"Señora Albeniz, I smelled your empanadas while I shopped for fruit." He smiled at her and was rewarded with a large meat pie. She seemed to have forgotten the incident. He gave her his coins and bit into the pie.

The squatting woman looked up at him. "Ah, Señor Quinones, I can taste the scallops now." She laughed with her mouth wide open, revealing her empty gums. "Do you anticipate your trip to Barcelona? On the back of my beautiful Pedro?"

"Of course, Señora Albeniz, I shall leave tomorrow. I will come at dawn. Feed Pedro well today."

He left the señora, pulled his bicycle from the police station wall and pedaled slowly toward home. Tomas raked the dirt in front of the hacienda and waved. A dangerous smile that bespoke of troubles to come widened his face. *You must own a pistol, my friend, or you will end up in the cemetery on the hill.*

Unsettled, Garcia pedaled quickly up the mountain where he knew he could rest in the shade of his olive tree. His stomach began to ache. Was it the old woman's cooking or was it the thought of a spy stretched across a boulder with buzzards eating his flesh?

At the sound of a motor, Garcia turned and saw a shiny black Mercedes following behind him. The chrome of the automobile shone in the noonday sun. Its sleekness reminded him of a grand carriage.

He moved off the road to watch the long car pass, only to have it stop alongside him. The window glided down and the face of a woman who looked remarkably like Jordana's mother, only older and, sad to say, even less attractive, peered at him. It was Jordana's aunt. She had arrived to snatch the girl from her little village of Brasalia, a place where no husband could be found. Garcia shuddered at the thought of the lovely señorita in the clutches of some stranger whom her mother and aunt had deemed a perfect match for the young woman.

Garcia nodded at the woman. *"Buenos dias, señora."*

"And to you, young man." Her voice was shrill just like her sister's, like the braying of a donkey. The same offensive layers of fat lay along her cheeks, her chin shook as she moved. No doubt the rest of her was just as repugnant as her face.

"Would you be so kind as to direct me to the Rios hacienda?" She smiled, revealing mammoth crooked teeth, set one on top of the other as if they were confused about where they belonged.

"Si, señora." Garcia pointed up the road. "Go one kilometer until you see a road bear to the right and switchback up along the ridge by this gully." Garcia swept his hand in back of him to the deep hole of rocks, brush and trees. "If you cross the bridge, you have gone too far."

The window of the Mercedes silently glided up and the car proceeded in the direction of the hacienda. Garcia watched the car until it was out of sight. The next time it traveled this way, there would be a sad young woman inside, her face wet with tears.

At his cottage, Garcia placed the fruit on the table. His eyes found the bottle of *vino tinto* and thought of opening it. Another day, he said to himself as he walked outside to find his chair. He sat down and lifted his long legs to place them on a large rock.

He considered it his thinking chair. There, his mind was free to wander, to solve problems and, lastly, to dream of what could have been. As yet, he had been unable to dream of what could be. He closed his eyes and listened to the sounds of the mountains. He heard the wind in the trees. Again, the hawks circled above him and screeched their high-pitched calls, much like the sound of a crying baby.

His mind was troubled. Garcia hoped that Eugenio would keep their secret and leave the white parachute hidden in the hills. Their knowledge of the parachute was dangerous, its presence a link to some unimaginable subterfuge that reached out to ensnare them. How could he expect a mere boy to understand the significance of what he had found? Eugenio had said he thought a plane had crashed somewhere high in the mountains and the pilot had parachuted into the hills behind his farm to save himself. How could a young boy think in that manner? Even he, a mature man, had trouble understanding the meaning of it all.

Exasperated, Garcia stood up; his mind could take no more. The bicycle waited for him near the shed and he pedaled down the hill to the village, savoring the thought of a drink at the tavern to ward off his thoughts of impending doom.

Chapter Nine

T he village was quiet as the late afternoon sun touched the tips of the Pyrenees and sent shadows across the town square. Señora Albeniz had left her little corner, leaving it dark and empty. The courtyard of the Lanzarote hacienda lay in deep shadow, but Garcia could not help but notice a warm glow in the window. It was an omen. Never before in passing her street had he seen this small beacon of light, flickering and dancing like a wounded firefly. Was it for him? Was there some force in the universe that was pulling him toward the beautiful señora? For some reason he could not explain, he slowed his bicycle and looked through the sheer curtains, wondering if he might see her.

A voice from behind froze him in terror.

"Garcia, my friend. Are you giving the señora a piano lesson this evening? A very special lesson?" A sly rumble escaped Tomas' throat. The old man emitted a certain impishness and boyish grin, shifting easily from petulant behavior to childish gossip.

"Tomas! You must not frighten me like that. I…I was looking for you."

"For me, señor? Why are you looking for me?"

Garcia studied the old man's face in the fading light. "In the morning, I must travel to Barcelona to buy scallops for Señora Albeniz. Do you think…perhaps I may need a…a pistol for my journey?"

"A pistol? Why do you think it is unsafe to travel the road to Barcelona?" Tomas' suspicious black eyes searched Garcia's face.

Garcia hesitated. "I...I have heard rumors of a spy." Yi! Was he himself gossiping like the rest of the citizens of Brasalia?

"Rumors? You have heard *rumors* of a spy? My friend, they are not rumors. It is so. As I spit on the grave of a devil, I know it is so. Are you afraid? Of a spy?"

Garcia seemed stricken by a sudden paralyzing illness. Why did he ask about a pistol? Why had he mentioned the spy? His heart beat wildly. He could barely carry on a conversation with Eugenio regarding a spy and now here he was in the middle of the village discussing pistols and spies without the slightest hesitation. As though he were some connoisseur in the art of espionage.

"Of course not," he replied sharply to Tomas. "Never mind, I shall travel without a pistol and, if I am murdered along the way and Señora Albeniz does not taste her scallops, the burden will be on your soul, señor." Garcia angrily pulled his bicycle in the direction of the tavern.

"Wait, my friend. I would not want to see you murdered along the road to Barcelona." Tomas paused and studied Garcia for a long moment. He reached under his shawl and pulled an old pistol from its hiding place.

"Now, my friend, this is a pistol." The old Spaniard pushed the long barrel of the pistol into the flesh of Garcia's stomach. "It's very simple. You merely pull the trigger and it fires."

Garcia's body began to tremble as he looked down at the pistol, whose barrel rested menacingly in his navel. "Tomas," he said so quietly that even he had trouble hearing himself. "I have decided I do not want your pistol."

His eyes never leaving Garcia's, Tomas lowered his pistol and returned it to its hiding place.

"A very poor decision, señor. One that may result in your untimely demise." Tomas' throaty laughter permeated the air as he left a trembling Garcia standing in the middle of Alia Street, wondering what had happened to the serenity that was once his life.

He pushed his bicycle slowly toward the tavern, where he knew he could find some kind of solace in one of Miguel's whiskeys. When he arrived, he saw Luis Neruda's white mule in his usual spot by the tavern door.

Leaving his bicycle against the large malalucca tree, he went inside and breathed in the heavy smoke. He was relieved there was no sign of Lope and Jorge. In the corner, the brooding Luis stared at him as though he were some kind of threat. He ignored him and greeted Miguel.

"Good evening, Miguel. I am certain I would like a whiskey from your brown bottle over there." Garcia pointed to the tall bottle he knew contained a whiskey Miguel had purchased in Barcelona, the finest in the house.

Miguel looked at him. "Eh? No *cerveza*?" He reached for the whiskey and poured a generous amount in a short glass. " Señor Quinones, you surprise me. What is the occasion for whiskey?"

Garcia did not answer. Instead, he took a large swallow and set down his glass. After a deep breath, he leaned toward Miguel. "My friend, it has been a harrowing day. I must somehow find relief. It is too much for me."

Miguel's face reflected concern as he studied Garcia, noting the deep crevices forming a frown between his eyebrows. A shadow of a dark beard hardened his jaw, giving a haggard appearance to the otherwise handsome face.

"A harrowing day? Teaching piano?" He laughed. Garcia ignored Miguel and glanced at the table where Lope and Jorge usually sat. "Where are they?"

"I am sure they are in the mountains looking for the spy." Miguel sipped his own whiskey and looked at Garcia with an intensity that was unlike the amicable man he was. "It is troubling that they consider themselves members of the Nazi party despite the fact Spain is not in the war. I suppose it allows them to flaunt their hate for those who are not like themselves. They are dangerous, señor."

Garcia was quiet. "Do you think there is really a spy?"

Yi, yi! Here he was, gossiping again. Yet, from within him, there was a yearning to know, though he could not explain why.

"I am thinking it is so, my friend. We shall soon find out if they are successful in their quest. What then, I don't know. Will they turn him over to the Germans or will they kill him?" Miguel hung his head. "I do not want them to find the spy, Garcia." As an afterthought, "If, indeed, there is a spy."

Garcia shook his head and looked over to the dark corner where Luis sat, his head bowed, his large hands wrapped around the whiskey bottle. Did he eavesdrop on their conversations?

Garcia's glass was empty when he thought he might say something to Miguel about the parachute. The parachute. How he wished Eugenio had never found it, much less shown it to him. It complicated things even more. A talkative eleven-year-old boy had knowledge that could cause the death of this perhaps imaginary spy. He decided not to disclose the secret. He found the subject too sensitive in his present state of mind.

Chapter Ten

Garcia left the tavern late and pedaled his bicycle down the main street toward his cottage. The constellations hung in their familiar places and gave Garcia a feeling of peace. From childhood the sky had seduced him with its infinite mysteries.

His eyes were pulled away by a stream of headlights that swept the roadway ahead of him, an automobile, approaching at a dangerous speed. It was the black Mercedes that had passed him earlier in the day. The gleaming black and chrome chariot screeched to a halt in front of him. The back passenger door flung open and out poured Señora Rios, her face panic-stricken, her eyes wide and fearful. Perspiration drenched her body as she ran toward him, almost collapsing as she stumbled into his arms.

"Señor Quinones!" she screamed. "My Jordana has run away! She has left the hacienda. You must help me search for her!" Her lips trembled and a moan escaped her. "Gone. She's gone."

On the other side of the Mercedes, Señora Rios's sister pushed her large body from the car and echoed the words.

"You must help us search for Jordana!"

The two women waddled down the street wringing their hands and calling out into the night. "Jordana! Jordana!"

Garcia watched as citizens of Brasalia left their houses and gathered in the square to watch the two women as they ran from one side of the street to the other, calling out for the young señorita. It was all to no avail. Eventually, they returned to the Mercedes and slowly rode up the mountain to their hacienda.

Garcia watched the automobile climb the hill as he pedaled behind them. They had searched the streets of Brasalia until there was nowhere else to search. No one had seen her.

The beautiful Jordana had thought it better to steal away into the night than to succumb to the wretchedness of a stranger for a husband.

Pity, he thought, as he crossed the small stream and turned onto the lane to his cottage. The weariness he felt was like none he had ever felt before. His every bone ached with the weight of events that had, in a matter of days, filled his world with unending anxiety.

As he traveled down the lane toward his cottage, he heard the sad bleating of his darling goats. Again, he had neglected them and kept them from the soft hay in their sleeping places in the barn. He saw his petite Tia, her little slanted eyes questioning, her tail flickering in greeting.

"Ah, my precious. How could I neglect you so? My heart is broken that I could leave you out where the wild dogs could eat you." He opened the barn door and led his goats inside. They jostled him gently. He was their shepherd; they depended on him for protection and care.

He closed the barn door and walked to the cottage. Were he not so tired, he would sink into his thinking chair and lose himself in a happier place. If that place still existed.

He pushed open the door and walked into the darkened cottage. Rather than light a candle, he removed his clothing and crawled naked into his bed. He reached for his pillow, but instead found the warm body of young Jordana Rios, who slept contentedly, a soft whirring noise escaping from her parted lips.

He did not move as he watched the sleeping girl. Her face was peaceful, like an angel's. Slowly, like a flower opening to the sun, Garcia became fully aroused.

Horrified at himself, he eased from his bed, grabbed his clothes and burst through the cottage door. He dressed as he stumbled to the barn and collapsed in the hay where he fell into a fitful asleep, a goat on either side of him, their soft breathing a comfort to his ears.

Once more, the gods had mocked him.

Chapter Eleven

Tia licked the face of Garcia as he lay stretched in the hay. Soft light from the rising sun found its way through the holes in the barn's walls like miniature spotlights and fell on the handsome Spaniard's face. Around him, his goats stared at him and bleated softly, their tails flicking. Garcia opened his eyes, momentarily forgetting where he was, but remembered quickly enough. Jordana!

Hurriedly, he left the barn and returned to his cottage. Jordana was still in his bed, her body in the same position as it had been when he arrived home. In the early morning light, he could see her long hair, dark along the whiteness of the pillow.

His shoulders sank. Not only was it possible the Judge would kill him, but Jordana's mother would no doubt aim the pistol.

The gods had turned against him. This simple piano teacher whose only desire was an uncomplicated life in the mountains with his piano and his goats. How could it have come to this? Abruptly, Garcia turned and left the cottage.

He quickly pulled his bicycle from the side of the house. He could not be late for his journey to Barcelona.

Garcia considered the ride down the mountain to Señora Albeniz' house was possibly his last. The forces in the universe had decreed him cursed, a recipient of unending adversities that subjected him to trials of principle. His father had taught him that adversity was the first path to truth – that a man most easily becomes acquainted with his true self amidst the storm of difficulty. So in spite of everything, Garcia chose to believe that a noble spirit appears greatest when one is in distress. At all costs, he must preserve the highest of hearts.

The house lay in a deep crevice on the mountainside. Ramshackled and pocked with needed repairs, it harbored one of the most dreaded women in the whole of Brasalia—Señora Albeniz' sister. Inez was known to be somewhat crazed. Having been hit on her head with a falling rock some years ago, she was thought to be filled with the most poisonous venom and considered everyone she saw a victim to be devoured. She was called *un perro enojado*, a mad dog.

Upon his arrival, Garcia nervously pulled his bicycle into the yard and watched as a skeletal dog barked viciously from across the clearing. The mangy creature circled Garcia and snarled.

After a quiet observation of the wild dog, he asked himself – *could perhaps this be Blanka's sister*? The thought left his head as soon as he saw a blur of a form streak past him somewhere into the semi-darkness of the morning.

As he peered into the shadows, a large mass of spittle landed on his cheek. Disgusted, he reached up to wipe his face, wondering how spit had been able to travel some three meters from where he thought he'd seen the dark form.

Then a rock whizzed past his head. Garcia crouched down, only to be tackled by a mass of flailing arms and legs as well as the most putrid odor ever unleashed by a human form. He gagged, lashing out to protect himself from the frenzy that sat atop him and pounded his head. As quickly as the form had ravaged his body, it left in a whir of dust, disappearing somewhere on the hillside.

Garcia lay still in the now quiet of the yard. He heard birds singing and felt the mountain wind. When he opened his eyes, he saw Blanka standing above him.

"Señor, I see you have met my sister."

Garcia watched the bare gums move in the wide mouth and wrinkled face. With difficulty, he stood and brushed himself off. His shirt had been torn and his pants covered in dirt and brush. He looked angrily at Blanka. "Why do you not lock her up when you know someone is coming?" Disgusted, he slapped his pants to remove the dirt and twigs.

"Ah, my friend. My sister does not perceive that her assumptions are incorrect."

"Whatever do you mean?" Garcia spoke sharply, an edge to his voice that Blanka had never heard before.

"Ah, it is sad, Señor. Her wretched mind gave way; the wind entered her head." The old woman paused. "It is obvious she thought you some threat to her dog. Or, me. Or, our castle here."

Castle? Garcia's eyes scrutinized the house. The structure was built of every imaginable material that could be scavenged from the surrounding hills. A strong wind would blow it away; a heavy rain would dissolve it in a pile of mud. Castle, indeed.

"What if you had not come to my rescue?" Garcia's heart had finally quieted; his breath calm. But, still he was angry.

Blanka shrugged her shoulders. "I am sure my sister would have killed you, senor.

Garcia recoiled. "Killed me? She is mad! Totally without conscience."

Looking up at the dawn sky, Señora Albeniz squinted as if in deep thought. She nodded slowly. "Yes, she would have killed you and then cooked you."

The sound that escaped Garcia's throat was almost girlish. "How can that be?"

With a casual shrug of her shoulders, the senora nodded at the large black boiling kettle that sat on the far side of the yard. "My sister likes to cook, señor."

Again, the girlish shriek from Garcia. "Insane! Your sister is insane!"

"Remember, it is the wind, Señor Quinones. It is in her head and it speaks to her." Sadness crept over Blanka's face. Perhaps she was remembering her sister when she was a lovely young senorita whose only desire was to dance the sardana and kiss handsome men who wore fancy boots.

Garcia expelled a long, slow breath. "Take me to Pedro. I must leave for the port."

"Si, señor," Blanka said, as she led the way to the small barn where her prized donkey lived.

Garcia's eyes darted around, looking for the mad woman who had pummeled him and, no doubt, had diabolical plans to cook him in the black pot that was, indeed, large enough to fit his body. A shudder ran down his spine as he followed the old woman to the barn.

Inside, Blanka swept her arms wide and smiled her toothless grin. "Señor Quinones, I present to you my most beautiful donkey, Pedro."

Garcia's eyes fell upon Pedro and remained there. Before him was the most pitiful donkey he had ever seen. When the animal saw Garcia, he brayed loudly, exposing laughing teeth and emitting a screeching sound that lifted into the hills and wreaked havoc upon the ear. He grimaced at the sound and thought again of the gods who had cursed him and were now laughing hysterically at the donkey he was to ride to Barcelona.

"This donkey will never carry me to Barcelona," he said quietly, his body weak with disappointment. "I am sorry, Señora Albeniz. I cannot get you your delicious scallops." He looked at Pedro again. "This is the most pathetic animal I have ever seen. Look at his scrawny legs."

"Hush! My Pedro hears you. You must not talk of his legs. He does not know they are as they are. If he hears you, he will be sad and will not carry you to Barcelona. He thinks he is beautiful. As do I." Blanka paused and lovingly looked at her donkey. "If you tell him he is beautiful, he will carry you to the ends of the earth." She rubbed the coat of the animal and leaned in to nuzzle his nose. She spoke soft words to him as if he were her lover.

Garcia looked again at Pedro's legs and then into the deep, dark eyes set beneath the long, upright ears. Pedro blinked and noisily expelled air through his nostrils as if to proclaim his master to be correct in her opinion of him.

He reached out and ran his fingers down the long length of one of Pedro's ears and felt the softness of the hair. He then rubbed along the jaw and to the soft nose where he felt the warm heat of the animal's breath. He leaned closer to the animal's ear. "I will ride you to Barcelona, Pedro, but you must not falter."

Chapter Twelve

The sun was higher in the sky than Garcia had intended it to be when he began his journey to the Port of Barcelona. He sat atop Pedro, who tarried along at his own pace as if he were an unhurried sightseer on tour. "Go, Pedro. Do not dally."

The donkey stopped often to investigate any and everything that caught his attention; no amount of cajoling would hurry him along. "Come, Pedro, we must go faster."

Señora Albeniz had instructed Garcia to talk sweetly to her donkey and, incredibly and with much embarrassment, Garcia did as he was told. "You are a beautiful donkey, Pedro. Your legs are the strongest and surest of all the donkeys in Spain. Thank you for carrying me to Barcelona."

It was two o'clock in the afternoon by the time Garcia guided Pedro into Barcelona's harbor. He looked up and saw a cloud of sea gulls hovering over a boat that had just docked, spilling its catch over its decks.

Farther down, the fishmongers lined the bulkhead where they called in a lilting song, "Fresh shrimp. Beautiful and pink."

"Come here for your fat mussels." The fishwives scurried around their wares like doting mothers. The smells of the fish yard were pungent and strongly reminiscent of the sea. The salty air held an acrid sensation that stung Garcia's nose with a biting odor of fish guts, fish heads and scales.

Despite the noise and movement around him, the proud donkey continued his plodding until Garcia pulled gently on the reins of his halter and slid from the back of the sweaty burro.

"At last we are here, Pedro. Let us find you some water." Garcia looked around for a watering trough and saw one at the edge of the dock where a spigot spurted an unending stream of water. He pulled on the reins and led Pedro to the trough where he drank long and noisily.

After Pedro, Garcia leaned in and drank. From there, they ambled down to a stall where shrimp, clams, mussels and oysters filled the baskets along the tables, then rows upon rows of fish of all sizes, their eyes turned unseeingly watching the progression of passersby.

At first, he did not see scallops, but then his eyes found them, plump and milky white, in a large ceramic bowl resting on top of a barrel. He had a vision of Blanka devouring them with her toothless gums, without a fork or spoon.

"*Buenos dias, señora*. I would like to buy some of your fresh scallops."

"How many would like, my handsome friend," asked the woman whose skin was the color of a walnut shell, a woman who had undoubtedly been a beautiful señorita at one time. She winked at Garcia and smiled. Her teeth were a lovely white, like the scallops she sold.

"I am thinking ten *libras, señora*. Plenty of ice, too. I have a long journey ahead of me." Garcia looked away in case the woman winked at him again. He glanced at Pedro who blinked and snorted softly.

Garcia pulled the money Blanka had given him and paid the woman. Without responding to her wicked stare, he wrapped the sack of scallops around Pedro's neck and led the scrawny donkey toward the road to Brasalia. He hoped to return before the sun set behind the mountains. He would eat bread and some hard, salty Manchego cheese along the way, with perhaps a bite for Pedro.

As he turned to place the reins on Pedro's neck, his eyes caught the figure of a man and a woman walking leisurely down the docks, her hand resting on his arm. Her other hand held her hat while the brisk wind flapped its brim. He watched them a long moment, and within him a memory stirred. He stared at them until they became lost among the throngs of people who milled around the docks looking for the perfect delicacy from the sea.

Chapter Thirteen

Judge Felipe Lanzarote's chambers were located in the El People' Palacio de Justicia de Barcelona, a building that was architecturally one of Barcelona's finest. It stood tall near the harbor, which ran along the flatland of the Llobregat Delta, where the city flourished between the mouths of the Llobregat and Besos Rivers. There was little doubt to those who visited that this was one of the most beautiful cities in the world.

The tall windows of the Judge's chamber gave him a splendid view of the great ships and blue waters of the Mediterranean; but, on this day, Judge Felipe Lazarote was not interested in a view of the harbor.

He had not moved the entire morning, had canceled all his appointments and told his assistant he was not to be disturbed. The draperies on his windows were closed as he sat slumped in his chair in the semi-darkness of his chambers. The judge was in a deep melancholy and, within that melancholy, his thoughts roamed over the possibilities of its cause.

He had spent his entire life doing exactly what he wanted to do, all the money he wanted, all the women he wanted. And now, at age forty-eight, he knew somewhere deep inside him there gathered a heavy cloud of discontent. His thoughts wandered like a ship without a rudder, pushed this way and that, guided only by the whims of his mind, a total lack of focus and sense of worth.

Something had changed within him and he had not, as yet, understood what that something was. He seemed unfulfilled by anything, not even his work, which had always provided a sense of accomplishment in years past. His high birth in Catalonia had allowed him favors and positions with hardly any effort on his part. He became educated at the finest universities and quickly rose to the high court of Spain while still in his thirties. The fact that he was tall and handsome further promoted his success in life.

Mortality? Was that the cause of his unrest? Had he come to a point in his life that was the beginning of the end? How could he have lived his life with no regard to how it would end?

After a long while, he stood and pulled back a drapery from the window. As the sun shimmered off the waters of the sea, his eyes fixed on a ship that sat a kilometer or so away in the harbor.

A child, he thought. I want a child. After all the selfishness he had absorbed in his life, like a sponge on the ocean floor, he wanted more than just himself. He wanted a child, a child with his name, a child who would give him love while he faded away into old age.

Rosina. Lovely Rosina. He had seen her the night before and noticed a tranquil smile on her face as she moved through their bedroom, arranging flowers and humming a soft melody. He had watched her quietly and saw within her a contentment that he did not possess. What did she have that he did not?

It was true he had neglected her over the years, leaving her alone while he ran the courts. Seldom did he visit her and when he did, he saw a sad woman. But, last night had been different. Her eyes shone with happiness. Her skin glowed like a ruby.

He wondered why he had not made love to her but, rather, had enjoyed watching her, talking to her. She was a beautiful woman who had spent their fifteen years of marriage waiting; waiting for him to come home, only to stay for a meal, a glass of wine and a few frivolous words.

His heart sank with the realization he had left her on the fringe of his life, far behind his work, his money, his women. And now, in the depth of his thoughts, that realization jolted him into a place that was hollow and empty. Empty of... *love.*

He wanted Rosina to love him again. More than anything else he had ever wanted, he wanted her to love him.

Felipe opened the remaining draperies, sat on the ledge and looked out to sea, his eyes following the gulls that flew above the port. Did Rosina have a lover? Was that why she had smiled that mysterious smile the previous night? A lover!

He pounded his fist in the air. Of course, a lover!! Why else would she appear so content and...and...satisfied? Suddenly, Felipe began to pace back and forth in his chambers, his face flushed, sweat on his brow. Rosina with another man was unthinkable! Yet, he had seen for himself her glow, that knowing smile, the way she moved. Yes! He would confront her right away. Demand to know the truth. Demand to know the identity of this man. No! No, he would set a trap for them. He would pay Tomas a large sum to spy on them. To bring him information that would confirm their guilt.

And then he would kill this lover. String him up from the highest tree and aim his pistol to that most tender of places that had so gratified his wife. Yes, that was what he would do.

He took a deep, satisfied breath and again looked out at the harbor. The winds had picked up, the flags atop the three port identification poles snapping back and forth like bullwhips. The vendors' stalls overflowed as crowds walked the docks in search of delectable fish, large pink shrimp, and tender squid.

The sun's reflection on something metal caught his eye and he scrutinized its source. There it was again, coming from a man who strolled along the wharf, a woman at his side. It looked as though the man was in uniform, the rays from the sun catching his insignia. Felipe leaned over and retrieved a pair of binoculars he used for watching the ships and guided them through the crowd until he again spied the man and the woman.

Adjusting the lenses, he saw the woman wore a long, soft green dress, cinched at her waist, with sleeves that ran to her elbows. Her brunette hair was shoulder length and atop her head was a wide-brimmed hat the color of fresh cut hay. Her lips, painted the color of cherries, moved in gay conversation.

Felipe moved the binoculars to the man, who listened attentively, sometimes nodding his head, sometimes throwing his head back in laughter. They are intimate he thought, and began to move the binoculars across the man's uniform. He adjusted his binoculars once more and caught a full, distinct view of the man's hat, erect and imposing on his head. It was the silver insignia on the face of the hat that the sun's rays had caught, military insignia.

A Nazi!

Felipe moved the lenses to the uniform's shoulder boards, heavily braided with silver oak leaves. Felipe held his breath. Only one man wore those braids: The Reichsfuhrer SS, Heinrich Himmler. Germany's second-in-command, subservient only to Adolf Hitler.

Felipe's heart beat rapidly as he pressed his face to the window glass and squinted. He moved his binoculars to the two men who followed behind. German soldiers of a lower rank. Bodyguards?

Moving his sight back to the prancing SS officer, Felipe studied him more carefully, noting the mustache, the eyeglasses, the belt around his waist, the pistol in a holster. Even from such a distance, the German appeared imposing, his walk clipped and pompous.

Felipe put away the binoculars and picked up his telephone. There was someone who needed to know about his sighting of the Reichsfuhrer. As he dialed the number, Felipe put aside his personal dilemma; a much more important matter needed his every attention.

Chapter Fourteen

Twice, Garcia found himself asleep atop Pedro as they journeyed the mountain road on their return to Brasalia. The old donkey plodded along, perhaps thinking of his return to his little barn on a quiet hillside. The night sky was clear with abundant stars, the almost-full moon providing a serene light that led them along.

It was late - much later than Garcia would like to have been traveling. There were wild dogs that would enjoy a tasty meal of a less than virile donkey whose skeletal legs may not be able to kick with a lethal blow. And perhaps even himself. How would he fight them off? All he had was a sack full of scallops.

His mind wandered. Ah, Jordana. His last glimpse of her had been in the early morning light as she lay across his bed like a sleeping flower, one hand entwined in her hair. The note he left her implored her to return to her mother. *Dearest Señorita Jordana. You must return to your family. I have traveled to Barcelona, but will return late this evening. You must return home. Your humble servant, Garcia Quinones.*

Though it distressed him that the young woman's life had become manipulated by the whims of her domineering mother, he felt he could not become involved. Still, he believed Jordana's only defense had been to run away. Both her mother and her aunt reminded him of circus fat ladies, ever jovial, but ever cunning behind their smiles. And, the poor *señorita* must, of course, escape the stranger who was chosen to be her husband. Despite his sympathetic view of her situation, he felt powerless to offer any solution.

The sound of a train whistle carried in the clear night air, wrapping itself around Garcia like a lonely embrace. He heard the turning of the great steel wheels on the never-ending tracks and envisioned sparks flying and spreading upward like fireflies. Train fire flies. Maybe there was such a thing. Perhaps the real fire flies thought the sparks were also fire flies and followed them in hopes of a chance meeting. Garcia slapped his head. *I am ridiculous. A train fire fly, indeed.*

He stretched and yawned and shook his head to ward off his lingering drowsiness. During the last mile, the pace of the weary donkey had slowed. Garcia became alarmed and held the reins tightly when he felt a falter in his step. Suddenly, beneath him, the little animal stumbled, sending Garcia and the sack of scallops sprawling onto the narrow road.

"Pedro," he whispered as he crawled to the donkey and leaned over his body. "What is wrong, my donkey friend?" No breath came from the large nostrils, the stillness of his body a sign of the ebbing of life. He grasped Pedro's head in his hands and buried his face into his warm neck. His words were muffled. "Pedro, you have been so faithful." He held the donkey to him with such strength that he felt his own heartbeat. Then, a harrowing thought rushed into his head. *Senora Albeniz's beloved donkey was dead.*

In the still of night, on the lonely road to Brasalia, came a voice, deep like the sound of rolling thunder. "May I be of assistance, señor?"

Garcia jumped and looked up. "Señor, you have frightened me."

"I am sorry. I did not mean to. May I be of assistance to you?" The man leveled his calm eyes at the piano teacher.

"I...my donkey is dead, señor." Garcia lifted his hands in a helpless gesture, his eyes fixed on the still donkey. "And, I don't quite know what to do."

The stranger looked intently at Pedro and then Garcia. "It is my advice, señor, that you move your donkey off the roadway."

"Off the roadway? Señor, there is no place to put him. I have no shovel with which to dig a grave."

The stranger pointed to the dark valley below. "You must roll him off the side of the mountain, my friend." He looked at Garcia, then at Pedro. "It is the only way."

Astonished, Garcia raised his voice. "Roll him off the side of the mountain? This faithful donkey that has carried me unfalteringly to Barcelona and back? That is impossible, señor."

The stranger eased to the side of Pedro and squatted down. His hand rubbed along the animal's coat as if confirming Garcia's words. *A faithful donkey.* The wasted legs did not go unnoticed.

"It is better to roll him off the side of the mountain than expose him to the comings and goings of the road. He would not want to be seen like this. Donkeys have their dignity just as we do." He continued rubbing the dark, wiry hair that ran like a whisk broom down his spine. The corn-stalk ears remained erect.

Garcia reached out and gently touched Pedro's soft nose. The little donkey with the thin legs had served him well. With no complaints, he had carried the one hundred seventy-five pound body of Garcia as well as the scallops almost forty kilometers. And, now, here he lay, his heart still, his eyes closed, his spirit somewhere in the universe.

"Si, señor, I suppose the wild dogs and buzzards will get him no matter where he is." Garcia sighed deeply. "It just seems so cruel."

The stranger shook his head. "I agree, but we must do it. Come, señor, I will help you."

He stood, then leaned over and grasped Pedro's two front hooves. "You take the two back hooves. We'll pull him to the edge."

Together, they dragged the poor beast to the edge of the road where the mountain fell below them. Gasping for breath, the man said: "Now, let's get behind him and shove him over." He braced his shoulder against the backside of the donkey and motioned for Garcia to do the same. "Push, señor! Push!"

At last, with a final grunting effort, the men pushed the donkey over the edge of the mountain and watched him fall, only to land just two meters below on a small ledge covered with low brush. They stood silently watching the prostrate donkey as though he might rise up and hurl himself down the mountain as they had intended.

"I feel bad," Garcia said. "He was a good donkey."

The man nodded in agreement. "Would it ease your heart if we said a prayer over him? You know, like 'we send you to heaven with blessings'?"

Garcia nodded hesitantly. "*Sí*, that would be good."

Garcia closed his eyes. With solemn reverence, he began. "Pedro, you were a faithful servant and we send you to heaven so that your hooves may fly and your manger may never be empty of hay."

Garcia cleared his throat. "That is all I can say, señor." He turned and picked up the sack of scallops and began walking toward Brasalia. The stranger caught up with him and kept pace for a while before he spoke.

"That was a good prayer. I'm sure your donkey is happy now, wherever he may be."

"Actually, it is not my donkey. It is Señora Albeniz'. She gave him to me to ride to Barcelona to buy her scallops. And, now, I must return to her without her donkey."

A slight chill crept over Garcia's body. He thought of Señora Albeniz' love for her little donkey, thinking him beautiful as she whispered sweet words into his lofty ears. It was her love for him, she declared, that made him strong and virile. He wondered how the old woman would take the news that Pedro had died. No longer could she push her worn face into his wiry coat. "Somehow, I must tell Señora Albeniz that her donkey has died and we pushed him over the mountain."

The stranger hesitated. "Senor, it would be in your best interest if you do not tell her we pushed him over the mountain. Just tell her he died and had a proper burial. That you met a stranger who had a shovel and together we buried him near the beautiful peaks of the Pyrenees. I believe that will be more acceptable to Senora Albeniz."

Garcia walked a few steps. "You are right. I do not want to lie to Señora Albeniz, but neither do I want to tell her the truth."

"It is settled then?"

"*Si*."

The moonlight followed the men as they rounded the final bend in the road before descending the hill into Brasalia, where the village lay in hushed slumber, unlike places across the mountains where the aeriel bombings of French railway yards and bridges by the Allies obliterated any semblance of peace. Occasionally, the far-away drone of Allied aircraft skirting the German Luftwaffe and heading to targets deep within Europe rode the winds of the mountains, a reminder that all was not well.

It was the moonlight that enticed the beasts of the mountains from their caves and into places they would scavage and declare their own. As a cloud covered the moon, a wail permeated the mountainside, a reverberation filled with such agony that the two men froze in their places, wondering if it was the devil himself. The sound continued, so full of sorrow that Garcia fell to his knees and covered his ears. *It was Pedro. It was Pedro come back to life.*

The two men turned away from Brasalia and began to run down the road toward the terror-filled cries of the donkey, the mournful braying filling their ears. Had there been a translator of the donkey language, they would have interpreted Pedro's cries as *"How could you leave me when I carried you all the way to Barcelona? How could you throw your faithful donkey over the edge of the mountain for the buzzards to devour?"*

With only the moon to light their way, the two men found where they had rolled the body of Pedro off the side of the mountain, found the small brush-covered ledge on which the carcass had landed, but no Pedro. Leaning out into the brush and rocks, they searched the mountainside.

"Where is he?" asked Garcia, mostly to himself. "It cannot be." He shook his head and looked at the stranger, who himself, stood puzzled and thoughtful.

"Señor, is my mind playing tricks on me? Did we or did we not push the donkey over the side of the mountain?"

Garcia's next words teetered on the edge of sarcasm. "And, señor, was the donkey dead or was he not?"

The stranger stepped closer to the edge of the mountain and once again surveyed the rocks and brush.

"Perhaps the donkey was not dead, but in a donkey coma, a debilitating trance, maybe." He nodded his head slowly in affirmation. "I am thinking he will bray again and then we will be able to determine exactly where he is."

The men squatted and looked out over the valley and waited.

Garcia was curious. "Señor, who are you? You never told me your name. What are you doing on the road to Brasalia?"

The man lit a cigarette and tossed the match down the mountain. "I am visiting a relative."

"In Brasalia?"

"Near."

"Who is your relative?"

The stranger paused and looked up into the sky, directly at the Big Dipper which hung constant in the star-filled sky. "I'm sure you do not know him."

The stranger's hesitation heightened Garcia's curiosity. He pursued his questioning.

"What is his name?"

Without answering, the stranger stood and stretched and looked around them. Finally, he said. "Luis Neruda is my cousin."

"Luis?"

"Yes. Luis."

"Luis is your cousin?"

"*Sí*. Do you know him?"

"Of course. And his mule, too."

"How do you know him?"

"Ha! He is at the tavern most every night, but he talks to no one. Some say he talks only to his mule."

"Is that so? I find my cousin very companionable."

"That is good." Garcia looked up at the man. "You never told me your name."

"No, I did not." With the slightest hesitation, the stranger looked steadily at Garcia. "My name is Juan."

"Ah, Juan. Thank you for your assistance with Pedro." Garcia stood and offered his hand to Juan. "My name is..."

"Garcia. Your name is Garcia."

Garcia's eyes widened. "How did you know my name, señor?"

"Because I have been looking for you."

Garcia studied the man carefully, his eyes traveling to his battered fedora and scuffed leather jacket. Somehow, he saw him differently. Light from the moon revealed his intelligent eyes, the careful, almost military, stance, the caution with which he spoke. In some way, Garcia knew this was not an ordinary man, that this was not a chance meeting, that their encounter had been planned and orchestrated for a specific reason.

The harrowing sound that rose up from the mountain fell on the two men like the cold breath of a demon. It was Pedro again. He called to them. *Help me, help me.*

"Come, señor. He is over there." The two men slid a few meters down a slight grade onto a large rock that jutted out like a pancake wedged into the side of the mountain. From there, they dropped to their knees and looked under the edge of the rock. There, looking up at them with large eyes that glistened in the moonlight, was Pedro. When the animal saw the two men, he lifted his head and brayed in such a prodigious manner that one could be drawn to tears.

"Pedro, you precious donkey, you! You are alive!" Garcia laughed robustly and slapped the rock with his hand. Pedro snorted through his nostrils and shook his body fiercely, as if warding off evil spirits.

"*Sí*, señor, he is alive. Now, we must get him back up the mountain."

Garcia frowned. "I am not quite so sure just how to do that. He seems to be in a rather isolated spot."

"That is true, but it stands to reason if we show him the way, he can travel back up the mountain. It is only a short distance."

"And how do we convince Pedro that he must climb back up the mountain?" Garcia hung his head. "After all, we rolled him down the mountain and I'm not so sure he trusts us."

"That is possible, but we must try." Juan slid from the edge of the rock and dropped down into the brush close to Pedro. The donkey merely blinked his eyes, his long lashes fluttering, a soft guttural sound from deep within his throat hinted of his awareness.

Garcia dropped from the flat rock into the brush beside Juan. Behind them the mountain whispered of long-lost souls. Garcia looked up and saw it was only a matter of two or three meters back to the top of the road.

"If we could lead Pedro back over there," Juan pointed in the direction of brush and rock where it tapered up in a stair-like direction to the edge of the road, "then perhaps we could get him to the roadway again."

Garcia shook his head and became thoughtful. "Since Pedro still has his halter, we should have no trouble leading him. Let us try."

Both men jumped when Pedro again lifted his head and brayed soulfully into the night. Was he telling them he would not move from the safety of the rock?

Garcia picked up the reins and gently tugged in the direction of the rock stairs.

"Come, Pedro." Amazingly, the donkey followed, his hooves navigating carefully. Once they reached the spot where they intended to ascend onto the roadway, Pedro stopped and looked up, as if knowing what was expected of him.

Juan patted Pedro on the nose. "Just a few more steps, my friend, and you will be safe."

Juan looked at Garcia. "Let me climb first, then hand me the reins. While I tug on the reins, you can pull on the halter."

Garcia nodded and pulled out the length of the reins and handed them to Juan. He then slipped his hand through the leather straps of the halter. "Ready," he said.

"On the count of three, señor." Juan braced his feet on the roadway. "One. Two. Three." He gritted his teeth and tugged on the reins while below him Garcia pulled the halter.

It was to no avail. Pedro dug in his hooves and reared up with his head. He was going nowhere. After all, he seemed to say, these men pushed me over the mountain. He flicked his tail in anger.

"He will not move, señor." Juan eased on the reins, as did Garcia on the halter. "There is nothing more we can do."

"Let us try one more time." Garcia planted his feet firmly. "Come, Pedro, you must move up the mountain." Juan wrapped the ends of the reins around his fist and bent his knees in a staunch position.

"One. Two. Three." Both men pulled. Pedro, staunch and relentlessly stubborn, did not move.

Exasperated, Garcia released the halter. "How could this be?"

"Si, señor. It is no use."

"Tomorrow, I will bring a friend and rope and we will tie ropes around Pedro and drag him up the mountain onto the roadway."

"Good idea. The donkey is afraid and, out of fear, he is staying put."

Garcia rubbed Pedro on his nose and spoke gently into his soft ear. "We will return tomorrow, Pedro, and deliver you from this quandary. I shall leave you now." Garcia placed his boots on the rocks and climbed to the roadway. When he reached the top, he cast his eyes around for the stranger, but saw only the stars in the sky and heard the winds blowing in the treetops. Garcia took a deep breath. How did the stranger know his name? And why had he been looking for him?

Chapter Fifteen

A weary Garcia Quinones walked down the last hill that swept gently into Brasalia to the spot where he left the bag of scallops, only to find they had disappeared. His frustration mounting, he looked around and could see no evidence of them ever being there. Again, the curse of the gods; the death of the donkey, the rise of the donkey and now the disappearance of Señora Albeniz' scallops. He shuddered and wondered how he could survive the old woman's wrath when she learned of the plight of her donkey and the loss of her scallops.

In the depths of despair, he continued his walk through the tiny village and up the road toward his cottage. His body sank into a deep weariness as he turned onto the lane. Clouds had covered the once-bright moon, leaving the walk as dark as his sense of pending doom. He heard his goats bleating anxious cries as he approached the barn. Little Tia greeted him as usual. Always forgiving, she pushed on his leg and stuck out her tongue as he opened the barn door and led them inside.

Garcia's bones ached unmercifully, fatigue consuming his body like a poison. He opened the door to the darkened cottage and removed his clothing – the smell of Pedro, the sea air and the docks of Barcelona permeating the air around him. Another strange odor seeped into his nostrils. Of course, the Albeniz sister – the one who had pummeled him, leaving the scent of madness to linger on his body.

He fell into his bed with a weary groan, only to feel the warmth of Jordana Rios's body underneath the blanket. *Impossible.* She had not left the cottage as he instructed her to do. Weak with despair, he crawled from the warm bed and picked up his filthy clothing. In the barn, he fell onto the hay and pushed a goat away from him before he fell into a deep sleep.

Chapter Sixteen

The bleating goats awakened Garcia before the sun had even tipped the mountains. A scant five hours had passed since he had returned from his harrowing trip only to find Jordana still at his cottage. Not only in his cottage, but in his bed, her naked leg stretched across the sheets. He pulled his tired body up from his bed in the hay and walked through the barn door. His goats were scattered throughout the barnyard, only little Tia stood near the door waiting for her master.

In the dim early morning light, Garcia weaved himself through his goats, wondering how they had been able to escape when he distinctly remembered closing the door the previous night. He need have wondered no more, for sitting atop a large rock was the stranger from the night before.

"Ah, I was wondering when you would arise on this beautiful morning, Señor Quinones." He left his seat on the rock and lit his third cigarette of the morning. "Your goats and I have been having some very deep conversations, but I am ready to converse with a human." He laughed, a low, friendly laugh.

Garcia watched the stranger with mounting trepidation, observing the same drab, rumpled jacket and worn fedora hat from the night before. The mystery of his appearance and then just as quickly his disappearance disturbed Garcia. How did he know where Garcia lived?

He told him he had been looking for him, an unsettling thought as Garcia stepped closer.

"Señor, you are baffling to me. Who are you?" Garcia was surprised at the gruffness in his voice.

Juan removed his fedora and the shadow across his face lifted. Again, Garcia noted the intelligent, dark eyes, eyes that watched him intently. It was abundantly clear he knew many things about Garcia. Another thing was quite clear: the stranger had some questions to answer.

"Señor, I am Juan, as I told you last evening."

"Your name means nothing to me. What I want to know is who you are and what exactly you want. Your clandestine ways are annoying me."

Juan smiled, exposing straight teeth, the color of the cigarette paper in his fingers. "I understand. You have every right to be. Let us talk, Señor Quinones."

Reluctantly, Garcia motioned for Juan to sit in a wooden chair that leaned against the barn. He positioned himself on a nearby rock. The curious goats followed them as if they, too, wanted to know the answers to their master's questions. They stood in waiting, Tia at the forefront, their slanted eyes blinking. When this conversation had concluded, their shepherd would take them to the brush on the mountainside.

Garcia waited as Juan placed his fedora back on his head and expelled a long breath, a troubled breath as if what he was about to say was of great importance. He studied his profile and considered him a handsome man, not like the American movie stars, but with a worn, intriguing look that promised an interesting fellow to talk with. Gray tinged his black hair, his skin color somewhat lighter than the tobacco in his cigarette. He wondered if Juan was from the province of Catalonia, as he was. His dialect seemed familiar, with a lilt to it from the Catalonia of long ago. It was as though this man had lived a hundred years. A sad sort of wisdom emanated from his pores.

Suddenly, Garcia jumped up from the rock and pointed an accusing finger, scattering the goats in every direction. "You! You, señor, are the spy!"

While Juan contemplated his response, he placed a cigarette between his lips and inhaled. He waited while the smoke expelled from his nostrils and curled, oddly, into the shape of a question mark.

"The spy? What do you hear of a spy?" he asked.

"I hear the same thing everyone else in Brasalia hears. There is a spy roaming our mountainside." Garcia shrugged. "Of course, no one knows what kind of spy, whether German or British or even French. But surely, he is one of our Allies."

"Allies? The only ally to Spain is Germany."

"Not true, señor. Spain is and will continue to be neutral in this war."

As if to reinforce his belief, Garcia nodded emphatically and raised his voice. "It is my understanding that Generalissimo Franco has been reticent regarding his commitment one way or the other, but rest assured, he will never side with Germany."

Where had those words come from? Had he swallowed lies and repeated them until he believed them? Where was the passive pianist who herded goats?

The alleged spy gave Garcia an ironic smile. His words held a calculated precision.

"While I appreciate your belief that Spain shall remain neutral, it is only for appearance's sake. You must understand that they maintain the image of neutrality for the world to see, but in reality they are providing funds as well as supplies to the Third Reich. I would surmise that Franco believes Hitler will win in this horrific war. Then again, only Franco really knows what he will do." His stance was firm: "Franco is merely a proxy for Hitler. And fascism."

He paused as he picked a bit of tobacco from his lip. "And what about the soldiers Spain sends to fight along the Eastern front, alongside the Nazis?"

Garcia studied the ground and thought of Lope and Jorge. "That may be true. But I, a simple piano teacher, can only hope that Spain remains neutral."

He hesitated, then looked directly at Juan, each word laden with resignation. "I feel you are the spy, señor. What I don't know is why you are here, talking to me, a Spaniard who knows very little of the war."

"You have good intuition, señor. You really have no proof that I am a spy, yet your gut tells you so. It is quite a powerful skill you have, you know. To be able to feel things and know things. As if you have direct access to the knowledge of the universe."

The spy became philosophical. His voice softened, as if he were addressing the innocents of the world.

"The war effort would benefit from men like you, men who are willing to conduct themselves with honor and commitment." Juan looked up at the peaks of the Pyrenees. The trees leaned in the brisk wind and brought the fragrance of evergreen. He tread slowly. He had received a briefing from MI6. *Approach the pianist gently; he is an artiste.*

"Of course, honor and commitment are not innate, they are learned," Juan said. He smiled and turned toward Garcia, an eyebrow raised, waiting for a response from the self-proclaimed pacifist who looked at him with obvious doubt.

Garcia spoke with frustration. "*Pasmoso*, señor! You have avoided telling me what you want and yet you tell me the war needs men like me! Your words are laughable. I teach piano. That is all I do."

Juan watched a nervous Garcia pace back and forth. His voice soothing, he said, "Sit down, my friend, and I shall tell you a story."

Garcia ceased his pacing and faced Juan suspiciously. He felt himself waver, falling toward an undisclosed danger. He also felt something else: a defiance that pressed him to challenge the spy.

The men stared at each other for a long moment, their eyes unwavering, their faces set with an understanding that each of them must, from this moment on, speak words of truth. With an infinitesimal nod, Garcia spoke. "Your story had better be true, señor."

"Only the truth." Juan closed his eyes, pulling from his mind the words he wanted to say. "It is my belief, Señor Quinones, that we must fight against all tyranny and oppression. You see, I bear no grudge against the German people." He lifted his hands, shaking them as if to bring forth the answer to an inexplicable puzzle. "It is Adolf Hitler, whom I abhor. How could the German people have fallen victim to such insanity? How could he indoctrinate the minds of intelligent and resourceful Germans so successfully? I must do what I can to turn the tide of the war and—"

"One man cannot make a difference," interjected Garcia.

"You are wrong, my friend." Juan took a deep breath, "When I learned of the little colonel's plan to annihilate the Jews and his quest for a supreme race, I knew neither mankind nor I could tolerate such evil. That is why I fight against this injustice with the weapons at my disposal."

Garcia looked at Juan with surprise; he felt himself shiver.

"Weapons at your disposal? The Jews? Whatever do you mean, señor?" Hesitantly, he leaned closer. "You are a Spaniard. Why do you want to involve yourself against the Germans when we are not even in the war?"

"Ah, a difficult question to answer. But I shall try."

Juan leaned back in his chair and felt himself in another place, black and still. When he opened his eyes, it was with a start, like he'd heard a gunshot. He looked at Garcia, his eyes solemn. "There are many in the world who do not know that Hitler has extermination camps which are used to murder the Jews. If I were a Jew being persecuted, would I not want the good men of the world to rescue me?

"We are not alone in this world or in this war. Spain may be neutral, but her people think as I do. We must do what we can to rescue those who cannot rescue themselves. Franco has used poor judgment in choosing Hitler as his friend instead of leading his people with honor. With the Allies."

Garcia was quiet as the famous winds of the Pyrenees gusted around them, chasing the gray clouds and leaving blue skies behind. He grappled with the words he had heard. "You have not answered my question. What are these weapons at your disposal? You must explain."

"Ah, and therein lies the purpose of my visit to you." Juan stood and stretched. "Let's take a walk, my piano friend."

The two men left the barnyard, the goats trailing behind them. At the end of the lane, they turned up the path that took them farther into the hills.

They walked quietly to the top of the first rise. Juan stopped to light a cigarette.

"The SIS sources of Great Britain tell me there is a high-ranking German officer on holiday in Barcelona, along with his mistress and a few other Germans. They appear at the German Embassy daily, but their true purpose is to holiday.

"SIS's information also tells me that his mistress is a friend of yours. That she heard your music quite often while in Brussels and Paris. It seems she was an ardent fan of yours while you studied in Brussels at the Conservatory." Juan continued walking without speaking, letting Garcia absorb what he had said.

"Go on," Garcia said quietly, an anxiety in the pit of his stomach.

"Our intelligence sources tell us that the German officer has tracked your location to Brasalia and plans to pay you a visit."

"A visit! An officer of the Third Reich is paying me a visit? How preposterous. Why would he do such a thing?"

Juan laughed quietly. "It seems his mistress wants to hear you play the piano, señor."

Garcia jumped and threw his hands in the air. "His mistress? Who is this woman?"

"Her name is Hedwig Potthast. Sound familiar?"

Garcia became still. "Hedwig Potthast?" The pianist's brow furrowed as he nodded slowly. "I remember her well. She followed me around at the Conservatory like a lovesick schoolgirl. Said my playing made her feel *alive*."

"You must have made quite an impression on her if she's followed you to Brasalia."

"That's ridiculous! I cannot imagine her desire to hear me play is anything but a joke. In all of Spain, there has to be at least a hundred pianists who play better than I." Garcia shook his head. "Unbelievable. Your intelligence information is faulty, my friend."

"I'm afraid not. You underestimate your genius, my friend. Nonetheless, my sources tell me this officer is going to seek you out and demand that you play for his mistress."

"Who is this high-ranking officer?"

Juan picked up a rock and threw it high in the air and watched as it tumbled down the mountain. "Heinrich Himmler, Reichsfuhrer of Nazi Germany. Subservient only to Adolf Hitler."

Garcia stared at Juan, his face frozen in disbelief. "Heinrich Himmler and his mistress desire to hear me play the piano?"

"That is so." Juan looked up into the sky, toward the higher peaks where wisps of see-through clouds weaved their way across the mountains toward the sea.

"Tell me about this fraulein, Hedwig." he said.

Garcia blew out a breath and shook his head. "Hedwig Potthast. How I wish I had never known her."

"Wish you'd never known her? Why?"

"Many reasons. Perhaps reasons you will not understand."

"I would like to know."

Garcia remained still a long while, his mind turning over his memories of the fraulein. Finally, his eyes scanning the ridges above them, he spoke.

"She came to all the recitals we had. Followed our tours like a puppy dog. I found her to be obsessive in everything she did. She insisted on carrying our instruments, cleaning them. She became such a nuisance that I spoke to the Kapellmeister about her."

Garcia stretched and watched his goats wind their way through the rocks. He was hesitant to continue – these were memories from another time, a time that embraced his beautiful Maria. It was difficult to continue, but he did.

"Going to the Kapellmeister about her was not a good thing to do. He admonished her and afterwards, she went crazy. Broke into the music room and poured petrol on all the instruments. Would have burned the place down had it not been for a security guard on patrol."

"A perfect mistress for Himmler, eh. Someone who destroys with ease and, of course, with no conscience." Juan motioned for Garcia to continue. "What happened then?"

Garcia shook his head, bewildered. "Nothing. Absolutely nothing. She was never accused of anything. But, I must say, señor, from that moment on, I feared for my life. I was not sure if she knew it was I who complained. I certainly did not want to take any chances."

"Do you remember anything else of importance about her?"

A tiny chuckle eased from Garcia. "Ah, yes. Yes, there is something else. You see, Hedwig Potthast idolized me. Thought I was the most handsome man at the Conservatory. Perhaps in all of Belgium and Paris. I feel she not only has a desire to hear me play after all these years, but she also may have…shall we say…a lingering infatuation."

The two men were silent, their thoughts their own. Finally, Juan spoke. "How convenient for us. Her yearning to see you will ensure their visit.

"How do you know this information?"

"Sources at the Embassy. We'll find out how much influence Fraulein Potthast has on her German lover."

He pulled another cigarette from his jacket pocket. "More about the fraulein. Did she continue to come to the recitals?"

"No. I never saw her again. And, now, here she is. Back in my life." Garcia seemed to shudder. Wryly, he looked at Juan. "Because of you, señor."

Juan smiled. "I feel she would have found you no matter what the circumstances. The fact Himmler is her lover is why British Intelligence has involved themselves in this very opportune situation.

"Your story becomes even more ludicrous. I am afraid your credibility has diminished, señor." Garcia turned toward the high rocks on the mountainside and his little goats followed.

Juan climbed behind Garcia, picking his way carefully among the rocks. "It is so, Garcia. You will be hearing from the Germans."

The sun glinted off the slight gray streaks that ran through the spy's dark hair.. He stopped and watched Garcia walk away from him. He had not told the piano teacher everything; the rest of the story would have to wait until he was more receptive. "Adios, señor," he called as he walked down the mountain. "We will talk again."

Chapter Seventeen

A frustrated Garcia Quinones left his goats on the mountainside and returned to his cottage. He muttered to himself the entire way home; *Germans visiting him, Garcia Quinones, a simple piano teacher. How could that be*?

He slammed the door to the cottage behind him as he came into the room that served as a kitchen and sitting area. Standing at the stove with a teakettle in her hand was Jordana. She half smiled at him, her eyes large with surprise. She did not expect him to return so soon.

"*Buenos dias*, señor. Did you sleep well?" Her eyes were languid, full of the despair that filled her life. She had cried when she read the note he left her; but found she could not leave her refuge.

"*Buenos dias* to you, señorita. I see you have found the tea and the tea kettle." His voice was gentle. He looked at her with kindness and concern. Perhaps he did not want her to leave.

"*Sí*" she said. "And, also the crackers in the cupboard. They are delicious." She paused and almost smiled when she added, "As well as the cheese."

She looked at him with such beseeching eyes that Garcia turned away, not wanting to fall victim to her exquisite beauty.

"I am glad you have made yourself comfortable here, but we must talk about your leaving. Perhaps you did not take my note seriously."

He walked to the small table and sat in the wooden chair that rested in the sunlight by the window. *The tea kettle.* He rested his eyes on the pot, all its dents, discolorations and saw his mother. It was all he had left of her. *Garcia, have some tea. You have been at the piano for six hours.* How he missed her. *Yes, mama, I will have some tea.*

He found Jordana watching him. Like a butterfly resting on an apple blossom – *should I stay or fly away.* When he continued, his words were stern.

"What you have done is impossible. You have run away with no thought to the consequences. What do you intend to do, Señorita Jordana?"

She looked at him for a long moment, willing the universe to pluck her from the dilemma in which she found herself.

"Señor Quinones, I only know what I cannot do and that is to return to my home where I will be chastised and then sent away to Madrid to marry. Otherwise, I have no idea what is to be done."

Garcia studied her face. Sadly, he saw mounting fear in her anxious eyes. Along the line of her mouth, a hesitancy, as if holding back words that, if she said them, would cause her to shatter, like a wayward comet exploding into the universe. Still, he had no doubt that she had a clear understanding of her difficulties. How could he possibly send her into a world that would take advantage of her beauty? Then again, how could he possibly allow her to continue to stay with him? He stood and walked to the stove to reach for a teacup, only to have Jordana take it from him and pour him tea.

"*Gracias, señorita.*" He sipped the hot tea and tasted the sweetness of honey, with perhaps a little sassafras. "Ah, very good." He returned to the table and continued to sip his tea while his mind raced for solutions to the problems set before him.

Slowly, her feet making no noise on the floor, Jordana came to him. Once at his side, she slid to the floor and laid her head in his lap. Her hair, mussed from a night's sleep, tumbled across his legs. Her arms wrapped around his waist and there she lay while Garcia sipped his tea and thought again of the gods who had cursed him so abundantly.

He could not help himself. He reached out and plucked a strand of the long, dark hair toward him. As if her hair were the most prized treasure in the world, he caressed it with his fingertips as gently as he played a Chopin rhapsody. "What is it you want to do, Jordana?"

She lifted her head and her eyes fell upon his with such pleading that he was momentarily breathless. Her lips parted and with a voice as soft as an angel's, she spoke. "I want to stay with you."

Garcia quickly looked away, afraid that the longing in her eyes would capture him and render him helpless. With a steely resolve, his eyes found hers again.

"I'm not so sure that is possible."

Jordana's lips trembled. "Why is that?"

"What about your family? Your mother?"

"What kind of family would give me away to a stranger?" Garcia saw immediate tears form in the brown eyes. He nodded. Of course, she was right.

"I don't know what to say. Perhaps you can speak with your mother and tell her how you feel."

"It is impossible to talk with my mother. You see her. You hear her. You know how she is."

"That is true." He looked across the room and saw dust motes floating in a ray of sunlight that pushed through the window that faced east. "Jordana," Garcia's black eyes spoke the truth. "I think it is important to let your mother know you are safe."

Jordana jumped from the cottage floor and began to cry. She looked at Garcia as though he were an enemy. "If I go back, I will never see you again."

Garcia's eyes opened wide as he looked into the tearful face. "See me?" Then, as though lightning had struck his body, stopped the beating of his heart and made him a lifeless stone statue, he drifted away. He felt nothing, saw nothing, heard nothing. Then, as if a warm breath whispered on his cheek, he felt himself come back, back to his little cottage, to the beautiful woman who looked up at him, her lips parted, a half-smile waiting for him. Garcia stared at her for a long moment, a moment that revealed Jordana's feelings for him. How had he missed it? Her adoring looks? Her tender care of him? In a daze, he rose slowly from his chair and left the cottage. *How could they? The gods, of course.* They had had a meeting and decided to add one more dilemma to the mounting trepidations in the piano teacher's life: Jordana was in love with him.

Juan Castillo, MI6's consummate spy, left the goat herder, who also happened to be one of Europe's most famed pianists, and picked his way west, farther into the mountains, through a green mènagerie of trees whose conical tops looked like hats worn at the *desfile de payasos en el circ*, the parade of clowns at the renowned Barcelona Carnival.

Juan, whose Catalonian heritage had begun centuries before, knew the myth of the mountains well. His great grandfather had told him the Pyrenees were named after a princess, Princess Pyrene, who was brutally raped by the dark and drunken Hercules. When Hercules became sober, he learned the beautiful princess had died. Heartbroken, he cried out to the mountains, demanding the mountains mourn and preserve her name forever. In response, the mountaintops shuddered and echoed back to Hercules "Pyrene," over and over again.

Juan felt the famed winds of the mountains blow across his face, ceaseless winds, winds that, through the ages, played tribute to Pyrene. As a little boy, trailing his grandfather in the higher elevations, he had heard the agonizing voice of Hercules calling Pyrene's name. Now, as he climbed higher, he tilted his head and listened for "Pyrene."

Once he'd traveled a kilometer west, he turned north, even higher in the elevations, and found his small camp. It lay nestled in the fissure of a large perpendicular rock whose shape reminded him of a large dagger, its point embedded in the rocks. When he arrived, he found Luis and his white mule hovering in the recesses of the rocks, Luis leaning on his mule for warmth.

"My friend, you are guarding our humble camp?"

Luis laughed, then rubbed the neck of his mule. "*Si*, my mule and I are most honored to protect these rocks and trees where you live."

"My gratitude to you both." Juan removed his fedora and looked around the camp; a small valise with a change of clothing and personal items – a comb, his razor, cigarettes – and, best of all, two bottles of Scotch. His love of the distinctive smoky flavor kept him in touch with a louse of a man who supplied it on a regular basis. He'd heard the man had been arrested and charged with treason, a petty charge really, considering the man's life was at end anyway – destroyed liver – from too much whiskey, of course.

"Too early for some fine whiskey?"

"Never too early."

"We must talk."

"Of the pianist?"

"But, of course. The pianist." Juan pulled the dark bottle from his valise and unscrewed the top, a long, appreciative sip before handing it to Luis. He settled himself on a nearby rock and lit a cigarette. His conversation with Garcia Quinones had stirred memories of his own entry into spyhood. He had seen the crumbling of Europe – had listened to the BBC in October 1939 when Britain refused Hitler's offer of peace. Had been there in May 1940 when Churchill flew to Paris and learned the French were burning their archives and preparing to evacuate the city. Had witnessed the heartbreaking capture of *La Ville-Lumière*, the City of Light, the Germans parading down the streets of the Parisian arrondissements like peacocks, absorbing the culture of Paris, then urinating in the Seine. From there to Calais, where he watched the German bombers crisscross the Citadel. He continued to wonder why Churchill or the War Office had not ordered the evacuation of Calais. So many lives would have been saved. He, himself, had left in the middle of the night in a small boat secreted into the water by the French Resistance. He remembered watching the bombs explode in the distance, one after the other. Even as he crossed the Channel, his eyes never left the smolder of fire, as Calais became a mere orange dot on the horizon of the night sky.

If he had wondered then about his view of the world and the war, he wondered no longer. Truth and love must prevail over lies and hatred. "It is like this, Luis. Though a somewhat worldly man, our friend has been in a cocoon for some years now. You know, isolating himself. And, I wonder why."

Luis nodded. "Depression, perhaps?"

"Could be. From the information we have gathered, we know his wife died some years back. We also know his last public performance was in Paris. Been in the mountains since."

"Si, a recluse."

The Pyrenees winds gusted and the swaying trees whined with the voices of ghosts who sat atop them and proclaimed the mountain theirs.

A recluse, yes. Garcia was an artiste, not a politician. What did he care of the war?

Juan stood and paced the small camp. "So much depends on the pianist. I must be assured of his ability to do what is asked of him. Perhaps we are asking too much of this man."

Luis watched as Juan paced. He knew the spy warrior would turn over every detail of the mission, dissecting it until it was perfect. "Your instinct has always been good, Juan."

Finally, Juan slowed his pace and looked into the blue of the Spanish sky. It was clear to him that the pianist must begin living in truth and rediscover his suppressed identity – it was fate that would cause his life to be more than a pianist who herded goats.

Quietly, he said, "We will proceed cautiously. It is my belief that the pianist will be cooperative. If not, we must abort the mission. As well as Senor Quinones."

Chapter Eighteen

Garcia pulled his bicycle from the side of the barn. It was barely noon and already he'd had a confrontation with the spy and a lovesick girl. Juan divulged to him harrowing information about the Germans, the War, the Jews. He looked toward the mountains, then upward into the blue of the Spanish sky. *What am I looking for*, he asked? As the mountain wind swept over the rocks and trees, Garcia felt the unveiling of a single truth; he had kept the war on the periphery of his life deliberately – with no thought of the consequences on his soul.

And now, it would be the piano that would throw him into that which he had kept at bay. He would come face to face with the Germans, because of his piano.

And what of Jordana? It dawned on him that his cottage had not been a simple refuge for her to escape a planned marriage to the old man in Madrid. It was more than that. Much more, and again, he could only blame his piano.

Garcia felt weak. The morning had sucked from him every bit of strength. Still, he had to face Señora Albeniz and deliver the news of her donkey.

The dread he felt as he pedaled to her house was immeasurable. He knew she would not take it well and that knowledge caused him to pedal more slowly toward her place on the hillside.

How would he tell her that her donkey was stranded on the side of a mountain? How could he say that the scallops, too, were lost? He shuddered at the image of her face when she learned of Pedro's predicament.

He did not consider Señora Albeniz to be a forgiving woman. Of course, she would blame him for everything. His breaths became shallow as he readied for the onslaught of the old woman's wrath. He also cursed the gods.

He turned the wheel of his bicycle toward Blanka's house, gritted his teeth and braced himself for an unpleasant encounter. He saw her in the yard, preparing to leave for the village where she would sell her empanadas.

Right away, as he leaned his bicycle against a tree, he saw that her face was stern. Nervously, his eyes darted around for her sister whom he knew lurked somewhere out of sight, waiting for an opportune moment to throw herself upon him, cackling her way through incessant punches to his body.

Blanka stood still and waited for Garcia to approach her. She said nothing, but her cold eyes watched him carefully. Could she already know what had happened to her Pedro? Her scallops? Hesitantly, Garcia edged toward the woman while keeping an eye out for the loco sister.

"*Buenos dias*, Señora Albeniz. I see you have made your meat pies for the village." He smiled and watched her face for any indication of warmth. There was none.

"Where is my Pedro?" Her gravelly voice lashed out at him with a vengeance that stunned him. Should he jump on his bicycle and ride until he could pedal no more? His need to flee was so great he felt his toes squirm in his boots. He held his breath until he could gather the strength to speak.

At last, his voice, cajoling and sweet, crept out of his mouth. "Ah, my dearest Blanka, your Pedro is doing very well. He waits for me on the side of the mountain. He became very weary on our return from Barcelona and I felt it best to let him rest in a peaceful spot outside of the village. I go there now to retrieve him."

There. All the lies he had ever told in his life were contained in these few words.

"Señor Quinones," she hissed, "you must return my beloved Pedro without delay. Bring him here now." Then the most evil of grins consumed her toothless mouth, "Or, I will have my sister cook you in her boiling pot."

Boiling pot! He felt the blood drain from his body. "Of course, of course," he soothed her. "I shall return in haste to bring Pedro to his stall where he can drink and eat fresh hay." Garcia backed away toward his bicycle. Sweat formed on his upper lip.

"Good day, señora."

Blanka held up her hand. "Where are my scallops?"

"Your scallops?" Garcia raised his eyebrows and smiled.

His mind raced. "Of course, your scallops." With surprising ease, he began to tell another lie, a lie that would surely send him to hell. "Ah, Señora Albeniz, it saddens me to tell you that in the black of the night a wild animal jumped from the mountainside and stole your scallops." Garcia shuddered. "I was so frightened, I told your beloved Pedro to run for his life and he ran like the wind. If it were not for his speed, surely we would both be meat for the buzzards."

Blanka said nothing as she listened to Garcia's tale. Finally, she shot him a cynical look that caused Garcia to tremble.

"It seems you are an unlucky man, Señor Quinones. Bring me my Pedro and we will talk of the scallops."

The speed with which Garcia went down the mountain was unheralded. Never had he pedaled with such force and intensity. At all costs, he must retrieve Pedro and bring him home.

The village was quiet as the sun bathed the streets and warmed the stones of the police station and the Church of the Holy Father. He rode past Señora Lanzarote's house and saw only a rooster scratching in the dirt.

He was relieved there was no sign of Tomas. The man instilled in him a feeling of dread, of the Judge and of the cold cemetery on the hill. He decided the Judge's jealousy was just a figment of Tomas' imagination. No more would he discuss these subjects with the old caretaker. Instead, he would continue to give Señora Lanzarote her piano lessons as always, with no thought whatsoever of the Judge and his pistol.

As he turned the corner at the police station, his heart stopped. The blood drained from his body in one rush, leaving his spirit to float above him as though he had died. He gasped for breath as he read the large poster plastered to the stone wall of the police station.

REWARD
FOR INFORMATION ON THE WHEREABOUTS OF
JORDANA RIOS. POSSIBLE KIDNAPPING. GUILTY PERSON
WILL BE PROSECUTED AND HANGED. 100,000$ PESETAS
FOR INFORMATION LEADING TO ARREST AND
CONVICTION.

Garcia gripped the handlebars of his bicycle, gasping for air. Again, the gods. In their quest to punish him for his many sins, they were providing the means for his inevitable demise.

A helpless laugh escaped him. Death by hanging, death at the hands of Blanka and her sister, death from the Judge's pistol. What did it matter? One way or the other, he was a doomed man.

From the door of the police station, Capitan Torres called to Garcia. "I am sure we will find the culprit and hang him from the highest tree. No?"

"Yes, of course, Capitan."

The policeman's belly fell over his wide leather belt, holding up pants that were too short. A strap ran diagonally across his chest, where a gun rested in a holster at his waist. He had been Brasalia's peacekeeper since before the Spanish Civil War, appointed by the Judge himself.

"Tomorrow we begin a house-to-house search for the señorita. It has been forty-eight hours since her disappearance. Someone is hiding her."

"House to house search? I'm…su…sure you will be successful in your hunt, Capitan."

Lifelessly, he pedaled to Miguel's little rooms, which were tacked on the back of the tavern. When he knocked on the door, it was opened slowly by Miguel himself, sleepy-eyed and partially dressed. Behind him, Garcia saw the naked body of a woman flash past the doorway and into another room.

"Eh, Señor Quinones, you are here very early. The tavern does not open for business until one o'clock." Miguel rubbed his eyes and yawned.

"Yes, yes, I know. I must talk with you, Miguel. It is urgent."

"Urgent?"

"*Sí!*"

"Come in, my friend. I shall make us some *cafe*."

"No, no, Miguel. No coffee. We must talk right away." Garcia paced in the small room

"What is the matter, Garcia? You act as though the devil is chasing you."

"That may well be, Miguel. It is Señora Albeniz. She is very upset with me."

Miguel laughed his robust laugh. "Ah, so it *is* the devil after you. I pity you, Garcia. She and that sister of hers are forces to be reckoned with." He paused and became serious. "What is it that is happening, Garcia?"

Garcia stopped pacing and sat at the small table by the window. "It is such a small thing, really. I have lost her donkey."

"Lost her donkey? Pedro? Señor, you have cut into the very heart of the old woman."

"I know, I know. That is why I need your help. We must retrieve Pedro. Do you have ropes?"

"Ropes? Why do you need ropes?"

"It is like this, Miguel. Pedro collapsed on the road from Barcelona and I thought he was dead. So, I pushed him over the edge of the mountain." Garcia did not want to mention Juan; that was another dilemma.

"I am confused. If Pedro is dead, why would you want to return him to Señora Albeniz?"

"Therein lies the problem, Miguel. Pedro is not dead."

Miguel's brow furrowed. "Why did you push him over the edge of the mountain if he was not dead?" Miguel began to laugh.

"Please, Miguel. You must treat this with the utmost importance. Pedro is, indeed, alive and stranded on a ledge just below the edge of the road. We must pull him up onto the roadway so I can return him to Señora Albeniz."

He glanced through the doorway to where he had seen the naked woman. "That is why we need the ropes."

"I see," said Miguel. "Let me dress and we will go to my cousin's house for some rope. Then the three of us will rescue Pedro."

"You are a good friend, Miguel. I shall wait outside for you."

Garcia left the small room and leaned against a post outside the door. In a few moments, coming from inside, he heard the rhythmic pounding of flesh on flesh along with groans and whimpers. "*Mi pequena puta*," he heard Miguel say in a hoarse whisper over and over again. Garcia did not move, but listened to the fury of their passionate lovemaking.

The door opened at last and Miguel appeared, fully dressed, his hair combed and a sheepish expression on his face. He shrugged, "Ah, Garcia, there is nothing like a woman in the morning." He said no more as they walked in the direction of his cousin's house.

Ropes in hand, the morning air was cool as Garcia, Miguel and Miguel's cousin, Paco, rounded the bend in the roadway that led to the spot where Pedro waited. They arrived at the edge of the roadway where the donkey had been shoved down the mountain, Garcia surveying the brush and rocks with a discerning eye.

"Stay here. I'll shimmy down the rocks to the ledge. Pedro waits for me there." Garcia braced his boot on the first rock and began to lower himself to the large pancake-shaped rock under which the donkey stood in safety. He leaned over the edge of the large rock only to see an empty space. There was no Pedro. *It was the gods again.*

The three men returned to Brasalia without the donkey. Garcia, despondent over the events of the past few days, retrieved his bicycle and pedaled past the police station, a sense of impending doom washing over him. Sleep. He needed sleep. Wearily, he pedaled to his cottage. When he arrived, he left his bicycle in the shed and walked to the barn, where he fell into the hay and slipped into a deep, dreamless sleep.

Darkness had settled over the mountains when Garcia opened his eyes. Where was he? At that moment, Tia licked his arm and butted her head into his shoulder. He reached out and rubbed her neck. "Ah, my Tia. My faithful Tia."

Under a full moon, he left the barn, pulled his bicycle from the shed and steered toward the village. Around him, he heard the call of a nightingale and the blowing of the mountain wind. *Why can I not find peace*? he thought, as he lifted his boots from the pedals and glided down the steep mountain road.

The darkness of the tavern was soothing. Garcia wanted nothing but whiskey. And more whiskey. His life as a contented pianist was over. It was just a matter of time before Señora Albeniz and her sister dug his grave and rolled him into it, much like he had rolled Pedro over the mountain's edge.

He said nothing when Miguel set a large glass of whiskey in front of him. He picked up the glass and felt relief as the fiery liquid ran down his throat.

The mysterious disappearance of Pedro devastated him. Had the wild dogs devoured him? Had he fallen down the mountainside into the depths below? The fact remained that he was still missing and, again, he must confront Señora Albeniz with the news.

The two men drank quietly for a long while. Hesitantly, Miguel spoke in a quiet voice.

"Garcia, we must talk of the spy." He leaned over the top of the bar. His earnest eyes swept the sad face of his friend. "Please, señor. It is important."

After another sip of whiskey, Garcia looked up at Miguel. "What is important?"

"The spy is important. I have it on good authority that Lope and Jorge are closing in on his capture. As we speak, they are setting a trap."

Miguel's voice lowered as he moved closer to Garcia. "We cannot let those two Nazis capture the spy." He let his words sink in while he poured himself another whiskey.

Garcia nodded and continued to drink in silence, his thoughts tumbling in his brain as if he had a delirious fever: the spy, Pedro, Señora Albeniz, Jordana, the Judge.

Garcia emptied his glass and motioned for more whiskey. Perhaps now was the time to tell Miguel of his encounter with the spy. He saw that Miguel's hand trembled as he lifted the bottle of whiskey and poured carefully into his glass. He leaned forward.

"My friend," he said, "I am in contact with the spy."

"What? You? How?" Miguel's eyes blazed with surprise.

"*Sí.* We had a long conversation in the mountains."

"A conversation? What of?"

"Mostly philosophical."

"Did he tell you his situation?"

"Somewhat. He is safe."

"Why is he here?"

Garcia emptied his glass for the second time and pushed it toward Miguel. "More whiskey," he said.

Miguel obliged, pouring the whiskey to the rim of the glass. "Go on, Garcia."

Garcia bowed his head and looked into the glass of whiskey set before him. He was flushed, an expression of pure helplessness covering his face.

A desperate man.

"I merely listened as he told me his opinions of the war, Franco, Hitler."

The ringing in Garcia's ears became louder; perhaps he had had enough of Miguel's whiskey. He stood abruptly and steadied himself.

"I must go home to sleep, my friend. The day has been torture for me. We will talk again tomorrow."

"But, Garcia, what about the spy?" Miguel watched as his friend walked unsteadily to the door of the tavern. Garcia merely shook his head, none of Miguel's questions answered, and stumbled into the night.

Above him, the moon cast light along the streets of the village and on the mountaintops in the distance. He stood a moment and breathed deeply, acknowledging the whiskey had caused a deep melancholy within him.

He knew he must recover what he had lost. Life was, indeed, like music; it must be composed by ear, compassion and instinct, constant with hope and serenity.

Somehow, he could not quite grasp the whole of it, only pieces here and there.

His gait was unsteady as he walked a few steps to Luis' white mule, which faithfully waited for her master. He patted the mule's nose and untied the reins. After two attempts, he climbed on top of her broad back and pressed his heels into the sides of the large animal, whispering into her ear, "*Mi casa.*"

The mule obeyed without hesitation and carried Garcia down the streets of Brasalia and up into the mountains where the wild dogs howled and the night birds called. They moved along in slow rhythm over the mountain road, Garcia hugging the mule's neck and whispering over and over, "*Mi casa. Mi casa.*"

The mule's slow plodding brought them to the fork that led to Luis' barn. There was no hesitation as Garcia pulled the reins in the opposite direction to his own cottage and again whispered, "*Mi casa, mi mula encantadora.*" *My house, my charming mule.*

At midnight, the mule and her rider arrived at the cottage where Garcia unceremoniously dropped from the mule's back onto the ground and watched as the white backside and the long tail slowly traversed back down the mountain. He lay unmoving, watching the night sky. Thin clouds passed over the moon. Finally, he stood and found his way into his cottage.

Inside, he undressed and did not hesitate to fall wearily into his bed where again he felt the warm body of Jordana. As he watched her, the soft moonlight spread across her face and revealed such serenity that tears formed in Garcia's eyes. Slowly, he reached out and pulled a lock of hair from her face.

Jordana opened her eyes and smiled at him, a knowing smile, a woman's smile. Hesitantly, she reached out and ran her fingers across his face and into his hair. The smell of her was as sweet as ripe mangoes, as desirable as the fragrance of the flowers that bloomed on the loquat trees. He ran his thumb across her lips, and felt her hips move slightly toward him in the moonlight.

His words were soft. "You must go home, Jordana."

Chapter Nineteen

The goats. Always the goats. In his half-sleep, Garcia heard the sound of their hooves prancing above him on the roof of the barn. He knew it was Tia. She had a way about her, like a woman, always wanting attention, becoming demonstrative if she didn't get it. He heard her bell ringing in quick bursts as he visualized her running from one end of the barn roof to the other, the ballerina goat jumping so high that the weight of her landing caused the barn to shake.

He grimaced as he stumbled from the pile of hay and entered the barnyard, his head aching from too much whiskey. From atop the roof, as suspected, Tia looked down at him with her pale blue eyes, eyes that wondered if he would shepherd her and her companions to a place covered in delectable brush.

"Ah, good morning, my pet. You have been a bad girl. Come down so I may reprimand you." Garcia walked toward the path that led to the hills, knowing the goats would follow. He saw the tall figure of Juan leaning against the trunk of a tree.

"Ah, the spy. *Buena manana a usted, espia,*" he said casually. *Good morning to you, spy.*

"I have been waiting for you since the moon rise." The spy's words chided the pianist.

"That would have been mostly all night, señor." Garcia stopped and looked into the face of the spy. "I have been wondering where you were. The village gossip tells me that Lope and Jorge are close to your capture. Then, they will stretch you over the rocks and let the buzzards eat you. "

The corners of Juan's mouth twitched with amusement. "No, Señor Quinones. I am a careful spy."

"That you must be, since Lope and Jorge have been searching for you for four days now. They are Nazis, you know."

The spy grinned and lit a cigarette, lazily blowing smoke into the early morning mist. "I am aware of Lope and Jorge, but I'm not concerned about two Nazis, amigo. I am more concerned about what is to come."

"What is to come? I do not follow you." Garcia scanned the face of the spy and was again struck by his air of mystery, an inscrutability that made one watchful. He was thin and agile and Garcia envisioned him running with the greatest of ease, leaping and twisting away from his enemies.

Juan took the cigarette from his mouth and flicked it into the rocks. He was quiet as he watched one of the goats trot to it and examine it with its tongue. Momentarily, he looked at Garcia. The spy's eyes burned with such intensity that Garcia almost turned away.

"What is to come?" said Juan. "What is to come is the Allied invasion."

Garcia's head snapped forward. "An invasion? Señor, I tremble for Europe and all those who fight in this war, but I am a piano teacher. What do piano teachers care of invasions?

Juan's face turned to steel, the muscles flexing hard in a way that forced his mouth into a grim line. It was as if another man materialized in front of Garcia. His eyes swallowed the young pianist like quicksand.

"It is my duty as an agent of British Intelligence to impart information to you that you must keep secret until your death."

"Death! I implore you to give me no information that results in my death, señor. You are insane to think I could assist you in any way!"

Garcia stiffened and raised his chin. "I ask you to leave, señor."

"That I cannot do, Señor Quinones." It was clear he had no intention of leaving.

He moved a step closer to Garcia. His words were solemn, an authoritarian edge in his voice. "You are hereby appointed as a member of British Intelligence and you are to carry out my orders without hesitation." He paused and then spoke with such gravity that Garcia held his breath. "If you do not comply, amigo, I shall have to kill you."

Garcia's intake of breath was so loud the goats turned and peered at him. *Kill me? The spy is going to kill me? Me, a piano teacher?*

On the rock-covered hillside, the hawks soared above them. Garcia spoke in a desperate whisper. "You have gone mad. You cannot expect this of me. I have nothing to give you."

Juan stood his ground. "Ah, but you do, my friend. You have much to give the Allies. Let me tell you in detail."

"No! I will not listen!" Garcia backed away.

"Your life depends on it, señor."

Moments passed while an anxious Garcia paced the hillside trail. "Mad. You are mad," he muttered, his heart pounding with fear-filled blood.

Finally, in a voice weak with capitulation, Garcia spoke. "I cannot deny the importance of this moment." He raised his hands in question. "Though all of this confuses me, I shall not throw my life away. You may tell me about this Allied invasion."

The men left the hillside and returned to the barnyard without speaking. They settled in the two wooden chairs that sat under the eaves of the barn. Garcia watched the sky while Juan placed a cigarette in his mouth and struck a match.

The spy spoke almost casually. "You know, Garcia, the deception in which you are about to participate would never have happened had you not become such a virtuoso pianist." He looked at Garcia and smiled. "But, of course, those who have heard you play are glad you did."

The spy became sober. "Our man at the German embassy in Barcelona has kept us well informed of the activities of Germany's number two in command. The German's desire to please his mistress is prevailing, to say the least. We expect Herr Himmler to visit you any day. He knows exactly where you are."

Garcia interrupted. "So the German finds me and I play for his mistress. How does that help you and the Allies?"

"Ah, good question, indeed. Let me ask you a question. Have you ever acted? You know, like a part in a play?"

"An actor? A play? No, never."

"Do you think you could play a role, a role in a great deception?" Juan smiled at Garcia and even winked.

"Señor , I am not a deceptive individual so it would be very difficult for me."

"I see." The spy rubbed his chin in thought. "What if you were groomed for the role? *His instructions from His Majesty's Secret Service came rushing forward: He's an artiste. Appeal to his creative side.*

Garcia became more confused. "I am not following you. What is this great deception of which you speak?"

"Ah, you are curious, no?"

"Of course, I am. My life is at stake here," said Garcia, a distinct edge to his words.

"I see you have not forgotten that."

"How could I? My life is very precious to me. You must continue – I am very anxious to know my future."

The spy leaned back in his chair. "The parachute."

"What about the parachute?"

"The boy, Eugenio, found the parachute and showed it to you. There was something else which the boy and his dog did not discover, but is important that it be found. You must return to the farm where the boy lives and together you will find what was there along with the parachute."

"My confusion continues. Explain."

"I did not parachute into Spain, señor . I entered through the Port of Barcelona. Another member of MI6 was dropped into Spain and buried the parachute and a document pouch with the intent that it be found. It was also planned that his parachute would be seen in the sky for a brief moment before he left your village and became lost among the citizens of Barcelona, thus beginning rumors of a spy in Brasalia. Part of the plan, you see.

"And, of course, as you know, the boy and his dog unwittingly found the parachute. Be that as it may, it is you who will find the document pouch that was buried near the parachute. This is where we must begin the first part of this…play."

Garcia's face was a mask of confusion. "There are two parts?"

"Yes, two parts. The first part is finding the document pouch." Juan continued, stifling a yawn. "The second part is giving the document pouch to Herr Himmler." He leaned back and stretched.

Garcia could not believe what he was hearing. This man, this so-called spy, was going to pitch him into the very depths of hell, all in the name of the Allies. And, here he was, a neutral citizen of Spain, not given to the inner workings of the war or, for that matter, British Intelligence, caught in a web of espionage.

"You are mad! It is clear to me that you have lost your senses. I cannot possibly do what you suggest. I refuse to participate in anything having to do with the Germans, most particularly Heinrich Himmler."

Juan waited while Garcia spouted all the angry words he could muster. He acknowledged to himself that part of the success of the Allied invasion depended on this one man, a man who was neither a spy for the Allies nor a German sympathizer. He was a simple piano teacher who happened to be sought out by the Reich Leader of the entire SS, a man subservient only to Adolf Hitler.

"Of course, you can. I will show you how. But, not today."

Garcia looked at the spy with a new-found curiosity, pondering what he had been told. "How do you know your information is reliable? Who is this man in whom you have placed so much trust?"

Juan flashed a surreptitious grin that promised a rare look inside the workings of MI6. His eyes, however, were cautious, as though he were unsure about divulging too much. Having made a decision, his shoulders relaxed. "His name is Blackeye. His code name, of course. Come to think of it, I don't think I even know his real name. Nonetheless, he and I have worked together for years. Quite a fellow. You will meet him in the next day or two. He plans to visit Brasalia."

"Ah, another spy in our little village." Garcia rolled his eyes.

Juan straightened his fedora and nodded.

The spy had known since the previous evening that the Germans planned to visit the pianist in a matter of days. Blackeye had met him and Luis mid-way between Barcelona and Brasalia. They discussed the details of the well-planned, extensive operation that involved many SIS agents, even the newly acquired apprentice spy, Garcia Quinones. The success of Juan's mission weighed heavily on the outcome of the Allies' impending invasion onto enemy-occupied soil and, hopefully, the demise of the German army.

The three men had met on the steps of a church and talked while they watched the pigeons chase imaginary specks of food.

"So you see, Juan," said Blackeye, "being the totally charming fellow I am, I engaged in conversation with Hedwig Potthast while she and Herr Himmler visited the German Embassy in Barcelona in February."

"What kind of conversation," Juan had asked, whose ears perked up when learning of Blackeye's encounter with the Germans.

"It was so comical. I knew the fraulein was not married to Herr Himmler, but she masqueraded as his wife despite the fact she was his mistress. And there he was, Himmler, introducing her to me as his wife, not his mistress, an indication of his elitist and supercilious view of rules, as if they did not apply to him."

Blackeye grinned at Juan. "I am so handsome, my friend, that even Himmler's mistress would chance a rendezvous with me."

He became serious as his voice lowered and he leaned into Juan.

"The two of them visited the German embassy one morning. Himmler left the fraulein in my care for a few moments while he conversed with a nearby officer. The fraulein casually mentioned that a friend had been a student of the Brussels Conservatory some years ago and she had heard he had left the Conservatory in the late thirties and moved near Barcelona.

"She said she dreamed of hearing this pianist play again, especially a piece by Beethoven, which was her most favorite. She said no one in the world could play like Garcia Quinones. She would *die* to hear him once again."

Therein, began the search for one Garcia Quinones. It also inspired the planting of a seed that would grow as part of the Allies' over-all secret operation: dispensing erroneous wartime battle plans to the enemy, namely the Third Reich's number two man, Heinrich Himmler, who they knew regularly dined with Hitler. MI6 had given the code name "farmer" to Himmler. Not many people knew the Reichsfuhrer was once an agriculturist and even raised chickens.

When Blackeye contacted his superior, the plan materialized quickly. MI6 knew every move Himmler made while in Barcelona. They knew he liked to holiday there while winter lingered in Germany.

He was due to return to Barcelona at the bidding of *Mrs. Himmler*, who, despite the enormous burden of the war on her dear Heinrich, cajoled him into returning to Barcelona so she could find the virtuoso pianist, Garcia Quinones.

Garcia watched the man walk away, picking his way over the rocks that led to the higher elevations of the Pyrenees. The spy turned and called out.

"The señorita must go. It is dangerous here."

Soon, Juan was a speck in the distance, the fedora a dark dot eventually lost among the rocks and trees. Garcia stared into the empty space as if questioning the very existence of the man. Had he imagined it all? Had he become delirious for some reason, like Señora Albeniz' sister? Had the wind blown through his head and taken with it his only means of reasonable thought? A parachute? A spy? A document pouch? Himmler? Allied invasion? MI6?

He sighed heavily, the weight of one quandary after another weighing on him like giant boulders, burying him, taking away the very air he breathed. He rose from his chair and headed down the road to Brasalia to retrieve his bicycle, his mind overwhelmed; his body exhausted.

His troubles seemed insurmountable. There was the matter of speaking with Señora Albeniz about her missing donkey.

What of Jordana? Her family? The posting of a reward for her alleged kidnapper? When he returned, he must speak to her about her return to her mother. Somehow, restitution had to be made and made quickly, before the noose was placed around his neck.

And Señora Lanzarote's husband, the Judge. Was gossipy Tomas telling the truth when he said the Judge was a jealous man? For that matter, did the Judge even know he existed?

He felt as though every step down the mountain was a step closer to his grave. He plodded on in a paralyzing stupor, his brain dull, refusing to acknowledge the truths before him; truths that, like the soldiers who marched on the other side of the mountains, were marching toward him.

To his left, Garcia heard the crunch of footsteps on the small rocks above him. He turned quickly and peered through the trees. The sound was close by. Again, he heard a step toward the roadway. He eased forward to the edge of the trees and saw slight movement in the thick shrubs. He felt fear, a prickling on his skin and a coldness in his chest that reminded him of when he was a child and he believed monsters hid beneath his bed. Too frozen to move, he simply stared into the woods and listened.

A small rock tumbled toward him like a warning, landing only a few feet from his boots. He stared at it. He wanted to run. He wanted to lift his feet and fly down the mountain, leaving behind whatever prowled the mountainside. Sweat ran down his back as he tried to lift his boot. Fear would not let him.

Another rock rolled down the mountainside. When it hit the roadway, Garcia broke into a run, his boots pounding the earth like pistons, gaining ground, faster than he had ever run before. *I am a coward*, he thought to himself, as he rounded the bend in the road that brought him to the village.

Chapter Twenty

Garcia skirted the corner of the police station, shrinking past the ominous reward poster and stealthily passing behind Blanka, who already squatted in the shade with her meat pies. Before he discussed the missing Pedro, he wanted his bicycle, which still leaned against the tree outside Miguel's tavern.

He passed Señora Lanzarote's house, glancing at the tall windows under the portico. Tomas sat beneath the olive tree, his hat pulled low on his forehead, obviously asleep. Continuing down Alia Street, he turned onto Communion Street where the Church of the Holy Father sat in the early morning sun and spoke of life and all its blessings.

He cringed when he saw Senor Zaragosa and his burro leaving the gates of the church. He felt he did not need another tongue-lashing from the old goat herder so he melted into the shadow of a nearby tree.

Only a few paces from the church, the tavern came into view. His bicycle was leaning against the tree. Luis Neruda's white mule was nowhere to be seen. Garcia pushed his bicycle back toward the police station where he knew the wrath of Señora Albeniz awaited him. He steeled himself for what was to come, consoling himself with the idea that, at least, she was not loco as was her sister. Mean, but not loco.

His eyes searched the shade where she squatted, her meat pies piled in a basket by her side, flies around her head and a smoldering cigarette in her yellow-brown fingers. She looked up at him and to his surprise, smiled. "Ah, Señor Quinones, I have been expecting you. When I awoke this morning, I found my Pedro waiting for me. It must have been very late when you returned him to his little home."

"Pedro?" Garcia's eyes darted around him. Was this a trap? Was Blanka's sister hiding somewhere waiting to pounce upon him? Was Blanka's news a tactic to keep him in conversation until her sister could tie him up and take him back to the black pot where she would boil him to nothing?

Again, "Pedro?"

"*Sí.* Pedro. He tells me you whispered sweet words into his ears and he likes you very much, señor." The old woman cackled, her eyes bright with happiness. Indeed, her Pedro must have returned.

"Ah, Señora Albeniz, it pleases me to hear it." Garcia moved closer, a little wary, but relieved. "He is a good donkey. In fact, I consider him the finest donkey in all of Catalonia."

Señora Albeniz laughed and nodded her whiskered chin. "Now, all you need to do is bring me my scallops." She scrutinized Garcia's face, looking for some kind of acknowledgement that, indeed, he had not obtained the delicious scallops she so desired.

Garcia faltered. His relief at hearing of the return of Pedro was short-lived; now, in the midst of his relief, he was again reminded that he must bring Blanka her beloved scallops. Would his agony never end? He looked over his shoulder, again wondering if the loco sister lurked nearby.

"Ah, the scallops," he said. He hesitated. Another trip to Barcelona? Atop Pedro? His mind raced for an answer that would appease her. He saw her watching him, knowing he dare not tell her *no.*

The thought of another trek to the sea was unthinkable; yet, he knew it was the only way. He looked down at the basket where flies covered the piece of cloth that covered her meat pies. "But, of course, since the wild animals stole your wonderful scallops, they must be replaced."

He paused. "I shall journey next week to Barcelona." Then, as if the devil had placed himself on Garcia's tongue and moved it around to ensure his punishment, he said, "And I shall take you with me, Señora Albeniz."

The Señora threw her head back and squealed with delight. "Bless you, Señor Quinones. Bless you."

Garcia turned away, cringing. *Strike me dead. Throw my body out for the buzzards and wild dogs. I shall find no peace in this life. I beg you, end my misery.*

Beneath a cloudy sky, with the wind blowing briskly across the Pyrenees, a disheartened Garcia pedaled his bicycle back to the tavern. Only a whiskey could diminish his anxiety. Again, he leaned his bicycle against a tree and entered the dark tavern.

"Ah, Garcia. I have been thinking about you." Miguel called across the room. He automatically reached for the brown bottle and poured his friend a drink.

"You must come and sit a while. We have much to talk about." Miguel leaned across the bar and looked at his friend, detecting the apprehension in his face.

"Ah, amigo, it is true. We must talk. But, first, let us drink a whiskey together." With that, Miguel poured himself a glass and moved outside the bar to sit with his friend.

"I am doomed," he began. "I am to help the spy. If I don't, he will kill me."

"*Kill you*?"

"*Si.*" Garcia snapped his fingers. "Just like that." He drank long and set his glass on the bar, giving Miguel a piteous look, his dark eyes unwavering.

Miguel studied Garcia's face for a long moment before he spoke, his words resigned, holding no ambiguity. "It's simple, then. You must help the spy."

In the dark of the tavern, it seemed as if the air between them was laden with a palpable perdition. The war had reared its ugly head in their lovely village and, no matter how gentle their hearts or kind their souls, life would never be the same. Garcia considered it. Had he known all along that he would do exactly as the spy had asked? His entire life he had believed his destiny had been the piano - the notes, the composition of beautiful music, the joy of eighty-eight keys, from treble to bass, filling his life. There was no incongruity in that.

And yet, here he was. A pianist turned spy. Perhaps the same allegiance he felt for his music had transformed itself into a man who had become a spy. A patriot in memory of his father; perhaps for himself. One thing was very clear; his destiny had changed.

He looked at Miguel as he lifted his glass to his lips. His words were solemn. "Of course, I will help the spy."

By the time Garcia left the tavern, the sky had darkened and the same clouds he had seen earlier, black like billows of coal dust, galloped across the sky. He guided his bicycle onto the street and pedaled like a man being chased by hornets toward home, the wind gusting as if to blow him off the road. His leg muscles burned as he pushed into the wind, up the incline that led to the barn. And, all for his goats, the little divas who disliked rain and wind and would be clamoring for the safety of their barn at the first lightning strike.

At the end of the cottage lane, the unforgiving rain began to pelt him like bullets from a gun, hard, large drops that were as cold as ice. In minutes, he was soaked to his skin. He threw his bicycle to the ground and ran to where his little goats huddled at the barn door.

Gratefully, they ran inside, anxiously bleating and switching their little tails. His Tia was the last to enter. Her belly swollen, she turned and looked at him with her soft blue eyes. *Soon. Soon I will kid. You must stay near.* He patted her head as if in reply. Soothingly, he spoke to her. "You must not worry, Tia. I will be here for you."

From the barn, he ran to the cottage door. Behind him, lightning, writhing like a snake, lit the sky, followed by fierce thunder that boomed like cannons across the mountains. Shaking from cold, he stepped inside and looked across the room where he saw the flames of a small fire, its warmth a welcome as he shivered in his wet clothes. Jordana rushed to him with a towel and dried his face. He smelled her hair, the fragrance of lavender.

Her delicate fingers unbuttoned his wet shirt and pulled it from his body to place it beside the fire. When she reached for the button at the top of his pants, Garcia caught his breath. He watched her tiny fingers move slowly to each button until she was able to pull the wet trousers down his legs and place them by his dripping shirt.

Her face, iridescent and glistening as if covered in morning dew, held a slight smile. She knelt and pulled down his underclothing and left him standing naked in front of her. His body shivered from the cold, but the chill did not keep him from becoming fully aroused in front of the beautiful señorita. Quickly, he placed the towel in front of him.

He stood a moment before backing away from her. His eyes were pleading as he looked into her questioning face. "You must return to your family, Jordana."

The room stilled as Jordana's black eyes flashed with anger. "Return to my family? Return, only to be sent away to marry an old man I do not even know. I cannot do this." Tears filled her eyes as she hung her head. "I shall run away."

Garcia remained still, speaking softly. "But you have run away. You are here."

She lifted her face and looked at him for a long moment, a thousand thoughts expressed in the quivering lips and wet cheeks. "I shall run away from here."

Garcia moved a step closer. "From here? But, where would you go?"

"There is no place to go. I shall just go. Maybe to Barcelona."

"To Barcelona? That is impossible, Jordana. You cannot subject yourself to the dangers of the journey or to the troubles that may befall you. You must not."

Garcia saw the deep intake of breath. Lifting her chin, she seemed to become taller. She looked at him with such a resolute stare that he faltered.

"Señor Quinones, while I value your concern for my safety, it is I and I alone who carry the responsibility of what I do and where I go."

The two looked at each other a long while. At last, Garcia, searching his mind for words, spoke.

"Señorita, it is my concern for you that will allow you to stay." He turned and looked at the sheets of rain beating against the window. "We must, however, at some time in the very near future, speak with your family." Slowly, he pulled on dry underclothing and a pair of heavy cotton pants.

He lingered for a moment, listening to the rain beat upon the cottage roof. He did not want to tell her it was dangerous for her to stay at his cottage. Yet, he could not find the words to tell her that his life had changed, that he was no longer an innocent pianist who herded goats.

Chapter Twenty-One

The winds blew from the Mediterranean and brought with them a slight taste of the sea. The crisp air carried the sound of bells from the Church of the Holy Father, where Father Eduardo held Sunday mass. Garcia's ears rejoiced at the sound of the echoing bells. He tilted his head and clung to every melodious note.

His place of solitude on this particular morning was a few meters behind his old barn, under a beech tree, where he watched the March sun ease over the mountains. His goats grazed a half kilometer above him, their bells tinkling softly. Occasionally, the billy bleated loudly, proclaiming his dominance over his few nannies.

Garcia looked up to the peaks, wondering if his sensitive ears could hear the sounds of war, the bombs that destroyed cities and took away the lives of the innocent – those who wanted only to milk their cows and feed their children.

He closed his eyes and heard the wind, but no marching footsteps of Nazi soldiers, nor the report of their rifles. He breathed deeply, wanting to lift himself away from the turmoil of his life and into a place of no uncertainties.

When he opened his eyes, he saw movement in the trees above him, near his goats. He remained still and watched as two figures maneuvered their way around rocks down the mountain. After only a few moments, Juan's familiar fedora came into view. Garcia breathed easier and waited for the spy, wondering who his companion was.

"Garcia," Juan called. "Your goats tell me you are sleeping under a tree and, alas, you are!" The spy laughed and removed his hat as he sat under the tree alongside Garcia. Behind him, his companion remained standing, aloof in an immaculate white suit too fine for him to sit on the ground. He seemed out of place, too impeccably dressed to be standing on the side of a mountain. Tilted to one side, a Panama hat sat on top of his wavy black hair. The navy silk scarf around his neck fanned in the morning breezes.

"Garcia, let me introduce you to Blackeye, my trustworthy source at the German Embassy."

Garcia looked up at the stocky figure whose frame was silhouetted by the bright sun behind him. *So that's who he is, the other spy. The spy who said he had spoken with Himmler's mistress. The spy who said the mistress' name was Hedwig Potthast. The spy Hedwig told she would die to hear Garcia Quinones play again. How utterly convenient*, thought Garcia. *A chance meeting with the mistress of Heinrich Himmler who just happened to mention Garcia Quinones' name.*

"Señor," Garcia nodded.

The white-clad figure smiled. A Hollywood smile, the kind Garcia had seen at his concerts in Paris and London. "It is my pleasure to meet you, Señor Quinones. Juan tells me you two have joined forces against the Nazis."

Garcia looked at Juan. "Is that so?"

"But, of course, Garcia. Blackeye is an integral part of our mission and comes with important information."

Garcia turned his eyes from Juan to stare at Blackeye. He saw his manicured nails, a diamond ring on his little finger. He compared him to Juan, Juan's worn fedora, tattered leather jacket and scuffed boots. He became uneasy.

"And what is this important information?" Garcia asked, not moving from the shade of the tree.

Blackeye removed his Panama and squatted down beside Juan. "The Germans. They have sent six divisions and four Panzer groups to Pas de Calais, along with field hospitals and supply trains. This information tells us they believe the Allies will land at Calais – all this based on the German's belief that a large invasion force is being amassed across the English Channel at Kent – an illusion, of course. The Allies' implementation of one of the greatest deceptions in the war has placed an entire bogus military build-up, headed by Patton, on the Dover coast.

"However, the Germans vacillate between two possible landings. The intelligence you pass to Himmler will further enhance the German's belief that the invasion will be at Calais. If you are successful in the passing of this bogus intelligence, the Germans will send even more troops and artillery to Calais and away from the intended landing spot."

Garcia never took his eyes away from Blackeye – his expression hardened into deep skepticism. "How do you know what the Germans are thinking...and doing?"

Blackeye looked at Juan and shrugged. "How do I know? I am a spy. That's what spies do – gather information." He seemed irritated.

Juan cleared his throat. "Garcia, it is Blackeye's duty to report to me what he hears at the German Embassy. Not only at the Embassy, but in all of Barcelona. Let's just say he is a social man who mixes well with others."

Garcia's lips eased into a smirk. "So he eavesdrops?" Garcia raised his eyebrows. "Snoops?"

Juan pulled a cigarette from his pocket and tapped it on his boot. "Yes. Snoops."

"How credible can his information be if he acquires it by snooping?" Garcia asked, while examining Blackeye's fancy shoes.

Juan sighed heavily. "Garcia, your caution is good. You must, however, rely on our judgment. I simply ask for your trust."

Garcia continued to stare at Blackeye's shoes. They were full-brogue Spectators, made of fine leather, brown and white and not a speck of dirt on them. Finally, he looked at Juan. "Trust?" he said softly. "I have no choice but to trust."

Both men watched Garcia as he rose from his spot under the tree and brushed off his pants.

Garcia placed his straw hat firmly on his head and looked at Blackeye. "So, I am important to the mission, you say?"

Blackeye stood and became eye level with Garcia. His handsome face seemed to be mocking him, looking as if he were amused by Garcia's questions. Blackeye stole a quick look at Juan. "The success of your involvement is crucial to the success of the Allied invasion."

"I see." Garcia looked at Juan and nodded, then back to Blackeye. "I do not plan to stumble in this game we are playing." He paused. "You know, this spy game."

Blackeye nodded. "It is not a game; your life may be endangered."

"So I am told." He turned to Juan and sent a look of dutiful compliance.

His eyes again fell to Blackeye's brown and white shoes.

The two men left Garcia standing under the beech tree and made their way up the mountain, back to Juan's hidden camp.

"He's trouble," said Blackeye.

"Trouble? What makes you say that?"

"He's smarter than you think he is."

"It is good that he is intelligent. How else could he perform as he must? Meet with the Germans? Remain credible?"

Blackeye walked without answering. Finally, he stopped and turned to Juan. "He will fail us."

Chapter Twenty-Two

In the east of the city, near the docks, Blackeye weaved through the crowd at *Estació de Franca*, Barcelona's grand train station, on the avenue *Marquès de l'Argentera*, his white linen suit a sharp contrast to the dark fabric of war that raged north across the Pyrenees. Casual and unconcerned with the events around him, he seemed preoccupied. But, that wasn't true – he was focused and deliberate as he walked along the boardwalk where the arriving trains lined the tracks.

His eyes searched the throngs of people and spotted the navy blue hat he'd been searching for – a smooth velvet hat resting on the head of a very tall woman who stood impassively at the entrance of a small café.

From his position near the tracks, he could see her thin body and the dark leather handbag slung over her shoulder. A signal. She had not been followed. Still, he hesitated and scoured the crowd, his eyes darting from face to face and finally back to the tall woman. She seemed at ease as she lifted her hand and brushed a lock of hair from her shoulder. Her hair was her best feature. Thick and coarse, it framed her face like the winter pelage of a Russian sable. Blackeye smiled to himself and walked toward the café.

She saw him immediately and smiled. When she turned and walked into the café, he followed, his eyes still searching for something or someone out of the ordinary.

"Ah, the train was on time."

"Yes, to my delight." Her lips were full. She had painted them a deep claret, a color that contrasted sharply with her pale, poreless skin.

The waiter came and took their order for coffee and Danish. She removed her hat and placed it on a chair beside her. "I've missed you."

Blackeye reached across the table and touched her hand. "That pleases me."

He pulled back his hand and leaned closer. "Things are going as planned. Just a few details to handle."

"Good. No problems?"

"None that I can see. He doesn't suspect anything – why should he – I pose no threat to him."

Their conversation stilled as the coffee and pastry were placed on their small table. When the waiter left, Blackeye continued, his voice just above a whisper. "Of course, we must be cautious. We are dealing with a very cunning man. You know very well his reputation."

"You must be careful."

"But, of course." Blackeye smiled, his eyes washing over her face. "Shall we go? I've made reservations at the Hotel Duquesa de Cordona."

Chapter Twenty-Three

R ain began well before daylight on Monday morning. Not a gentle rain, but a blowing, howling rain that beat upon the roof of the barn like marching soldiers. Lightning cracked from one peak to the other and thunder rattled the windows and shook the small cottage where Jordana lay sleeping.

Garcia watched the rain from the barn door. The goats huddled behind him, knowing their master would dare not take them to their brush today. In only a few long leaps, Garcia ran from the barn to the cottage where he stood in the dark and listened to the rain as it ran from the pitched roof and splashed to the ground below. Only a few feet away, Jordana slept on.

He lit a candle and found his way to the corner where his piano waited. For a long while, he simply stared at the woolen blanket before he pushed it back and gently touched a key. He wondered if pianos could be lonely, if they wept when no one played them. When he sat down on the bench that overflowed with his sheet music, he was soothed as though a balm had been poured over him and healed his every hurt.

From the universe, he thought he heard voices. Yes, they were far away, but he heard them. *Play, Garcia. Play your beautiful music and be happy again.*

Garcia smiled to himself. *Happy again? Easier said than done.* He lifted his hands and placed them on the keys. They warmed from his touch, then spoke to him. *Play.*

Hesitantly, he placed his thumb and index finger on the C and E notes, the sound lifting high, suspended until his little finger found the A note. All at once Liszt's *Eleventh Hungarian Rhapsody* filled the cottage, shutting out the sound of the rain, the thunder, the blustering wind. Garcia laughed out loud – Liszt was the master today, not the Germans nor the war. And he played on.

At last, with his heart pounding, Garcia's hands stilled. He bowed his head and waited until his breathing quieted. *I cannot play for the Germans. The ears of devils do not deserve to hear beautiful music.*

Chapter Twenty-Four

On Tuesday morning, after leading his goats to a place high in the mountains, Garcia returned to his cottage. He pumped air into his bicycle tires and rode slowly down the mountain to Brasalia, the sun warming his back and the mountain breeze blowing across his face. Señora Lanzarote was waiting for him in her beautiful yellow stone house on Alia Street. He felt she would play for him as she had never played before; that she had found solace in her music, a comfort, an easing of the loneliness in her life.

When he arrived, Tomas was sitting on the wide steps smoking a cigarillo. Garcia watched the smoke swirl from his mouth in little wisps that settled in the crevices of his skin. He hoped the old man would not gossip and tell him of his impending demise at the hands of the Judge.

"*Buenos dias*, Tomas," he said as he leaned his bicycle against the side of the steps and walked onto the portico. "It is a beautiful day, no?"

"That it is, Señor Quinones. That it is." Tomas turned and looked up at Garcia. "She waits for you inside, amigo. I feel she has waited for you all week." He grinned at Garcia, his eyes narrowing. Garcia ignored him and knocked on the wooden door.

It opened at once and Pipeto, the housemaid, welcomed him inside. As always, he brushed his boots free of any dirt and walked to the red brocade chair that waited for him. Señora Lanzarote was seated at the piano, her back erect, her head in profile. Unbelievably, she turned and smiled at him. He nodded and smiled in return, removed his hat and sat in his designated chair. She remained still, but watched him with the black eyes he knew so well.

"Señor Quinones. I hope you are well."

"Indeed, señora. And you?" Garcia noticed a distinct warmth that caused a pinkness in her cheeks, a brightness in her eyes. It was as if she were another person. He wondered where the cold and rebuking woman of the past had gone.

"I am very well, señor. I have practiced long this past week and am ready for your instruction."

Garcia nodded and looked down at her hands. No longer were they white with cold, but pink and alive and ready to perform. "And, I am so pleased that…"

At that moment, Garcia hesitated. He heard a disturbance in the street and rose to look out the window, where he saw a cream-colored Packard limousine, the long hood projecting out as if it were a turret on a tank. Four erect headlights and a massive chrome grill made it appear quite ominous, weighted at the front.

I know this car. Sleek and as beautiful as the chariot of a king, it had once belonged to the King of Spain. His apprehension mounting, he observed a heinous detail that sent his heart pounding. The two flags above the headlights were emblazoned with the German swastika, the insignia of the Third Reich.

Before he could move, he watched four German soldiers leave the military jeep that followed the limousine and bound up the steps of Señora Lanzarote's house. He froze in place as they pushed open the heavy wooden door without knocking, the sound of their boots on the stone floor as threatening as the resonance of cannon fire. In an instant, he heard the prophetic words of the spy: *you will receive a visit from the Reichsfuhrer, the number two man in Germany, subservient only to Adolf Hitler.*

Garcia turned to see Señora Lanzarote rise from the piano in anger.

"How dare you enter my home uninvited," she shouted. Moving toward the Germans as if protecting her home and all within, she swung her arm toward the door. "Leave at once!"

A German officer, dressed in full regalia, braids and insignia on every part of his tunic, walked toward the señora and removed his hat. He studied her through his small spectacles as if she were a specimen in a test tube. "My apologies, Señora Lanzarote. Let me introduce myself. I am Heinrich Himmler, an officer of Germany's Third Reich."

When she did not respond, he turned to Garcia. "Señor Quinones." He smiled, his eyes cold and calculating. Then, back to Señora Lanzarote. "Please do not let us disturb you, señora. I am here to have a word with Señor Quinones." He bowed slightly and walked toward Garcia, his hand resting on the pistol that protruded from the black leather holster on his belt. He stopped just a few feet away.

"Señor Quinones, I bring you greetings from Hedwig Potthast." The German looked intently at Garcia.

"Hedwig Potthast? You will have to refresh my memory, Herr Himmler." He ignored the German's stare and walked casually to the red brocade chair and sat down, crossing his legs. Perhaps he was an actor after all; there was no outward sign that terror ravaged his body like a flesh-eating bacteria.

The German's irritation was obvious. "I repeat, Señor Quinones. Fraulein Hedwig Potthast. Of Brussels. Where you trained at the Conservatory. A close friend of one of your classmates."

"Hedwig Potthast? The Conservatory? Perhaps." Garcia left the red brocade chair and walked deliberately to the tall windows, his back to the Reichsfuhrer. He tapped his boot on the stone floor as if in deep thought. Quickly, he snapped his fingers and turned dramatically. "But, of course. Hedwig Potthast. She also played, but not as a student of the Conservatory. The violin if I recall."

"*Nein, nein, Sie tauschen.* "*Sie spielt die Harfe*! The harp! The harp!"

"Ah, it comes to me now. Hedwig Potthast. Plump, rather plain woman?" Garcia smiled his handsome, charming smile as he looked across at Himmler, who watched him in funereal solemnity. Indeed, if looks could kill, he would be dead.

The German stiffened. Grim-faced, he stared at Garcia. When he expelled his breath, his voice was hardly above a whisper.

"Nein, Señor Quinones. *Sie ist nicht prall, noch ist sie plain.*" With his last word, his small chin dipped low while his eyes peered over his spectacles. "She is neither plump, nor is she plain."

Garcia pondered this.

"Ah, of course, now I remember. She is the beautiful Hedwig of Brussels. How could I forget her lovely hands as they played the harp?" Garcia smiled widely at the German. "My apologies to you, Herr Himmler."

Himmler's face softened slightly. "Hedwig would like to hear you play. She remembers your brilliant compositions from the Conservatory. We shall return on Saturday. At three o'clock." He half-turned toward Señora Lanzarote who, pale and shaken, had almost disappeared into the shadows of the music room. "*Unser kleines* – he paused, then continued through unsmiling lips. "Our little recital shall be here at your home, Señora Lanzarote. With your permission, of course."

Without waiting for a reply, the Reichsfuhrer left the house as quickly as he had arrived. He hesitated at the front balustrade and turned abruptly toward them, the ominous death-gray uniform of the Third Reich proclaiming his superiority. "*Heil Hitler*," he shouted, clicked his heels and strutted to his waiting car.

Rosina stared at the closed door for a long moment before she turned and faced Garcia. "I don't know what is happening." Her voice broke. "Germans. Germans in my home."

Garcia placed a reassuring hand on the señora's shoulder while he watched through the window as the Germans left the village square, taking with them the last remaining morsel of his inner peace. When he turned to the señora, he began to tremble. She stared at him with such loathing that he wanted to shrivel into nothing. When she spoke, her voice was ice. "You may not play for the Germans in my house."

Garcia stepped down from the portico and into Señora Lanzarote's courtyard. The sky was still, as though a storm had passed, taking with it every breath of life-sustaining air. He paused and looked up and down the streets of Brasalia. Somewhat dazed, he tried to calm himself, stunned that the señora would have no part of the Germans and the recital that was to be an integral part of MI6's misison.

His encounter with the Germans had left him cold with fear. In no way could he diminish the importance of what had just happened. The war and the Germans were no longer obscure apparitions that had only occasionally flashed across his mind while he played his piano and herded his goats. He, Garcia Quinones, had spoken to the Third Reich's second-in-command as if he were a street vendor. What possessed him to be so cavalier, he did not know. What was clear to him was the fact Himmler would return on Saturday as promised and, at that time, Garcia would have to give the performance of his lifetime; not only as a pianist, but as a spy, one who had been recruited in a matter of moments on a mountain hillside by a member of Britain's infamous military intelligence.

But, how could he conduct a recital for the Reichsfuhrer if Señora Lanzarote refused to allow Germans in her home? Garcia saw the Allied mission to pass bogus intelligence to the Germans fade into failure.

And the spy. Juan. Was that his real name? Or one devised simply for conversation. *Infierno y condenacion*! *Hell and damnation*! He was trapped, lashed to the Allies' conspiracy simply because he played the piano.

Garcia glanced to a corner of the courtyard where, in the deep shade of a mango tree, he saw the orange spurt of a match flame. It was Tomas. The old man seemed to be cowering as he sat on his heels, puffing on a cigarette.

"Amigo, you are hiding?" Garcia walked to the hidden spot and looked down at Señora Lanzarote's *manitos*.

"I am not hiding. Can you not see that I am smoking a cigarette?"

"I've never seen you huddled in a dark corner smoking." Garcia hesitated a moment and then smiled at the old man. "The Germans have gone."

Tomas' eyes widened. "I do not like these Germans."

"Why is that?"

"They are smoldering with evil."

"How do you know?"

"It is very apparent to me, señor. In their eyes."

"In their eyes? What do you see in their eyes?" Garcia squatted down in front of Tomas. Tomas was afraid of nothing. Yet, the arrival of the Germans had spooked him.

"They are animals, like the *bestias* that roam the mountains." Tomas' face twisted in anger as he spat the words. He then looked at Garcia, his face transforming into a child-like softness. "It is true. I am afraid of the Germans, amigo."

Garcia said nothing as he stood and leaned against the courtyard wall, watching the old man. He saw Tomas' gnarled fingers tremble around his cigarette.

The old man continued with mounting resignation. "Señor Garcia, when the Germans came, they asked me if I knew where the pianist lived. I told them. But, I also told them you were over there, in the señora's house. I saw them push open the door without knocking. I apologize, amigo, if I did the wrong thing."

The humility Garcia saw in the old man was rare, as though he had recently dined with angels who had admonished him for his gruffness and enticed him to be more kind. It was quite apparent the old man had been alarmed by the arrival of the Germans, their intimidating speech, their imposing uniforms, the shiny black boots they wore; but, most of all, the imposing pistols that sat menacingly on their hips. "No need to be anxious, Tomas. We are safe here."

Tomas spat. "Not even the Church of the Holy Father will survive the Germans, Señor Quinones. It is just a matter of time before their armies swarm the entire continent." With difficulty, the old man stood. "I shall go home and drink whiskey." He walked a few steps. "It is the only thing I can do now."

Garcia watched as Tomas shuffled away. It was possible the old man's prophecy was correct. Hitler boasted of his greatness to the Spanish dictator, but he detested Franco and Franco's dominion over Spain and its people. There was no doubt that Spain was as vulnerable as Poland, as Belgium, as France, and all the other countries that had been crushed by the mighty Third Reich.

Chapter Twenty-Five

Juan shifted in his hiding place on the mountainside. His little nest, concave and snug, provided him with a perfect vantage point from which to observe the activities of the village.

He had seen the Germans arrive, the haunting gray of their uniforms a warning, perhaps even a prophecy: we will rule the world. They walked across the village square toward the Lanzarote hacienda, almost comical in their mannerisms. They pranced like peacocks, thinking themselves untouchable, invincible, prone to the belief that they were protected by the Aryan gods who proclaimed them the purist of the pure.

And, here he was, a master spy, watching their every move, recording it in his mind as though it were a photograph, and realizing a rifle aimed at the breast of dear Heinrich could mean the end of Germany's Reich Leader of the SS. There was, however, a much larger plan in play; one that, unfortunately, needed the presence of the repugnant German.

Next to him in his mountainside observatory, Luis Neruda watched silently as he, too, thought of sending a well-aimed bullet into the head of Heinrich Himmler. "There they go, the bastards. I shall ask God to guide the bullet, eh?" His finger on the trigger, Luis placed Himmler's head in his sights.

"His time will come. But for us, his purpose has yet to be fulfilled. Sadly, we must wait." *Though it will be difficult,* thought Juan, as he placed his binoculars next to him and lit a cigarette. It gave him a small pleasure to imagine his own gun aimed at Himmler, a slow squeeze of the trigger, a bullet bursting the skull. His index finger twitched.

"That is what you do best, eh? Waiting? It seems much of your life has been waiting and watching. You have been a spy since the beginning of time. I recall our first mission together. Munich?"

Juan placed the cigarette in his mouth and again lifted the binoculars. One last look at the departing Packard. "Yes, Munich. You were another Spanish patriot MI6 had trained. We Catalonians get around, don't we?"

A hawk screeched overhead and momentarily both men looked up and watched it soar across the hills toward the west into the lowering sun.

"I befriended a German who happened to be a spy. He was stupid and thought he could cultivate me as a spy for Germany. He taught me many things, but he did not teach me to love Hitler. I must admit he did teach me a lot about the game of espionage, though."

Juan leaned forward from his resting place and placed his binoculars back into their case and attached it to his belt. He struck a match and placed the flame at the end of another cigarette. He knew he smoked too much. The set of his jaw was firm while his eyes searched the horizon as though an army of enemy lurked behind every rock and he must kill them all.

"And it is because you are a spy that you are here in this little village in Spain." It was more of a statement than a question as Luis looked at Juan.

Juan shifted where he could see Luis' face. "It is here that we may turn the tide of the war, my friend." Both men looked up into the March sky when they heard the drone of engines. Lancasters. British bombers. A formation of six heading perhaps to Hauté-Savoie to help the Maquis, the guerrilla bands of the French Resistance. "We shall see how our piano friend performs in his new position." He laughed quietly and picked up a pebble and threw it down the mountain where it bounced from rock to rock.

Juan pulled his binoculars from their case and saw Garcia step from the portico of Señora Lanzarote's house. He held him in his sight and watched while the pianist's eyes roamed the village square, then lifted into the Spanish skies, seeming to focus on passing clouds that raced toward the sea. Juan recognized he had formed an affinity for the pianist in just a few short weeks, weeks he had spent gathering information on this man of thirty-six who, as it turned out, had been groomed for espionage without the slightest hesitation.

Next to Juan, Luis Neruda leaned forward.

"There he goes. I think I shall take the back road down the mountain to the tavern. I have a feeling our friend will need a whiskey after his encounter with the Germans."

Juan watched Luis descend the mountain as he himself left the large rock and melted into the trees. Still, his thoughts remained on Garcia. He had no qualms about Garcia's capabilities as a newly-made spy, but, he also knew the Germans. They were relentless and, if they suspected any falsehood in Garcia's performance, they would shoot him on the spot.

Chapter Twenty-Six

Shaken, Garcia left Alia Street and walked to the tavern though it was barely one o'clock. Upon his arrival, he saw the white mule and wondered if Luis had even missed his companion from the night before. It would not surprise him if the mule had obediently returned to the tavern and waited late into the night for her master.

Miguel poured generously into Garcia's glass and also into his own. "Another tortuous day for you, Garcia?"

"*Sí*. More tortuous than you can imagine." Garcia drank from his glass and then turned toward the dark corner and watched as Luis poured from the bottle on his table. The man's face sat in shadow on a thick neck and wide shoulders. Just once, Garcia thought, I'd like to see the man in the daylight, look into his eyes and see if, indeed, he has a soul. It occurred to him that he had never heard him speak, even after all these years. The man was mysterious, leaving Brasalia months at a time and returning to drink whiskey in Miguel's tavern. But, Garcia was more curious about Luis' relationship with the spy. A distant relative, the spy had said.

Miguel moved closer to Garcia and spoke in a voice laden with curiosity. "So, I see you are not dead."

Garcia raised his eyebrows in question. "Dead?"

"*Sí*, my friend. The spy was going to kill you."

"Only if I did not cooperate," he said and then paused to watch Luis again. He turned his eyes back to Miguel. "Because I value my life, *amigo*, I will cooperate."

"I am relieved." Miguel laughed and refilled Garcia's glass.

At the sound of the heavy wooden door opening, the two men looked up. They watched Lope and Jorge enter the tavern and lumber to their usual table, glancing sourly at Garcia and Miguel.

Lope pounded his fist on the table. "Whiskey."

Jorge repeated. "Whiskey."

Miguel looked over at Garcia and smiled. "I see our spy hunters have returned, amigo." Casually, he turned, picked up two glasses, the brown bottle of whiskey from Barcelona and walked unhurriedly to the table where the two Spaniards- turned- Nazis sat, watching Miguel with obvious contempt.

Miguel said nothing as he poured the smooth gold liquid into their glasses. Lope reached out and placed an enormous hand on the bottle. "Leave it"

Miguel nodded and returned to the bar where he glanced at Garcia. A message that said *beware*.

The tavern fell into an intense quiet, a silence that triggered an anxiety in both Garcia and Miguel as they sipped their whiskey.

Lope stretched out his long, heavy legs and stared menacingly at Garcia. He refilled his glass and yelled across the room, venom in his words.

"My political friend drinks whiskey tonight. Is there a celebration of some kind?" he taunted.

Garcia ignored him and pushed his glass toward Miguel. "I am finished, *amigo*. I shall see you tomorrow. My goats await me on the mountainside."

Miguel nodded. "*Manana*."

Garcia felt Lope's hot breath on his neck before he saw him, his body becoming one long shiver as he turned and again was face to face with the brute. He saw the same long dark hairs across his eyebrows, the same dirt-filled crevices on his face and, on his jutting chin, the same knife-inflicted scar. He smelled whiskey mixed with Lope's putrid breath. His stomach lurched.

Though the same height as Garcia—his bulkiness could smother a man into submission. He should have sent Garcia into a place filled with unfathomable fear. Yet, the pianist, tall and lean with fragile hands that played luminous ivory keys with the gentleness of a butterfly's wings, did not flinch. Rather, he moved closer to the man he knew was capable of killing him with one blow.

"I am celebrating my love òf Spain, *amigo*. My appreciation of our freedoms."

Then, the most antagonistic words floating in the universe slipped past his lips.

"Of course, my biggest hope is for the eventual demise of the Nazis armies and, of course, *el bastardo*, Adolf Hitler. Then, the celebration of all celebrations." Why Garcia smiled he did not know. And that was all it took for the *el gigante* to lift Garcia's body and sling it across the room with amazing ease.

Garcia's body slid into the chairs surrounding a table and remained there. In no hurry, Lope walked over and stood above him, watching as Garcia lay on the floor, a trickle of blood at the corner of his eye, his breathing shallow.

Slowly, Lope pulled a long knife from his belt. "Ah, Señor Quinones, I do believe it would pleasure me to cut off your fingers. No longer will you be called the virtuoso pianist." He laughed wildly and moved toward Garcia.

Garcia and Miguel drank whiskey late into the afternoon talking of the flying Luis Neruda, of how his form had shot through the air like a bullet and landed on Lope's back. How, in the swiftest of movements, Luis' arm circled Lope's neck and the big man crumbled to the floor like air released from a balloon. They laughed again at the speed with which Jorge ran from the tavern, abandoning his friend for the safety of the streets.

When Luis returned to the tavern in the early evening, Garcia and Miguel merely stared at him, their eyes round with amazement.

"I am speechless," said Garcia for the hundredth time. "Luis Neruda. Like a comet falling from the sky, you destroyed Lope. Did you notice, Miguel, how effortlessly he moved? Like a boxer, but with a ballerina's grace."

Garcia laughed again. Your hands, Luis. They are fast like the wind." He caught his breath. "I was not so sure how many hands you had, they moved so quickly."

"Yes, yes," said Miguel. "You have incredible hands, my friend." He paused and looked into Luis' eyes. "You have saved the life of the pianist, no?"

Luis' returned his stare, his eyes full of a wisdom balanced between fear and courage. Indeed, had Garcia seen Luis' eyes in the daylight, he would have recognized immediately the depth of the man, who without hesitation pummeled Lope and threw his unconscious body out into the street.

Luis had then unceremoniously piled the *el gigante* on top of his faithful white mule and carried him to the mountainside. There, he staked Lope onto the rocks and left him. He knew his friend, Jorge, would release him eventually.

Ningunos Nazi permitieron en la taberna. No Nazis allowed in the tavern.

Luis leveled his solemn eyes at Garcia. "My friend, your life has been saved because you have a mission, no?" Then, with a steadiness that belied the bottle of whiskey he had consumed, Luis stood and left the tavern to find his mule.

Chapter Twenty-Seven

S till reeling from his confrontation with Lope and Jorge, Garcia left the village with little daylight remaining and steered his bicycle toward Señora's Albeniz's house where he hoped to talk with her about their trip to Barcelona on Thursday.

On unsteady legs, he shuddered at how closely he had come to being split open from end to end by Lope's long-bladed knife. The threat still remained for another day; a day Garcia felt would come. He must be watchful.

He was calm by the time he arrived at Señora Albeniz'. The old woman was making soap in the large black pot that, at one time, most certainly had held the body of some unsuspecting soul captured by the señora's deranged sister. For all he knew, it was not soap in the pot, but the remains of some helpless creature that had fallen prey to the Albeniz sisters.

"Señora Albeniz, I am here to talk with you about our trip to Barcelona," he called across the rocky path that led to the yard. He leaned his bicycle against a tree and glanced over his shoulder for any sign of Blanka's sister.

"Señor Quinones, that is good news. I am anxious to taste the delectable scallops. I have been dreaming about them every night," she grinned at him, unembarrassed at her lack of teeth and the shiny pink gray gums that greeted him.

"We shall leave Thursday morning. I'll be here at daylight. We must be on the road and back again before night falls."

"Pedro and I are ready, señora. I shall pack us something to eat. I cannot wait to see Barcelona. I have not seen the sea since I was a young girl. The gods will bless you for taking this old woman to the beautiful blue sea where sea gulls fly and shells cover the beaches. All this before I die, my good friend."

Garcia smiled and regretted his earlier reluctance to take her with him. How could he deny her her one desire: to eat scallops from the sea and to gaze upon the blue waters of the Mediterranean once more. He admonished himself for his lack of compassion.

"Of course, señora. Remember, daylight."

Once again keeping an eye out for the crazed sister, Garcia retrieved his bicycle and pedaled the road toward his cottage. The sun dipped lower in the sky as nightfall spread across the Pyrenees.

Juan was waiting for him in the shadows of the barn, the burning of his cigarette beckoning Garcia to come hither and conspire with him. It seemed he never moved, just watched – watched with a spy's brilliant ability to calculate, to analyze and to ultimately snare whatever served his mission. Garcia shivered involuntarily as he felt the snare encase him, pull him into a precarious place that held nothing but danger. *What did he care about intrigue?* He had lost his quiet, unblemished life the instant the spy had spoken to him on the road from Barcelona. He braced himself for what was to come.

"You move slowly, Garcia, as if toward the gates of hell."

Without speaking, Garcia went into the barn, settled himself on top of the hay and leaned heavily backwards on the wall of the barn. He groaned as he adjusted his bruised body into a more comfortable position and let out a deep sigh.

Juan followed and sat near him.

"Indeed, a devil tried to kill me, my friend. It is a miracle that I am alive."

Juan studied Garcia carefully. He saw blood at the corner of his eye, a swelling around his temple.

"It appears someone's fist found your face."

"Ah, you are once more correct. I suppose it is a spy's talent to notice every detail. Can your genius tell you who inflicted this pain upon me?"

Garcia's sarcasm did not escape the spy's power of observation. He chose to respond with humility. "I only know that I am concerned that you have been injured and it is important to me to know how I may help you."

Garcia shrugged. "No need to concern yourself. It was your cousin, Luis, who prevented my untimely demise as well as the amputation of my fingers; therefore, leaving me alive to participate in your plan."

In the darkness, Juan did not need to see the face of Garcia Quinones to know he was angry. His words confirmed the pianist knew what was expected of him: a cunning, deliberate lie to the Germans, a lie that could very well see him in the cemetery. He did not want to lose the pianist. He was too important.

Juan pulled from his pocket a flask of whiskey and drank heartily before handing it to Garcia.

"Come, my friend. Let us discuss the visit from the Germans today."

Garcia laughed quietly before he turned the flask up and drank, the whiskey burning his throat and promising him a short reprieve.

Garcia wiped his mouth and returned the almost empty flask to Juan. "Ah, the Germans. Just as you predicted, they arrived while I was at Señora Lanzarote's house. Didn't even bother to knock. Barged in like the bastards they are. Why am I telling you this? I'm sure you observed them from somewhere in the foothills.

"And, it is ordained that Herr Himmler expects me to perform for his darling Hedwig at 3:00 o'clock on Saturday." He paused. "I don't think the Reichsfuhrer likes me."

"What makes you think that?"

Garcia laughed. "I'm afraid I was not kind regarding his Hedwig. Said I remembered her as being plump and plain."

"It was not a good time to flaunt your acting abilities."

"What difference does it make? He must please his mistress whether he likes me or not."

"Tell me about the Reichsfuhrer."

"A murderer. He smelled of murder. It was in his eyes."

The two men sat unspeaking, their thoughts their own.

At last, a slight slur in his words, Garcia spoke.

"I am thinking of my father and what his opinion would be of my present circumstances. Would he approve? Would he encourage me? Would he expect me to be a pacifist? A patriot?"

Juan saw the wetness of tears in his eyes. Fathers seemed to evoke in their sons a review of the principles and beliefs upon which their lives had been built. Garcia was in the throes of a decision, a monumental decision that would forever stand as a tribute, or perhaps a failure, to his father. Yes, his father was dead but he would know. Somehow he would know.

Garcia lifted the flask once more, high in the air as if it were a toast. His voice rose above the olive trees and floated into the universe for all to hear. "You Nazi bastards," he cried. "Be warned! Garcia Quinones is alive and well and you are no longer safe in Spain!"

The men sat quietly for a while. Garcia leaned forward and while slipping off his boots, said. "There is another problem. As I said, the Germans will return on Saturday for Himmler's mistress to hear me play. Señora Lanzarote refuses to allow the Germans back into her hacienda."

"This is not good news. She cannot know of the mission, of course. She must, however, be convinced of the importance of this so-called recital." Juan stood and paced the barn. "I shall have to pay her a visit."

"You? You will visit the señora?"

Juan smiled, a cryptic smile. "Yes."

From the mountains, a wild animal screamed, high-pitched, as though in the last breath of its life.

Garcia's words were harsh. "I will have to play for the fraulein. The passing of the secret documents to the Germans is your idea. The task haunts me and causes fear in the pit of my belly."

"You have no idea the consequences of passing the documents to the Germans, Señor Quinones. It will save thousands of lives when the Allied invasion begins."

The coldness of Garcia's words swept into the dark of the barn. "You must understand, señor, that it is *my* life I am concerned about."

Juan stood and walked slowly to the door of the barn. The waning moon was the color of old buttermilk, hanging high at the top of the earth. The Allied invasion was near, so near that every second of his mission was of paramount importance. He must ensure the safety of the pianist. Were anything to happen to his priceless fingers, their mission would fail. He smiled to himself.

Never before had he been assigned to protect the fingers of a virtuoso pianist.

He turned back to Garcia. "Of course, you are concerned. But, I am here to keep you safe." He paused and moved closer. "You must please the fraulein. If you please her, you will please Himmler." He squatted down in the hay next to Garcia. "Can you do that?"

The two men slept with the goats until little Tia awakened them with her antics on the roof of the barn. Again, she had squeezed through the broken boards at the back of the barn and pranced along the length of the roof as if she were a ballet dancer on a London stage, a dancer who happened to be a pregnant goat and who was, at this moment, ready for her shepherd to lead her into the hills.

Garcia turned over and spit hay from his mouth. When he opened his eyes, he saw Juan leaving the barn, a Pied Piper of sorts, as the goats obediently followed him. He sat up and moaned, newly aware of the bruises that covered his body.

"Ah, you are alive," called Juan as he returned to the barn and sat in the hay near Garcia. "Señor, you look as though you wrestled with a bear during the night. "

Garcia shook his head. "A restless night. I dreamed of someone chasing me, his hands reaching out and catching the edge of my shirt, only to rip my shirt from me while my legs struggled to escape."

"I see the reason why there is a hole burrowed in the hay where you slept. Your legs ran all night while demons slipped past your goat guardians and into your dreams."

"It is true. The demons were there," he said softly as he looked past Juan and into the barnyard. Painfully, he stood and walked outside where the early morning mist had obscured the cottage where the señorita slept, where the piano remained covered by a woolen blanket, and where, without a doubt, he would pray to the gods to save him from the Germans who waited in the bowels of hell for the lies he would tell them.

"Let us take the goats up the mountain."

They walked without talking, Juan's cigarette smoke lost in the heavy mist. The goats followed them, their bleating barely audible, subdued, as if they knew this was an important day and their good behavior a necessary ingredient to its success. Tia lagged behind, her belly heavy with kid, her slanted blue eyes remaining on Garcia; he was her shepherd.

"You, my friend, have awakened the gods," mused Juan, as if he were talking to himself.

Garcia continued walking, skirting a large rock and pulling himself forward by grasping the trunk of a small tree. He grimaced at the pain in his shoulder. "How so?"

Juan paused and gathered his thoughts. "It has occurred to me that while you are an accomplished pianist, famous for your compositions, as well as your passion for music, that you are guided by an even greater passion. A hidden passion perhaps, but still, it is there."

A silence followed the men farther up the mountain; even the goats tarried as if listening to the conversation. During their walk, the mist dissipated and left the mountain air clear as if it, too, wanted clarity of the preeminent events that awaited Garcia Quinones.

"Go on," prompted Garcia, his voice curious. "A greater passion? Explain."

As an afterthought, he added. "And, knowing how you possess an infinite wisdom, just how have I awakened the gods?"

Juan smiled. "While you are a passionate pianist, you are at heart a patriot, a patriot whose time has come. You spoke to the gods last night, my friend, and they heard you."

The seriousness with which Juan spoke was not lost on Garcia. He stopped on the mountain path and turned toward the Catalan. "You speak with such authority, Juan. Are you a brother of the gods?"

Juan held Garcia's stare with his own unresisting eyes. "I know what I know. That is all."

Neither man moved. Between them, duty prevailed. They were honor bound to offer themselves to the good of mankind. So simple. All along, this is what Juan already knew. Garcia discovered it in earnest as he screamed to the gods the night before; it was confirmed on the mountaintop as his eyes penetrated those of the spy.

"Where do we begin, my friend?"

The two men left the goats on the mountainside and approached the cottage. Juan eased himself into the dark shadows of the barn while Garcia entered the house where he found Jordana brewing tea and slicing bread and cheese. She looked up when she heard the door open. Her smile was hesitant but warm.

"It is you, Señor Quinones. I was wondering when you would return."

"Yes, it is I." He looked into her questioning eyes and sat at the small wooden table. "I smell the sassafras in the tea."

"I shall pour for you." Jordana reached in the cupboard and pulled two cups and saucers from the shelf and placed them on the table. She had barely poured the tea when he touched her hand and motioned for her to sit down. "We must talk, Jordana."

The girl sat demurely and waited. Garcia's eyes searched her face and saw in it a quality that he had somehow missed in their previous conversations. Her eyes were vibrant; in them an obvious intelligence, a knowing. He saw she breathed slowly, without anxiety. Across her forehead, wisps of hair had escaped from the ribbon that tied the dark tresses away from her face.

She looked at him curiously. "You wish to talk with me, señor?"

"Y…yes," he stammered. "We have discussed this before, but I would like to discuss it again. You have been away from your home for seven days. Your family thinks you are dead or kidnapped. You must let them know you are alive and safe. There is no other way." Garcia closed his eyes. When he opened them, he found her still watching him. "Another thing. El Capitan is planning to search the mountains for you. I'm sure he will include my cottage."

His eyes were so pleading that Jordana smiled and nodded her head. "I understand, Señor Quinones. We must let my family know I am safe."

She stood and retrieved the teapot from the stove and filled their cups. "I have decided to write a letter to my family to tell them of my good health and plead with them not to worry about me. That, I shall return home at a time of my own choosing."

"A letter? "

"But, of course. You see, Señor Quinones, I do not have to return home in order for them to know I am safe. A letter will do just as well."

The señorita's smile consumed Garcia and played with the sensibility of his thoughts. What of the dangers that had evolved in the days she had been at the cottage? What if Tomas had not told the Germans Garcia was inside Señora Lanzarote's house and they had come to the cottage searching for him and, instead, found Jordana? What about Lope and Jorge? At this very moment, they could be hiding in the mountains above the cottage, rifles in their hands, waiting for an opportune moment to kill him. Lope waiting to cut off his fingers. And, what of the spy? He visited Garcia every night with plans to thwart the Germans. No. No, indeed. The cottage was not a safe place for the señorita. Her life was in as much danger as his. *She just didn't know it.*

"I see," Garcia said quietly. What could he tell the girl? What information could he divulge to her that would not subject her to even more danger? None! She must not become involved. At any cost, her safety must not be jeopardized. He expelled a frustrated breath. "Write the letter and I will mail it for you."

He left the cottage and returned to the hidden corner of the barn, carrying with him bread and cheese for the spy. He must tell Juan about Jordana and her reluctance to return to her family. The spy had told him the girl must go as she would ultimately endanger their mission. Go? But where?

"I see you have brought some breakfast. My thanks to you." Juan reached out and took a slice of bread and a small wedge of cheese. "My stomach has been growling with hunger."

The master spy and his apprentice sat quietly and ate. Occasionally, they heard the tinkling bells of the grazing goats. As the last of the bread disappeared, Garcia cleared his throat. "The señorita has no plans to leave the cottage. She says she will write her family and tell them she is safe. There is no place else for her to go."

"She must go. The Germans will come, especially when our mission unfolds. If they find the girl, they will think she is involved in some way. We cannot allow the mission to be imperiled." Juan's glance at Garcia was inflexible. It was almost as if he had become another person, not the man eating bread and cheese in a goat barn – the set of his mouth, the coldness of his eyes, the slow deliberate way in which he spoke.

"She must be killed and buried in the mountains."

Garcia scrambled from his seat in the hay and stood above Juan, a sudden rage within him that threatened to boil over. It surprised him when he heard his own voice, calm and controlled.

"Señor, I will ignore what you have said, but I shall not forget it. Your ruthlessness amazes me. I shall attribute it to the fact that you are a spy, who operates with only one thing in mind—your mission. But, let me assure you, the mission that you and I are about to begin will not include the death of Jordana Rios."

Chapter Twenty-Eight

Garcia's young student, Eugenio, was expecting him at three o'clock. He was irritable. He had not slept well the night before. How was he to simulate a fictitious circumstance involving an innocent boy? How were they to find the bogus document pouch? He had spoken to the gods and now, if he was to be a successful patriot, he again needed help from those gods.

Juan folded his hands behind his back, his stance that of an instructor; the only things missing were spectacles on his nose and a book in his hands. Outside the barn, the wind blew and the resident hawk soared above the mountains. Juan levied his eyes at Garcia and began to speak. "The document pouch is an official leather pouch, about twelve inches square. It is folded and tied with a thin leather cord. Imprinted in English on the leather are the words: "CLASSIFIED TOP SECRET – NOT TO BE OPENED BY UNAUTHORIZED PERSONNEL.""

Garcia remained silent; his eyes attentive.

"The intent was for you and the boy to find the parachute and the document pouch together. As a result, its discovery could be verified by two people, making the find more credible. As we both well know, the boy, or should I say the dog, found the parachute before we could put our plan in place."

Garcia held up his hand to interrupt. "You involved me a little late, did you not?" His expression was cynical; this was not a perfect spy who stood before him.

"That is my fault, my friend. I was delayed while I hid in Barcelona's port, inadvertently locked in a cargo hold for over twenty-four hours before Luis rescued me. By the time I was freed, the parachute landing had occurred and the whole of Brasalia knew of the purported spy."

He ducked his head slightly, "Not exactly what was intended."

Garcia shook his head. "And what shall I do with the pouch?"

"You must convince the boy of the importance of the pouch and that you must take it to the authorities. He, however, must keep it a secret as before."

Garcia left the barnyard and pedaled down the road that led to Eugenio's farm. *I am no longer a piano teacher. I am a spy.*

There was no sign of the boy when Garcia leaned his bicycle against the wall of the large barn. He looked around for a sign of someone. His watch read 2:50 p.m., ten minutes early for his three o'clock appointment. Eugenio's absence was odd, and Garcia acknowledged his own uneasiness.

Even Pio was nowhere to be seen, the little dog a stalwart member of Eugenio's family. "Eugenio," he called, cupping his hands to his mouth. Inside the vast barn, a burro stood in the hay, looking at Garcia, its large eyes questioning. Garcia called into the depths of the barn, "Eugenio?" The burro snorted through his nostrils as if to say the boy was not here.

From behind, Garcia heard the sound of a motor and turned toward the road that led to the farm. It was the farm truck, loaded with farm hands. Leading the way were Eugenio and Pio.

"*Hola*, Señor Quinones," cried the boy. "I am sorry to be late. Shall you punish me by foregoing my lesson?" He ran toward Garcia, mouth open in laughter. He landed in front of his teacher; Pio barking along his side.

"Ah, my most promising student." Garcia tousled Eugenio's hair and then petted the small dog. "I am anxious to hear you play, my little friend. Have you practiced long?"

"Always for you, señor. I have played Debussy so much this week that I feel I am he. I feel I could win the Grand Prix des Enfants Prodiges."

"Ah, you tease me, Eugenio. You must prove to me you have practiced so diligently. Let us go to your piano and see."

The boy led Garcia into the music room of the sprawling stone house. Sheets of music lay scattered around the piano as well as composition notebooks by the dozens. Indeed, the boy had told the truth; his dedication to his music lay before them. Chopin, Mozart, as well as Beethoven's *"Moonlight"* Sonata *Opus 27 #2*, filled the room as if a mausoleum for the famous composers.

Garcia removed his hat and sat in the wooden chair beside the piano. Nodding to his student, he said, "I am ready to hear you play, Eugenio."

Garcia watched as the boy placed his small hands on the piano as if the keys were priceless jewels. His touch was gentle while his fingers found the notes of Debussy's ethereal *"Clair de Lune."*

Unmoving, Garcia's mind began to drift away. He lifted his eyes away from the boy's fingers and saw his own hands moving across the keys, finding the notes and, with ears whose hearing was so acute they could hear the laughter of angels, he heard music he himself was playing. He was at the Conservatory in Brussels, a mere boy like Eugenio. *So long ago.*

"Well, what do you think, Señor Quinones? Does my playing meet your approval?" Eugenio's large eyes watched Garcia and he hoped his lesson had pleased him.

From far away, Eugenio's voice pulled Garcia back to the wooden chair and the sheets of music that lay on the floor.

"You amaze me, Eugenio. In one week, you have mastered the art of the "C" scale. Never have I heard such tender playing, my little friend."

Eugenio nodded. "You must tell my mother how well I am playing."

"Oh, I shall. I shall."

Garcia rose from his chair. "Today would be a good day to take Pio for a walk in the mountains. The sun is beckoning us to feel the mountain wind upon our faces. Where shall we walk today?"

Delighted, the boy jumped from his piano bench and bounded out the door. Pio sat waiting for him under the shade of a small pomegranate tree, his long tail swishing in the dirt of the barnyard. "Come, Pio. It is time for our walk."

"We need a walking stick, Eugenio. Please retrieve two from the barn lest we fall among the rocks we are sure to cross."

"Sí, Señor Quinones. I have not forgotten our walking sticks." The boy ran to the barn and found a long stick for each of them and hurried back to Garcia.

"Here is yours. I will take the one that is the color of my mother's hair." He then left in a run toward the incline to the mountains, his Pio racing behind.

Garcia hurried to catch up with them, wondering if their path would take them to the hole where the parachute and document pouch lay hidden. He need have wondered no longer as Eugenio turned and waited for him.

"Señor Quinones, what of the parachute? Let us see if it is still buried." Without waiting for Garcia, Eugenio sprinted up the path at a fast pace, his dog leading the way.

Garcia hesitated. He glanced around the mountains, at the trees, the rocks. He felt the hairs on his neck prickle and his heart race. He turned and peered below them. There was no movement, only the mountain wind that lifted fallen leaves and threw them against the rocks. He had lost sight of the boy and his dog, but heard a cry.

"Señor Quinones, come! I have again found the parachute. It is here. In the hole."

There shall be no turning back. It is now at this very moment that I shall become cunning and deceitful. After all, those are the traits of a good spy, no?

Panting, Garcia approached the boy, who stood over the burial place of the parachute. "I see, indeed, you have remembered where the parachute is buried." Garcia looked from the hole to Eugenio. "Have you told anyone about the parachute?"

"Of course not, señor. You told me we must keep our discovery a secret and that is what I have done."

Garcia nodded to the boy and saw his feelings had been hurt. "I am sorry that I questioned you, Eugenio. Of course, you have kept the parachute a secret! You are the most trustworthy boy I have ever known. My apologies to you."

Pio began digging into the hole, perhaps considering it his parachute since he had made the discovery. It took only a few swipes of his paws to reveal the white silk.

"I am thinking it is time to take the parachute to the authorities. After all, the war is just across the mountains." Garcia looked upward toward the high peaks as if he could see an actual battle, a battle with German tanks swarming the fields of France and destroying what was once fields of lavender and the scurrying of honey bees.

"What about the spy? Where is he?" The boy's assumption there was a spy further solidified the story he would eventually tell the Germans.

"I'm afraid I do not know the answer to your question. I only know the existence of the parachute may be important. Let the authorities worry about the whereabouts of the spy."

Garcia fell to his knees and scooped away at the dirt that covered the mass of rope and silk. "Help me pull this out of the ground, Eugenio."

Together, their hands tugged until the yards of fabric tumbled out. "Ah, success!" said Garcia as he gathered the material together and placed it outside the hole.

The document pouch? Where is the document pouch?

In a surreptitious move, Garcia allowed his hat to fall into the hole, whereupon he leaned over and scrutinized the contents of the hiding place. His fingers dug hurriedly while above him Eugenio leaned forward in curiosity. "What are you doing, señor?"

"Ha! Trying to save my hat. Can you believe my clumsiness?" At last, Garcia's fingers found the smooth leather of the pouch. He continued his pasquinade while pulling it from its hiding place and exclaiming to Eugenio. "*Madre santa de dios! Como puede esto ser? Hay mas!*"

"More? There is more?" Eugenio peered over Garcia's shoulder into the hole. "What is it?"

The excitement in the boy's voice elevated. He would remember this moment in detail, would relay it to the Germans and when they interrogated him, he would relate to them exactly as it occurred. *They will, indeed, question this innocent boy and he must not falter.*

"It is a pouch," he said as he studied the words imprinted on the front. Just as Juan had said: "*CLASSIFIED TOP SECRET. NOT TO BE OPENED BY UNAUTHORIZED PERSONNEL.*"

"Maybe it is a document pouch of some kind." Garcia turned and looked at Eugenio with feigned curiosity. "Let us keep this a secret also, Eugenio. I must depend on you to protect the secrets of Spain. Together, we will be good Spanish citizens who help their country in time of need."

Eugenio nodded his head in agreement and licked his lips. "I shall keep our secret until the day I die, Señor Quinones."

Garcia squeezed his shoulder. "Your loyalty humbles me, Eugenio."

Chapter Twenty-Nine

Garcia leaned his bicycle against his thinking chair and walked slowly into the darkened barn, patting the pouch tucked away inside his clothes. Instinctively, he looked for the orange glow of Juan's cigarette.

"Are you looking for me?"

Garcia jumped and felt the man's breath upon his neck.

"Looking for the glow of my cigarette, are you? You must know a spy who is predictable is a dead spy." Juan's soft chuckle brought with it a soothing wash of calm upon Garcia.

He turned and looked into the smiling eyes of the master spy.

"I see you are learning well." The spy walked into the barn. "Tell me everything."

"I have the pouch." He pulled it from underneath his jacket and handed it to Juan.

"The boy?"

Garcia hesitated. The boy. The pure boy who knew no vileness, no maliciousness in his young life. He had no idea the part he was playing in the plot to deceive the Germans. Garcia felt his chest compress, his heart constrict. What had he done? He looked at Juan. "The boy…the boy was with me when I found the pouch. He saw me pull it from the hole."

"Excellent. So, no problems at all?"

"None."

Juan paused. "Then, we must go forward with the remainder of our mission."

"And that is?"

"You know the answer to that question. Your piano concerto for the mistress of Heinrich Himmler. Your presentation of the top secret document pouch to Himmler."

Juan smiled. "Perhaps 'presentation' is not a good word. Perhaps I should say 'your passing of top secret information to the enemy'."

Garcia looked at Juan for a long moment, never blinking, breathing quietly.

"It is my hope that it is as simple as you make it out to be – this passing of top secret information."

"It is my fervent desire that it will be a successful mission."

Garcia nodded and watched Juan light a cigarette. "I am tired. I must awaken early tomorrow to take Señora Albeniz to Barcelona for her scallops. I'll be away most of the day. When I return, I have more questions for you."

Juan touched the match to his cigarette and nodded. "We have much to do."

In a mock salute, he turned and left the barn through the small back opening and walked into the shadows of the approaching night, whistling a nameless tune.

How dangerous, thought Garcia. To whistle in the night. Who knew who waited in the gullies of the mountains?

Luis Neruda heard Juan's signal from his vantage point in the rocks of the mountain. He returned the signal by imitating the call of an owl. All was quiet along the peaks of the great Pyrenees.

A fatigued Garcia entered the cottage and sat heavily in a kitchen chair, the aroma of burning wood a soothing balm that seemed to calm his frenzied mind, bringing with it a desire to escape all that had happened to him during the past week. He reached for a bottle of sweet red wine, wine from La Rioja, he hoped would caress his body and erase the feeling of dread that so plagued him.

Behind him, he heard Jordana, her footsteps light and hesitant. "You have the letter?" he asked, without looking at her. He felt her move toward him and saw her slim hands lift the bottle of wine and pour a glass for him.

"Yes. I have the letter," she said, placing the wine glass before him.

"Sit," he said as he sipped his wine. "Let me pour for you. A beautiful señorita must have all the joys of life. Wine is certainly one of them." He finally looked at her and smiled, his eyes finding hers and holding her gaze.

She returned his smile and watched him pour wine into her glass. She tipped her glass toward him, "Salute."

Slowly, Garcia lifted his own glass and leaned it toward hers. "*Saludo. Es mi placer honrar a una mujer tan hermosa.*" It is my pleasure to honor such a beautiful woman.

"*Gracias, Señor . Es mi placer beber el vino con tan hermoso un hombre.*" It is my pleasure to drink wine with a handsome man.

"You embarrass me, señorita." He smiled.

Almost imperceptibly, in increments of heartbeats, Garcia began to feel the wine unlock something within him. His desire to be kind was almost overwhelming. Is this what men felt when they knew they were going to die? A tolerance and understanding of others? A deep love of life? An intrinsic awareness of a simple heartbeat?

He stared into the fire a long moment before returning his gaze to Jordana. He saw the smallness of her ears, the widow's peak where dark tresses pulled away from her face. He saw nothing but innocence exposed in the dark eyes that watched him.

"You must eat, señor. I have made a wonderful leek soup, with lots of onions."

"Soup? You have made soup?"

Garcia found he could not move; he was welded to the chair, the beating of his heart incredibly gentle, but yet he heard it. His musician's ears heard his blood pumping through his body, begging to stay alive, not to succumb to the inequities of life, to the adversities that awaited him.

"Yes, there is soup." Jordana rose and found two bowls and carried them to the stove. She filled them with the hot, creamy soup and returned to the table. She waited and watched as Garcia picked up his spoon and began to eat.

Outside, a heavy mist spread across the mountains where darkness had shrouded the rocks and trees and hid the animals of the night, the owls, and the stars. The light from the cottage fire dimmed, a flicker now and then that illuminated the body of Garcia, who stretched asleep across the table, his hand holding an empty bottle of wine.

The touch of Jordana's hand on his shoulder awakened him.

"Come to bed and I will warm you."

She tugged at his hand and walked him across the room. He lay down and quietly watched her undress before him. Her movements were so casual and natural that Garcia could hardly breathe. She moved to the bed and stretched her lithe body along his while wrapping her leg and arm over him. The warmth he felt was overpowering. She held him until the fire smoldered, the room melting into an inky darkness, a darkness that beckoned the piano teacher to make love. He felt her hand reach out and touch him where every man wants to be touched. It was the gods again.

Saying nothing, Jordana sat up, her nakedness like a thousand shining stars. The soft roundness of her breasts, on which sat nipples as erect as pistils on a flower, reached toward him. Hesitating only a moment, he leaned up and gathered the tip of her warm breast into his mouth. He was a lost man. His lips moved to hers and kissed her.

Just before daylight, Garcia pushed back the woolen blanket and eased out of the warm bed where Jordana slept soundly. As he watched her chest rise and fall in peaceful sleep, he smiled at the memory of her whimpering throughout the night. At first, timid and searching, their lovemaking was gentle. They explored each other without haste, emitting whispers and caresses that lasted until they could no longer wait for what was to follow. Without restraint, they devoured each other until they lay panting and content, falling asleep in each other's arms as if in a fairy tale.

In the darkness, Garcia dressed, quietly opened the door and stepped out into the cool early morning. He thought of Maria, their marriage. She had been his first love and, after her death, his heart had closed. His grief had diminished his desire to play the piano and, by his own choice, he had run away to the mountains and reduced his life to a simple existence. But, no more was his existence simple.

Like a tiny tremble within him, he felt the stirrings of hope, a resurgence of his soul. He looked up and saw the last remnants of nighttime stars fading in the light of the new day. *I'll always love you, Maria.*

Chapter Thirty

J udge Felipe Lanzarote arrived unannounced at his hacienda in the early afternoon, an afternoon that his court was closed. An embossed black cape covered his shoulders, which were wide and straight, like a bull's. He could have been a matador but, in his youth, he feared being gored, logical enough since his brother had been killed in his first bullfight. He never forgot his mother's anguished cries as they brought his brother's limp body home on a cart filled with cabbages, blood dripping from a gaping hole in his side.

Across the courtyard under the olive trees, Felipe saw Tomas and called out to him. "*Hola*, Tomas. What are you doing?"

Tomas looked up from his work and saw the Judge walking toward him. "I am weeding the señora's flowers, Señor Lanzarote. It is good to see you." Tomas thought it odd to see the Judge so soon after his last visit.

"*Gracias*, Tomas. Actually, I am here for several reasons. What is this I hear of the missing señorita? Capitan Torres apprised me of the situation and fears the worst."

"It is true, Señor Lanzarote. No one has seen the girl for a week. Many think she is dead and buried somewhere in the mountains." Tomas sadly shook his head. "Such a beauty, no?"

"I feel she is still alive. I also think it is possible she has run away. El capitan tells me she was to go to Madrid and live with her aunt. That she was to marry an old man." He laughed. "A good reason to run away, eh? A young beautiful señorita married to an old man."

"Anything is possible, señor. The reward will be claimed soon. Someone must know something." Tomas studied the Judge. He saw an uneasiness in him that put him on his guard. He had known the Judge a long time; he was a moody man.

"I shall talk further with Capitan Torres. A more extensive search is in order. The girl must be found and found soon." The Judge scanned around the courtyard as if looking for something.

"Tomas…have you noticed anything different about the señora? You know…a change in her?"

"A change?"

"Yes, a change. She seems…happier." The Judge moved closer to Tomas, and lowered his voice. "Happier. As if she is in love."

"In love?" Tomas gave a small smile as he watched the Judge's face and suddenly realized the purpose of his visit. "The señora loves you and only you, Señor Lanzarote."

The Judge's eyes widened. "Oh? I…I am glad to hear those words, Tomas." Still he hesitated. Tomas' statement did not erase the fact that Rosina was behaving differently, was more beautiful than ever. If there was another man in her life, Tomas did not necessarily know about it. Though, he could be protecting her, shielding her from the consequences of being discovered with a lover. He slowly kicked at a stone in the courtyard. "So, there is no other man?"

"Another man?"

"Yes. Another man." He stiffened and his shoulders rose beneath the cape. "I fear I am away so often that perhaps she has found someone. To…satisfy her…needs."

Tomas pulled at a stubborn weed while contemplating the Judge's question. It was true the señora seemed happier, but what did he know about her lovers or even if she had a lover? When he went home in the evenings and drank his whiskey, his thoughts were not of the señora and whether or not she was naked in the moonlight with a lover"It is my opinion, Judge Lanzarote, that you should ask the señora these questions. I am simply her gardener." Tomas stooped to the ground again and began pulling weeds, dismissing the Judge and his interrogation

The Judge looked toward the hacienda. "I see," he said, never intending to enter the large wooden door under the portico. He found himself unable to confront Rosina with his suspicions, not wanting to hear her tell him she was in love with another man. Still, he thought, why was Tomas so evasive if his wife had no lover? Of course! Tomas was protecting her. It was evident in the way he talked of the señora . *Bastardo*!

A frustrated Felipe Lanzarote returned to his automobile and headed for Barcelona knowing he could not live without knowing the truth. He could not live if Rosina loved another man.

He had traveled only one kilometer when he saw Juan step out onto the roadway from behind a large rock, his fedora in his hand in a slight wave. Felipe slowed and stopped only a few meters from the waiting Spaniard.

"Señor, you must live among the rocks along the roadway. I assume you saw me arrive?" The Judge gathered his unsettling thoughts regarding Rosina and hid them in a place where they would stay until he could mend them. Now, he must become the compatriot, the sub-agent, whose assistance to His Majesty's Secret Service was foremost in his mind.

Juan lifted his hat and placed it on his head as he leaned against the Mercedes. "No court today?"

Felipe nodded. "No court today, señor."

Juan studied the face of his friend, noticing a weariness around his eyes, a slackness in his face. "I planned to visit you at your apartment, but since you are here, let us find a place among the trees to talk." He turned away and disappeared into the trees.

The motor of the Mercedes turned over and Felipe pulled the long car to the side of the narrow roadway. "Wait up," he called as he followed the spy into the hillside.

The two men found a spot where rocks poked from the earth. They sat and pulled cigarettes, the sound of a striking match sharp in the quiet air. "The Germans visited your hacienda yesterday."

"What? So soon? Why didn't you tell me?" Felipe stood and towered above Juan.

"I'm sorry. You knew they would come."

Felipe returned to his rock. "I should have been there. I'm sure Rosina found their visit most unpleasant. She despises the Germans."

Juan lied. "She handled it well. Just a little shaken."

"And the pianist?"

"The encounter was unnerving to him, to say the least." Juan kept his eyes on Felipe. His friend seemed preoccupied. "We must continue to keep him focused and aware – sometimes I think he is too fragile. But, then again, I see an underlying strength in him. You know – the kind of strength you find in a man who rises to the occasion, when necessary."

"I understand. Though I have not met him in the years he has been teaching piano to Rosina, it is evident he is a good man."

Juan stood and walked a little farther up the hillside and leaned against a tree. "The recital is Saturday. Himmler and his mistress will arrive at three o'clock. The passing of the document pouch is crucial. I'd like you to be there. Observe everything you can. Not sure how things will go. Carry your pistol."

Felipe nodded. An alertness entered his expression as well as his body as he left the rock and walked toward Juan. He was in spy-mode – nothing else mattered. *Yes, I will carry my pistol.* Unconsciously, he reached inside his cape and felt the swell of his 9mm.

"I'll be there. Does Rosina know?"

"No, but I'll tell her." Juan paused. "Is there something I should know?"

Felipe looked up the mountain and watched the steel gray clouds rush east where the oceans would gather them into a wet squall. When he turned back to Juan, he shrugged his shoulders. "Nothing. Nothing at all."

"Do you have any questions?"

"No. I assume you have worked out all the details." He smiled. "You're the most perspicacious man I know. Why should I ever worry?"

Juan returned the smile. "I need you, Felipe. This is a dangerous mission – a lot is at stake. And, it's the apprentice spy who must perform perfectly."

"You can depend on me, Juan."

Both men looked west when they heard the roll of thunder. Far away, but sure to arrive before sunset. They shook hands and went their separate ways: Juan farther into the mountains, Felipe to his chambers in Barcelona.

Chapter Thirty-One

Long after Miguel had closed his tavern and the streets were deserted, Juan Castillo stood in back of the Lanzarote hacienda. He leaned on the courtyard wall and wished his flask was not empty. He pulled the collar of his leather jacket around his neck, then pushed his fedora low over his forehead. The passing rain had left the air cold and he longed for a warm bed with clean sheets. His camp in the mountains provided neither.

Across the courtyard, a candle burned in Rosina Lanzarote's living room, where the señora sat in a chair reading, a wrap around her shoulders. Her stillness was comforting to Juan. He was quite familiar with her regal poise and had always envisioned her with a crown on her head, majestic and elegant. She could easily have been a queen, he thought.

Juan eased to the hacienda wall where raindrops covered the glass in the long windows. Only a few feet away Rosina sat in her chair. "Rosina, it is I. Juan."

He watched her turn her head toward the window.

"Rosina," he said again.

She placed her book on a table and walked to the window. She looked through the glass and into the darkness of the courtyard. He moved in front of the window where she saw his face and the familiar fedora. For a moment, she just stared at him. Then, a smile.

"Come," she said, while opening the door.

Juan stepped inside and immediately the arms of Rosina Lanzarote wrapped around him and held him tightly. He heard a muffled cry as he pulled her closer. They stood a long moment together before she leaned back and looked at him.

"You look awful."

"Ah, what a greeting, my dear Rosina. I would rather have heard how wonderful I look."

"Ha! You are drenched and smell like a wet dog. When did you shave last?"

Juan pulled her arms from around him. "If you cannot be nice, I shall leave. It's been almost a year since I've seen you, yet you treat me unkindly."

Rosina laughed. "No, you can't get away that easily. I will take you any way I can get you, smelly or not." She grabbed his hand and led him to the sofa. "Come. I will pour us a whiskey and we will talk."

He obeyed and sat while she poured their drinks. His eyes took in the beauty of her long dark hair and the curve of her neck. He looked around the room and was reminded of the joy of having a home, a real home. With furniture, gleaming with polish, and photographs along the wall. Something stirred within; a sadness crept into his heart. He wished things had been different in his life. No. Not different. His duty as a spy was his life and he would not change his circumstances. Yet, a home. With a beautiful woman. Iliana. Children.

When she returned, he had removed his jacket and fedora. She picked them up quickly and placed them on the back of a chair. He knew she would clean them both before the sunrise. "I shall run you a hot bath later."

She sat and smoothed her hair and looked at him with her large eyes, a smile hovering at her lips. "On a mission?"

"But, of course. Always."

"I thought you were retiring from this spy business. How old are you now? Forty? Forty-five?"

"You know how old I am. I went to school with your husband and I've known you since you were sixteen."

"Ah, that's right. You're Felipe's age. I thought by now you would have asked Iliana to marry you and settled down with six children."

Juan said nothing as he sipped his whiskey. Across the room, an earlier fire had burned to embers, filling the room with the fragrance of oak.

Rosina waited for Juan to say something, but when he didn't, she probed further. "When was the last time you saw her?"

"A few days ago."

Rosina drank from her glass and looked at Juan closely. "Why don't you ask her to marry you?"

Juan turned and looked at the wife of his best friend. "I plan to at some future time."

"Why wait?"

"Why wait? Many reasons. First of all, I have to survive this war."

"Of course, you will survive. No one can harm Juan Castillo, spy extraordinaire."

Juan smiled. "I am glad to see you have a crystal ball, my dear, and that my future is bright."

Rosina's eyes narrowed. "Just how dangerous is this mission?"

"Who knows? It just takes one bullet."

"The war cannot do without you, Juan. Felipe and I pray for you constantly."

"Felipe? Felipe knows how to pray?"

Rosina shook her head. "Ever the comic, Juan."

"But only with you. The other parts of my life are much too serious. It is good you married Felipe instead of me."

The serene face frowned. "Sometimes our marriage is not what it should be."

"Oh?"

"He's never here. Always in the courts. And, other places, I assume," she said, drinking long from her glass.

Juan stood and walked to the decanter of whiskey where he saw the wedding picture of Rosina and Felipe. When he turned, he saw Rosina watching him closely. The woman had a knowing. She sensed things and now as she looked at him, he knew there were questions.

"Is there a particular reason you're here tonight, Juan?"

All Juan could do was look at her and nod. "But, of course, Rosina. There is a matter of importance that I must discuss with you."

"And that is?"

"The Germans."

He saw her face turn cold. "What of the Germans?"

Juan paced slowly to the end of the room and turned to face her.
"The recital," he said.

Rosina rose from the sofa and walked swiftly to where he stood.
As she walked, the fabric of her robe swished like the sound of an
oncoming wind. "What do you know of the recital?" Her voice was
sharp as he'd known it would be.

Juan chose his words carefully. "The recital is more than it seems."
He returned to the sofa. Rosina followed.

"Go on," she said, without warmth.

Juan's next statement would be even more perplexing to Rosina.
But, he had to say it. "Garcia Quinones is more than he seems."

Bewildered, Rosina simply stared at Juan and shook her head. He
could feel her anxiety as she deliberated over his words and wondered
how he, Garcia, Felipe and the Germans were involved. Finally, her
voice weak, she said, "I understand. All of this has to do with your
mission." She looked up quickly. "And, of course, you expect me to
allow the Germans to come into my home on Saturday." She hung her
head. "Juan, I am afraid of the Germans." Her hand shook as she lifted
her glass.

Juan merely nodded. The fear in her eyes did not go unnoticed.

Then, as he'd known it would, her anger surfaced. "Your audacity
infuriates me, Juan. How can you expect this of me?" She turned from
him. "All for 'the mission,' I suppose," she said with blatant sarcasm.
She left him on the sofa and walked to the windows and watched the
rain. Her back was stiff and unrelenting. She hated the Germans as
much as he did.

Chapter Thirty-Two

"Señora Albeniz, I am here," called Garcia from the lane that lead to the ramshackle house. It was unsafe to meander near their castle. Garcia knew the mad dog of a sister would attack him without the slightest provocation. He waited, only to hear Pedro bray loudly and wish upon him a good morning.

Soon, the shadow of the old woman appeared from the corner of the house.

"Señor Quinones, I hear you. So does Pedro. Come. Let us halter my precious Pedro and begin our journey."

"Is it safe to come to the barn?"

"Ha. You are afraid? My sister will not harm you as long as you can outrun her." The old woman's laughter filled the morning air and bounced off the rocks of the mountain. "She cannot outrun a man with legs as long as yours, señor." Again, peals of laughter.

"I am coming, but you must assure me your sister is not going to pummel me again."

A full minute elapsed. "I have locked her in a closet. You need not worry."

"I am coming." Garcia climbed toward the house and barn, still leery of what awaited him. Indeed, the mad woman would burn the house down to escape from a closet in order to maim him.

When Garcia arrived at the barn, Pedro had been haltered and packed with a sack of food for their noonday meal. Alongside him stood Blanka. He stared at her in astonishment. She had wound her hair into a chignon at her neck and pierced it with a long black, shiny piece of thin wire, the ends curled like a man's handlebar mustache. A pair of polished stone earrings, as orange as a sunset, swung on her huge, elongated ear lobes. Around her neck was a heavy chain holding a large ivory cameo of the Spanish king. She had tied a velvet sash the color of the waters of the Mediterranean around her waist. Beneath her sash, a long orange skirt fell to the ground, swishing as she walked. Garcia couldn't help but notice the package of cigarettes she had tucked in her sash. It was going to be a long day.

The old woman grabbed the hem of her skirt and pulled herself on top of Pedro. "*Va, usted burro hermoso!*" she cried as they left the barn and headed toward the road.

"Are you not going to release your sister before we go?"

Again, the toothless laugh. "You are so gullible, my friend. My sister waits for you behind the rocks of the mountain. You must be sure to duck."

Daybreak came slowly, poking through the gray mist a sunray at a time. They had passed through Brasalia seeing nothing but a chicken scratching in the dirt in front of the police station. By the time they reached the road to Barcelona, the sun had fully risen, the mist had dissipated and left the air clear, the sky bright blue. A perfect day for a journey to the blue of the Mediterranean Sea.

"Eh, I am so happy, Garcia. I have not been to Barcelona since I was a little girl. I remember my father placed me on his shoulders and together we watched the ships in the harbor. Big ships, small boats. And the sea gulls. They were everywhere, diving down like bullets into the sea for food.

"Where was your sister?"

"Inez had not been born yet. Until she came along, I was the only child and, of course, received all my father's love. When Inez was born, he hardly looked at me again." Blanka sighed deeply. "And I was such a sweet little girl, you know."

Pedro snorted in agreement as they rounded a curve in the road and climbed higher into the mountains.

"What about your mother?"

"My mother? My mother left us after Inez was born. Father told me she thought she was too beautiful to be married to a simple dock worker."

They plodded on in silence, a pleasant excursion into the mountains where the breezes from the east brought a slight taste of the sea, a saltiness that made one want to drink rum laced with fresh lime.

Garcia felt the bullet whiz by him before it hit Blanka and before he heard the retort of the rifle that had been fired. Before he could move, another bullet slammed into Pedro and sent him splaying on top of his mistress, who lay stretched upon the road. It was then that Garcia fell to the ground and hugged the dirt of the road. *My God, my God, what is happening?*

Two more bullets scattered the dirt around him before he frantically crawled into the relative safety of a rock wedged in the side of the road. A third bullet followed, grazing the top of the rock above him, sending splinters of stone onto his head. He pushed his body into the rock as closely as possible, and waited for another bullet. Ambushed, he had nothing with which to defend himself. He looked to where his friend and her donkey had fallen and his breath left his lungs at the massacre. One side of Blanka's face had been hit with the first bullet, obliterating her temple and brow, along with it, her eye. Unable to turn away, he began to wretch uncontrollably.

Pedro was still, blood pouring from the wound in his neck. His prone body lay partially on Blanka as if protecting her. She still held the reins of his halter as flies began to hover around them, bringing the maggots that would follow.

I must move from this place, thought Garcia. They will come down the mountain and kill me. He looked down the road from where he lay. If he could make it to the curve in the road, around a large protruding rock, perhaps there was a chance to run to the safety of the village. He moved slightly, only to have another bullet hit the rock above him. *They know exactly where I am.* Garcia belly-crawled to the protection of another boulder, much larger than the one behind him. If he could only make enough distance to allow him to jump up and run to the curve in the road, he might be able to escape.

He looked again at Blanka's body. The orange earrings hung grotesquely on her ears. Her lone eye, open in surprise, still watched him from the roadway, as if reminding him he must bring her scallops from the sea. He swallowed hard to keep the vomit from choking him.

Once more, he shoved his elbows in the dirt and pushed himself forward, a few inches at a time, to the safety of the curve in the road. He heard falling rocks above him and knew the killer was easing down the mountainside, aiming his rifle and preparing to kill him.

I must get up and run. There is no other way.

Again, the sound of falling rock. Garcia knew he had only moments before the bullets flew. With a grunt, he pushed himself up and, like a sprinter in a race, his legs pummeled the dirt and propelled him to the curve in the road. Behind him, he heard a bullet strike the roadway. Another. And finally, a bullet found his shoulder and sent him sprawling.

He rolled back to the side of the roadway and again lifted his body into a racer's stance, never taking his eyes off the curve in the road. Only a few yards more. He did not feel the pain in his shoulder; his blood pumped hard and his legs moved swiftly, he felt nothing but terror.

When he rounded the curve, it seemed the wind was pushing him toward the safety of the village. He passed the trees and the rocks as if he were flying, as if the gods had taken note of his predicament and said, *"Let us help the poor pianist."*

On the outskirts of Brasalia, the Church of the Holy Father loomed before him. Only a few yards more and he would be safe. He looked down at his shoulder and saw the pooling of blood in his shirt. He must not falter; he did not want to bleed to death in the beautiful church, he thought to himself, and decided to bypass Father Eduardo's sanctuary. Only forty meters farther, he collapsed in the darkness of the tavern, where Miguel stared at him in disbelief.

He was somewhere. He just didn't know where. As hard as he tried, he could not remember who he was. *I am asleep; I must wake up. I must open my eyes and wake up.*

"Garcia, can you hear me? Garcia." A cold cloth covered Garcia's forehead. Miguel shook him gently. "Garcia, you must wake up."

Garcia opened his eyes and was at once aware of the pain in his shoulder. He blinked and recognized Miguel. "Miguel, what has happened? Why am I here?"

"You have been shot. But, do not worry, the bullet passed through the muscle of your arm. No bones shattered." Miguel smiled at his friend. "You must tell us what happened." Standing in back of Miguel, Luis nodded his head in agreement.

"What day is it? What time is it?

"It is nine o'clock on Thursday morning."

"Señora Albeniz?"

"Señora Albeniz?"

"Yes. The señora and I were traveling to Barcelona together." Garcia closed his eyes and at once remembered everything. The bullets killed the Señora and her donkey.

"Tell us, Garcia."

"Help me sit up."

Miguel placed his arm behind Garcia's back and lifted him to a sitting position. Garcia grimaced as pain seared through his arm. "Here is some whiskey, my friend."

In a voice weak with the realization his life had been in unspeakable peril, Garcia spoke, "Someone shot and killed Señora Albeniz and her donkey. Their bodies are a kilometer away on the road to Barcelona." Garcia paused. "The bullets were meant for me."

Juan eased himself from a dark corner of Miguel's bedroom to where Garcia lay. He looked at the three men with a grimness that would shatter a star.

"Miguel, you go to the police station and tell El Capitan of the bodies on the road. Tell him Garcia was also shot and is here for questioning. Luis, you and I will go to the mountains and see what we can find."

The spy turned to Garcia. "As soon as you feel you are able and after you have talked to El Capitan, return to your cottage. Miguel will take you. Either Luis or I will be nearby. Stay inside until we are able to understand what has happened."

The eyes of Juan were black and foreboding. MI6's most formidable spy was in killer-mode. Even his fingers twitched, while the muscles on his face were frozen into a grim reminder to all who saw him that he was trained to kill.

Juan studied the blood that soaked the bandages on Garcia's arm. "How large is the entry wound?"

"Large. Most likely the rifle was a large caliber, probably a hollow tip considering the wound."

"What about the old woman? The donkey?"

Garcia closed his eyes and visualized the last moments of his leisurely walk with Blanka. She was almost beautiful with the orange earrings hanging from her ears, the chain around her neck and the colorful long skirt. Her desire for scallops, he realized, was a journey back to a time when she was young and loved by her father. If she saw the sea again, she would feel her father in the sea breezes, hear him in the sea gulls that called above the blue of the sea and find him in the smell of the fish that tumbled from the nets onto the dock.

"The señora was riding the donkey. I was to her left side when I felt the passing of the bullet just inches from my head. It appeared that the bullet struck her at the brow bone and the force of the impact tore a large portion of face away, including her left eye." Garcia paused, his breath shallow.

"The next bullet struck her burro. In a matter of seconds, they were both dead. There was nothing I could do. I fell to the ground and waited for the next bullet."

Juan saw the paleness in Garcia's face, heard the weakness in his voice. "Go on."

The words of the piano teacher were barely audible. "Then I knew I was going to die."

The three men looked at each other. Luis spoke, "But you did not die, señor. You are here. You are safe."

Juan prodded Garcia. "You saw no one? Heard no one?"

"I saw no one. All I heard were the sounds of the bullets and the falling rocks as they rolled down the mountain."

"Do you think there was more than one shooter?"

"I'm not sure. The bullets came rapidly. There could have easily been two."

"I suspect Lope and, perhaps Jorge, are at this moment hiding in the mountains, rifles warm. Have they been seen in Brasalia this morning?"

"No," said Miguel, "we have not seen them since two nights ago here in the tavern."

Juan turned to Luis. "Let's go." Then to Miguel, "Find El Capitan and bring him here so the murder can be reported officially, as well as Garcia's injury. The body of the old woman must be tended to, as well as the burro."

Garcia looked up sharply. "What about the Señora's sister? She waits for her return."

"Someone will need to tell her what has happened. Perhaps El Capitan should take her the news."

The sister whose mind heard strange winds would wait in the rocks of the mountains for her beloved sister to return. Her eyes would scan the hills for a glimmer of the orange earrings, her ears would listen for Pedro's slow plodding and her heart would beat like a hummingbird's as she craned her neck and watched the road from Barcelona.

"No. I will tell her." Garcia's voice was firm.

Capitan de policia Torres followed Miguel into the tavern and through the doorway that led to the entrance to his small house. When he saw Garcia, his eyes widened and went from Garcia's face to the bandages around his shoulder and upper arm.

"Señor Quinones, who did this to you? This is madness! Who would shoot a man as fine as you?"

Garcia responded with a chuckle, "I am afraid bullets sometime do not ask questions as to the integrity of the men they kill. Fortunately, it only struck my arm."

The Capitan moved closer and carefully touched the bandages. "My friend, you are in much pain?"

"The pain is easing." He looked at Miguel. "Miguel has been a very good doctor; he has provided me some of his finest whiskey."

Capitan Torres's face became stern. "Señor, it is my duty to find whoever did this to you. What can you tell me about what happened?"

"There is not much to tell. Señora Albeniz and I were traveling to the Port of Barcelona to buy scallops. All at once, bullets were flying through the air. Señora Albeniz and her burro were killed before we could take cover.

"I never saw who fired upon us. All I know is that whoever it was, was intent on killing me."

The Capitan nodded. "I will take my deputy and Father Eduardo to the road. We will remove the body and make arrangements for her burial."

El Capitan lifted his heels from the floor and puffed out his chest in a display of authority. "Then, I shall investigate this murder." He cleared his throat, "Of course, I will have to report the incident to the regional authorities headquartered in Barcelona."

"Capitan Torres, I will be responsible for finding Señora Albeniz' sister and telling her of her sister's death."

"Do you need Father Eduardo to accompany you?"

"No, that is not necessary. I'm sure you are aware that the sister is not in her right mind and…and is sometimes…violent."

"Yes, yes, I am aware."

El Capitan nodded to Miguel. "Miguel, please see that Señor Quinones is seen by the doctor. He is due to arrive next Tuesday for his usual stop at the clinic before he continues to Barcelona."

"Si, I will see it is done."

Juan and Luis climbed the rocks above the bodies of the old señora and her burro and peered down to the roadway. The mountain breeze ruffled the señora's long skirt, which lay in the dirt and mixed with the red brown of the burro's blood. The stillness around them lifted up into the hills as if inconsolable, weeping for the soul of the woman and questioning the universe as to the purpose of her death.

The two men studied the scene and pretended to be the killers, contemplating the best vantage point from which to commit a murder. Juan nudged Luis and pointed to his left where thirty meters away, a large bolder stood high and behind it, a smooth grassy area.

"A perfect view of the road, eh? A place to stand, to sit, to level a rifle barrel." Juan stood and walked toward the large bolder, ever mindful of the mountains as his eyes scanned every rock and tree around him.

Luis followed, both men scrutinizing their surroundings with studied proficiency. A footprint? A cigarette butt? Perhaps a shell casing?

Juan knelt down behind the boulder and examined the ground with such intensity that Luis knew the spy master had, with his intrinsic genius for seeing what others could not see, found something that did not belong behind a boulder in the mountains.

"Interesting," he said quietly. "A button of all things. Metal, brass." Juan rubbed it between his thumb and forefinger and studied the embossed design. "Military?" He showed it to Luis.

"Could be."

"I think so," Juan said thoughtfully as he placed the button in his shirt pocket. "I see boot prints, two sets."

"Lope and Jorge?"

"Most likely, but we need proof before we inform the authorities. Come, let us go. We need to protect Garcia no matter who wants him dead."

Only twenty meters down the mountain, the two men discovered the body of a dog. "Odd that a dog would be here, shot through the head. Do you know whose it is?"

"It is not familiar. Should we bury it?"

"We don't have time. We can come back perhaps."

They left the mountain and the bodies on the roadway only to take with them the realization that their assignment on behalf of MI6 had become a much more complex mission. The key player in the conspiracy to dupe the Germans must be kept alive.

Chapter Thirty-Three

The sun was inching toward the west when Garcia and Miguel left the tavern and walked the two kilometers to Señora Albeniz' cottage. Inside Miguel's shirt was a pistol, loaded, and, as he liked to say, amazingly accurate.

The wound in Garcia's arm no longer bled and, except for an occasional throb of pain, his injury seemed insignificant. The bandage was wound tightly; as an antiseptic, they had soaked it with Miguel's finest whiskey.

"I'm not quite sure how to talk with Inez. You know that's her name, don't you?"

"Sí. I have known the sisters for many years. Never, though, have I had a conversation with the sister who seems to talk to the wind. Only Blanka knew how to communicate with her."

"What will happen to her?"

"Who knows? It's possible she will be able to care for herself."

They approached the incline to the cottage, their eyes sweeping the rocks for a glimpse of Inez. "Señora Inez," called Garcia. He turned to Miguel. "Beware, Miguel. She is masterful at throwing rocks and spitting. I have seen her spit travel three meters or more."

"Señora Inez," he called again. "There is a dog, Miguel. I'm thinking she must not be here if the dog is quiet."

They stood at a safe distance from the cottage and waited.

"Let us go. She is in the mountains somewhere; hiding, hunting, I don't know." Garcia hesitated and looked one more time toward the hills. Something was amiss. Why wouldn't Inez be home waiting for her sister's return?

At Garcia's cottage, the goats grazed among the rocks nearby and bleated like children when they saw him.

"You are a good friend, Miguel. My gratitude is immeasurable." Garcia paused and looked at his friend for a long moment. "By the way, you know Juan?"

Miguel laughed quietly, his massive chest rumbling like distant thunder. "*Sí*, my friend. The collusion stretches deep and wide." He turned and began his journey down the mountain.

"Stay well, my patriot friend," he called from the roadway, "you are important in this quest for freedom."

Garcia silently watched him disappear into the rocks and trees. *Patriot? I am a wounded pianist who longs only for the sweetness of beautiful music.*

Inside the cottage, Garcia found Jordana sitting at the table reading, her hair swept back and piled on top of her head. When she saw him, she jumped from the chair and ran to him.

"You have been hurt? What has happened?" Her fingers touched lightly on Garcia's makeshift sling.

"It is a small injury." He moved slowly to a chair and looked at Jordana.

"I am afraid I did not mail your letter," he said, while pulling the letter from his shirt. "You will have to rewrite it. It has been damaged."

Jordana stared wide-eyed at the bloodstained envelope. "You must tell me what has happened."

Garcia sighed wearily. "I cannot. I can only tell you that you must remain in the cottage at all times. If you hear anything out of the ordinary, you must hide somewhere. Perhaps behind the piano." His voice softened. "I am sorry but I must lie down for a while. I feel very tired."

The señorita gently placed her arms around Garcia, "I will pour you hot tea."

"*Sí*. Tea would be good."

Garcia drank his tea without speaking and then eased himself onto the bed and closed his eyes. He breathed deeply as his mind heard the first notes of Bach's *12th Sonata*, his fingers finding the keys and sweeping him away.

The sound of a gentle rain on the rooftop awakened Garcia from a fitful sleep. Beside him lay Jordana, her body resting in deep shadows, her long hair flaring out on her pillow, a beauty not intended for the wealthy old man in Madrid.

With a painful slowness, Garcia sat up. He had slept for hours, dreaming dreams filled with someone chasing him. Always chasing him.

From his bed, he crossed to the window and looked out toward the mountains. It was midnight; a moonless, starless night that allowed the stealth of living things, whether man or animal, to wander the hills in search of prey.

He turned his eyes from the mountains and scanned the farmyard and the barn. He looked for the glow of Juan's cigarette where he knew the continuance of their spy game awaited him. He, indeed, found the orange ember under the eaves, in front of the barn near the olive tree.

"My friend, how is your arm?" Juan called from across the barnyard as Garcia left the cottage.

"Somewhat painful," said Garcia as he ducked the rain and walked along the eves of the barn.

"You are lucky to be alive, with only a bullet through your shoulder."

"That is so. I am quite aware, señor, that the bullets that flew all around me were looking for my head and not my arm. It is only by the grace of the gods that I am here talking to you."

Juan nodded and looked at a haggard Garcia. "We must assess what has happened," he began. "Luis and I found an area above the road which we believe was the hiding place of whoever shot you. There was evidence that someone was there. We did not find shell casings, but we found a few cigarette butts as well as this." Juan reached in his pocket and pulled out the small button. "I'm thinking this is a button from a military uniform. Maybe the Blue Shirts. Luis and Jorge have occasionally been wearing their uniforms while on leave. Though I can't imagine them wearing the uniform while committing a murder." He laughed quietly, "Of course, their stupidity runs deep."

"It wouldn't surprise me. What is our next step?"

"Our next step is to keep you safe. Our mission cannot be successful without its key player, and that is you, Garcia."

Garcia leaned out of the rain against the barn alongside Juan and thought about his integral role in the operation. "It occurs to me that it will be quite difficult to play for the Reichsfuhrer and his mistress."

"Your arm, of course."

"Yes, my arm. My injury will most likely prevent me from performing as Fraulein Potthast expects me to, like the pianist she remembers from the Conservatory." Garcia sucked in his breath and let it out slowly. "It seems I am doomed to fail in this undertaking."

Juan heard the call of an owl, knowing it was Luis, who crouched above them and watched for possible peril. His signal was comforting to Juan, who knew their safety could shatter in the blink of an eye.

"May I suggest we take one thing at a time? Between now and three o'clock Saturday, you must determine if you'll be able to play. We have less than forty-eight hours before you not only have to perform for the Germans, but you must also pass the document pouch to Heinrich Himmler."

There was sharpness in Juan's words; he was becoming the cold spy, steeling himself and, hopefully his infant spy, for what was to come. Their plan must be perfected before Garcia sat at Señora Lanzarote's piano and played better than he had ever played in his life. Before he stood close to the Reichsfuhrer and whispered in his ear that he must talk with him in private about an urgent matter. After all, written on the pouch were the words "Classified Top Secret – Not to Be Opened by Unauthorized Personnel."

"I know these things, Juan," said Garcia irritably. "And I also know it is I who has to please Himmler's mistress. It is I who has to convince the Germans that the document pouch is legitimate."

"Well said, my friend. But, do not forget what is at stake here. In the end, we are talking about the Allies and their offensive into the German fortresses. The success of your performance will affect many lives."

Together, they watched the rain. To the south, miles away, lightning lit the sky in code-like bursts. *Be ready for the Germans! Be ready for the Germans!*

"Get some rest, my friend. Morning comes quickly. We will need to spend the day going over our plan. It is vital that you are adequately prepared, despite all that has happened today."

There was no denying that Garcia's part in the overall ambitious deception of the Germans was critical. The mechanics of channeling bogus information to the Third Reich in concert with other secret Allied operations was difficult; a plan could not be successful if it was mounted piecemeal. Juan left the barn and climbed into the mountains to where he knew Luis waited. He was troubled. Too much had gone wrong. Above all, he must keep Garcia alive for his performance for the Germans.

Chapter Thirty-Four

G arcia returned to the warm cottage. A candle burned on the small table where a teacup with a spoon sat as though watching the flame nearby and daring it to dim. He sat in a chair and stared at the darkened corner of the cottage.

He left the chair and walked to the piano. With trembling fingers, he touched the edge of the woolen blanket and began to pull. Inch by inch, the rich mahogany wood revealed itself and beguiled him like the body of a naked woman, ever closer, until she smothered him with memories of past interludes.

My love, I have missed you.

Gently, he pulled out the piano bench where pages of music protruded from inside the seat and dared him to retrieve them. As if in a trance, he touched the corner of a yellowed page and tugged. Chopin's *Etude No. 1 in C Major. Yes, he breathed. Yes.*

He leaned over into the keyboard and blew his warm breath over the ivory keys. The piano was alive, willing him to devour its beauty. Slowly, with a gentleness as delicate as the beating of fairy wings, he placed his fingers on the seductive keys and began to play. The first note, a sixteenth note C below Middle C, with the C octave in his left hand, was followed by a sixteenth note Middle C. The music began to soar upward until it rested on the E in the highest register of the piano, music so entreating that even the gods listened. Then, amidst memories of his rapturous days in the concert halls of Europe, Garcia's fingers stilled, the notes ending softly. *I am a pianist, he thought. A pianist.*

Garcia closed the piano as tears fell on the dark wood, tears that held unimaginable grief. Behind him, he felt Jordana place her hands on his shoulders. She kissed his hair, the top of his ear, his brow.

"It is almost daylight. Come to bed," she whispered. "I long for you."

Garcia obeyed and fell into the warm bed. He pulled her body toward him and felt the softness of her skin. When he kissed her, she moved above him, where he watched her breasts sway to the rhythm of her movement. His hands held her hips as they lifted and proclaimed him as hers.

From the hills, Juan heard the notes of the piano, slowly at first. Then, a resounding of notes that swept up into the heavens and spoke to the gods with such clarity and intensity that the earth stood still. Garcia Quinones, virtuoso pianist, composer extraordinaire, had found his piano. He smiled to himself. If the pianist performed half as well as a patriot spy, he had every confidence their mission would be successful. He leaned back and lit a cigarette and waited for the sun to rise.

"Your coffee, señor." Garcia placed the hot cup next to Juan and sat beside him. He had slept well and felt his strength had returned despite his wound.

"Today is the day, eh? To rehearse, shall we say, for our great deception." Juan sipped his coffee and studied Garcia's face.

"*Sí*. Today."

"I heard your playing late into the night." Juan's face softened as he looked at Garcia. "You warmed my cold heart, señor."

Garcia said nothing as he drank his coffee and watched his goats meander throughout the barn where they sought shelter from the cold rain. He wasn't surprised to see Luis appear from the shadows. "Luis," he said, "I will share my coffee." He handed the large man his cup.

"Gracias, señor."

A silence filled the barn. There were decisions to make, details to discuss and information to share.

"There has been no sign of Lope and Jorge," said Luis. "I have searched the usual places, but they are nowhere to be seen."

"That is odd. Their leave does not expire until next week, then back to the Eastern front. It is possible their guilt at having killed the señora and her burro keeps them in hiding."

"They will surface in time."

Garcia spoke. "This afternoon I must go to Señora Albeniz's house to find her sister. She must be told of her sister's death."

"Of course," said Juan. "That must be done."

"What of this document pouch? The information? Himmler will most certainly question my knowledge of its contents."

"The document pouch contains intelligence, written in English, which provides pseudo information regarding the landing of the Allies on the beaches of France."

Juan paused to light a cigarette, his fourth of the morning. "I will refresh your memory of the information Blackeye shared with you earlier. Pas de Calais is the bogus landing site for the Allies. It is located directly across from England. Some thirty kilometers across the channel.

"The shortest distance actually, so it seems reasonable that the Allies would choose that crossing for an offensive. At least, we hope the Germans think so."

Garcia and Luis listened attentively.

Juan continued. "The documents you will hand over to Herr Himmler provides in great detail the particulars of the Allied landing. All bogus, of course, but highly convincing. The mere fact that a top secret document pouch was discovered buried in the mountains after a parachute had been spotted in the air above Brasilia adds up to a credible occurrence."

"Will I have looked inside the pouch and read its contents?

"No, not at all. After all, the pouch is deemed top secret. You, as a good citizen of Spain, would not dare to open such a pouch. Your duty is to hand it over to the authorities, whether it contains German or Allied intelligence. You are acting as a citizen of a neutral country and not involved on either side of this war; therefore, your sympathies are neutral."

"What about the boy?"

"The Germans will seek him out and interrogate him."

"What if he falters?"

"Falters? The boy knows only what has happened. The rumor of a spy. The finding of a parachute and the document pouch. He only knows what he knows."

"And their interrogation of me?"

"What of it?"

Garcia stared at Juan until his eyes became blurry. "You forget that I am supposed to deceive the Germans? That I am at the mercy of their probing? You treat this as if I am a master of deceit."

Juan nodded and began to pace slowly around the barn. He stopped in mid-step and turned toward Garcia. "Your concern is a valid concern. My suggestion is that you fervently believe your own lie."

"Believe my own lie? How is that possible?"

After deliberating a long moment, the Catalan slowly tapped his forehead. "It's all in the mind, my friend. All in the mind."

Highly exasperated, Garcia raised his voice. "Again, how is it possible to believe your own lie?"

Juan expelled his breath and moved so close to Garcia that Garcia felt the heat of his breath. He whispered in an alarmingly menacing tone.

"Your mind is a powerful tool, Garcia. Will yourself to believe you made a serendipitous discovery along with the boy. That the happenstance was real. Visualize it again and again in your mind until you believe it."

Luis nervously cleared his throat. He felt the tension in both men as they circled one another. He knew Juan's mind was capable of believing his own lies in order to deceive someone, to complete a mission. The piano teacher was a different man. Maybe he wasn't capable of masquerading as a teller of lies. And yet, he must. If he didn't, the mission would fail.

Garcia, in a voice weak with emotion, capitulated. His voice was low.

"Your tenacity amazes me. I feel as though I am being manipulated into doing something that I'm not so sure I can do." He paused and looked from Juan to Luis and back again.

"You have my word. I will not falter."

Juan saw it instantly, a flicker in the pianist's eyes so small that he almost missed it. It was fear.

The path to Inez Albeniz' house was deserted. There was no sign of the woman nor her dog. It puzzled Garcia greatly. "Señora Inez," he called, cupping his hands around his mouth. Only the sound of the mountain wind was heard in the late afternoon.

He saw her large black pot in the middle of the yard, empty, and no fire underneath. There was no rising smoke in the dilapidated chimney of the house. Even the front door was slightly ajar. Garcia wondered if he should go inside. He hesitated a moment before deciding it was fruitless. If Inez were there, the dog would be there, too.

Troubled, Garcia began to walk into Brasalia, perhaps a visit to Señora Lanzarote's, since her house would be filled with Germans at three o'clock the next day. He would tell her about the music he intended to play for Fraulein Potthast. Then, he would visit the tavern where he knew Miguel's whiskey waited for him.

Above the road to Brasalia, Juan and Luis watched Garcia with interest.

"The man is in turmoil, eh?"

"No doubt. But, he is intelligent. It is his conscience that weakens him."

"I am thinking he strives for perfection in all that he does."

"I agree. Perhaps his performance tomorrow will be perfect." Juan turned to Luis, his eyes serious and foreboding. "So much depends on it."

"I will keep a close eye on him. We must keep him safe. Let us go. We'll scout the ridge along the road. That will lead us to the village. Perhaps you can visit Miguel. It's possible he has seen the Blue Shirts."

The two men worked their way through the rocks and trees on the ridge above the road and searched for any sign of danger. They found nothing unusual and separated; Luis to the tavern and Juan to the hills above the road to Barcelona.

Chapter Thirty-Five

The rock was hurled from nine meters away, thrown at such speed and strength that its landing on the back of Garcia's head sounded like a batted ball. He crumbled to the ground, where his body rolled over, unconscious and bleeding, to the side of the roadway and into the tall grass.

Miguel looked up when Luis entered the tavern. A quick glance at the patrons seated at the small tables told him Lope and Jorge were not there. He walked to the bar as Miguel poured him a whiskey.

"Still no sign of them?"

"None. They are hiding somewhere or it's possible they have left Spain to return to their posts.

"Could be."

"Where is Garcia?"

"I thought he'd be here. We left him walking this way about an hour ago."

"Might have stopped at Señora Lanzarote's."

The two men drank quietly and watched the door. There was no sign of Garcia.

"Have you talked further with Capitan Torres?"

"*Sí.* I talked with him as he and Father Eduardo brought the old woman's body to the church. She is being buried today."

"Where?"

"In the old cemetery on the hill. I am thinking her sister is still in hiding. Garcia went to the cottage today to talk with her. I'm not sure if he was successful or not."

Luis drank the last of his whiskey. "I will take a look at Señora Lanzarote's house and see if he is there."

"Watch your back; the Blue Shirts are dangerous. Oh, by the way, your mule has been calling for you."

Luis laughed. "I plan to take her now. *Gracias.*"

Luis left the tavern and found his faithful mule waiting for him. Rather than mount her, he led her down Alia Street toward the large yellow stone house.

"Señor Neruda, greetings," called Tomas upon seeing the big Spaniard and his mule. The yardman leaned his rake against the olive tree.

"Ah, Señor Tomas, good to see you. Are the gods blessing you daily?"

"Always, my friend. Always." Tomas squinted his eyes and leaned in closer. His voice lowered to a conspiratorial whisper. "It is my belief, señor, that there truly is a spy in our village. Who else would have killed poor old Blanka?" He raised his eyebrows, "And her pitiful burro?" He continued with disbelief, "And I ask you, for what reason?"

Luis studied the old man whose reputation as the town gossip was well deserved. His eyes, though, were wise and filled with a shrewd intelligence.

"Who knows the truth, Señor Tomas? There is a war going on and brings with it unrest."

The discerning eyes of Tomas watched Luis with a penetrating stare. "You baffle me, Señor Neruda."

Luis raised his chin and looked down at the shriveled old man. "How so, señor?"

"When you are not in the tavern, I wonder where you are. Certainly not in the church with Father Eduardo."

Luis laughed quietly, his barrel chest shaking.

"Old man, your observation is correct. I am not in the Church of the Holy Father listening to the preaching of Father Eduardo or receiving Holy

Communion. I am, however, touched that you wonder where I am. May I assume that you are concerned for my well-being?"

"Ha! Your well-being is your own concern, señor. I am curious, that is all."

Luis patted the old man on the shoulder. "Your candidness amuses me."

Tomas sat on the edge of the stone portico and nervously rubbed his hands together. "Luis, I am concerned about Señor Quinones."

Luis looked at Tomas with surprise. "Señor Quinones? How so?"

Tomas struggled with his words. "I fear his life is in danger."

Luis felt his body stiffen, his adrenalin soaring.

"What is it that makes you think so?" he asked casually.

"The Judge."

"Judge Lanzarote? What about the Judge?"

Tomas seemed embarrassed as his gaze wandered around the courtyard. "The Judge came to me with many questions about his wife. He feels the señora has a lover."

"A lover? Why does this make you fear for Señor Quinones?"

"That is an easy question to answer. When the Judge sees that Garcia is so young and handsome, he will think that he is Señora Lanzarote's lover."

"I see. So, he has not actually accused Señor Quinones?" Luis sat beside Tomas, his ever-searching eyes scanning the courtyard and the street beyond.

"No, but I feel it is just a matter of time."

Luis breathed quietly and tried to sort what he was hearing. "What else?"

"The Judge tells me the señora has been smiling and singing. To him, that is evidence that she is being satisfied by another man."

"That is the only proof he has?"

Tomas raised his hands in question, "I am not sure, señor. I only know that the Judge left here two days ago to return to Barcelona. I feel he has gone to retrieve his pistol. Then, he will return and shoot Señor Quinones."

"Did he tell you he was going to kill Garcia?"

"No, he did not say so. But, he left here very upset."

The sun was easing down the Western sky. Alia Street was deserted except for a flock of chickens and one lone rooster.

"Señor Tomas, what did you tell the Judge?"

"I told him nothing! I told him nothing because I knew nothing!" Tomas quieted and began wringing his hands again. "Luis, Señor Quinones is a very handsome man. He spends time with the señora every Tuesday."

The old man paused a long moment. "Still, I do not believe Garcia is a man who would make love to another man's wife." He looked at Luis with pleading eyes. "I confess I have been telling Garcia that one day the Judge will find out how handsome he is and will kill him."

Luis nodded slowly. "Your prediction may come true, Tomas. Who knows what the Judge may do? Let us hope he is a reasonable man. Let us also hope he does not suspect Garcia as his wife's lover."

From inside the house came the faint notes of Señora Lanzarote's piano. Lilting, the music drifted into the hills like a lullaby.

Luis rose. "Tomas, have you seen Garcia this afternoon?"

Tomas also stood. "No. Señor Quinones has not been here today."

It was late when Luis left Alia Street. With a troubled mind, he decided to return to the tavern where he hoped to find the piano teacher drinking whiskey with Miguel. If he did not, he must find Juan and tell him of the missing Garcia as well as the jealous Judge.

Inside the tavern, Miguel sat at a table with Father Eduardo. When he saw Luis, he waved his arm. "Come, Luis."

Luis sat with the two men and declined a whiskey. His mind was filled with a portentous feeling of dread. He looked at Miguel and quietly asked, "Has Garcia been here?"

Miguel shook his head. "No."

Luis stood abruptly and nodded to Miguel and Father Eduardo.

"Father. Miguel. I must take my mule home. As you can tell by her constant braying, her belly is empty."

Outside the tavern, Luis quickly mounted his waiting mule and gently kicked her sides. "Come, *mula*. We must ride in the mountains."

The white mule snorted and picked up her hooves in quick response. She knew her master's commands as well as she knew her own heartbeat. She heard in his voice an anxiety that propelled her to gallop, a loathsome thing for a mule to do.

Traversing the hill behind the Church of the Holy Father, Luis guided his mule to the path on the ridge above the road to Barcelona. Once on the path, if he turned east, he would find the large rock that hid the killer of Señora Albeniz. If he turned west, he would find

Garcia's cottage. He was certain Juan would be stationed somewhere on this east/west path.

Luis cupped his hands around his mouth and emitted the call of an owl. Three hoots, pause and three more hoots. Nothing but silence in reply. His instinct told him to turn west, back toward the piano teacher's cottage.

Once he was one kilometer along the path, he stopped again and signaled for Juan. Three hoots, pause, three hoots. No response. He pushed his mule onward toward Garcia's cottage.

Chapter Thirty-Six

Even before he was fully conscious, he knew he was bound, his arms behind his back, his shoulders stretched in enormous pain, his feet together so tightly he could move nothing. He felt as though his body had been thrown from a mountaintop, over rocks and brush, until it landed in a heap of battered skin and bones.

Garcia was reluctant to open his eyes. He did not want to see what waited for him. His ears heard only the mountain breeze that whispered among the rocks. The night air rested in sweet moisture upon his face as he licked his lips.

He smelled her before he saw her, the stench unfurling in the air and reminding him who she was, a mad woman who cooked mysterious things in a huge black pot. His stomach lurched and he turned his head to vomit.

Hesitantly, he opened his eyes to the darkness around him. He blinked several times before his vision cleared and permitted him to see his surroundings. To his right, lying alongside him was a long, dark object, almost discernible, but not quite.

He squinted to improve his vision, drawing in more detail. The realization that the object next to him was a body surfaced in his mind. The body of a human, unmoving and stiff. He willed himself to remain quiet, though he wanted to scream to the heavens above. *What have you done to me?*

His fear forced perspiration from his pores; his dread a heavy weight upon his chest.

Clenching his teeth, he made himself study the body carefully, his eyes traveling its length and resting upon the face. He knew the face. He knew the deep scar in the chin and the heavy, hairy eyebrows that he had seen from only inches away.

Even in the night, the skin of Lope's face became clear, white and lifeless, as if it had been painted to perform as a circus clown, the expression on the dead man's face twisted in torment. Maybe he did not know he was going to die. How did he die? The woman, of course. The mad woman who lives like an animal and preys upon humans.

Garcia closed his eyes and breathed deeply and wondered why he was still alive. He knew implicitly that whatever had happened to Lope was soon to happen to him.

From his left side, about thirty meters away, he saw movement; a silhouette of the woman bent over and pushing wood underneath the large kettle. In moments, flames shot upward, smoke billowed toward the heavens and the furious sound of a crackling fire filled the barnyard.

His body began to twitch in a desperate attempt to run. But, how could he? The ropes that bound him would ensure his death before sunrise.

He lifted his head slightly to better watch her. The sight of her picking up a hatchet sent his body into spasms, a scream hesitating in his throat and his mouth opening to release it. .

In a tilted hobble, she walked toward him, the hatchet in her hand. He closed his eyes and feigned unconsciousness. He did not want to see the blade of the hatchet swing toward him and split his head in two. He quieted his breathing and waited.

A powerful swing struck the leg bone of Lope, just below the knee. It was a thud-like sound as the blade dug into bone with such force that the upper body of Lope rose up from the ground in silent protest. A few more blows and the leg was severed from the dead man, a grotesquely morbid sight as the woman lifted the leg and returned to the fire, where the water in the cooking pot boiled in delightful anticipation.

Through slitted eyes, he watched while the mad woman returned again and again and dismembered the body of Lope. As Lope's body slowly disappeared, he saw another body on the other side of where Lope had lain. Jorge, of course.

Nausea crept into his throat and he swallowed it back. Morbid thoughts exploded in his head. It was clear to him that the woman had followed him and Señora Albeniz as they traveled the road to Barcelona, followed them along the upper ridge of the mountain. He was certain she saw Lope and Jorge murder her beloved sister.

Garcia watched the removal of Jorge's body, limb by limb, until the spot was vacant. Two men, whose existence had been slowly sliced away, leaving nothing but bones in a cooking pot, had simply disappeared.

An acrid odor, more pungent than goat dung, filled the air and again he was holding down vomit. The stench from the cooking pot mixed with the constant rise of caustic smoke permeated his nostrils and lungs no matter how he turned his head.

He had remained as still as possible. If he vomited, the mad woman would become more aware of him. But, he knew she would come. He knew the hatchet would be in her hand and he wondered what she would remove from his body first. Would she kill him before she dismembered him? He shuddered and again turned his head to vomit.

As he suspected, the mad woman walked slowly toward him, holding the murderous hatchet and muttering to herself in an obscure language that was surely spoken by the devil himself.

Never had he known such fear; never had he been in such pain. Perhaps his death would be merciful. At the moment his heart stopped beating, he would not feel the removal of his feet, his legs. And his hands. Hands that all his life had played beautiful music, had caused him to weep with joy at the sounds of Beethoven and Chopin. Would his severed hands go to hand heaven where they could be placed upon someone else's arms to play once more?

He felt the presence of the old woman standing over him. As he looked into her eyes, he saw an amazing thing. Her eyes were dungeon black, depthless pools of nothingness.

"Where are your eyes, old woman?" he asked softly, almost tenderly.

She said nothing and continued to stare at him. The hatchet in her hand remained still.

He waited. "I am sorry your sister is dead." How ridiculous. What difference did it make that he expressed sympathy to the mad woman?

She would not understand his grief at having seen her sister's face shot away. Still, he was sorry she had died. That she had lain there lifeless with her orange earrings and long skirt pointing toward Barcelona, her scallops and the blue of the Mediterranean.

"Who will cook empanadas for you now, señora?"

Still she said nothing. He could see the faint light of the rising sun behind her, escaping the peaks of the mountains. Perhaps she did not kill after the sunrise, he thought. Preposterous. She was going to kill him no matter what – day, night. What did it matter?

"You know I play the piano? I play lullabies." He began to hum, softly at first, lilting and then raising his tenor voice in song, '… *kiss the morning with gladness, lift your heart to the sky. Give me your hand to go waltzing, waltzing in meadows nigh*'.

After a long moment, the hatchet fell from the old woman's hand. She dropped her body down near him and sat with her legs crossed and, in a voice cracked with age, began to sing, '*kiss the morning with gladness…*'

"Garcia. Garcia." Juan touched the shoulder of the pianist gently as he cut the cords from around Garcia's ankles and then saw with alarm his swollen wrists while he sliced through the bindings.

"He will never play for the Germans. Look at his wrists."

"And the bruising."

Garcia groaned and opened his eyes. Intently, he studied the faces of Juan and Luis, blinking repeatedly, confused, as his eyes went from one face to the other.

"Relax, my friend. You are safe."

Garcia nodded, still not sure who they were. Finally, as if lightning had entered his brain, he tried to sit up. "The woman? Where is the woman?"

"She is here, but she is dead."

"Dead? How can she be dead?"

Luis pointed toward the prostrate body of Señora Albeniz. "We found her there, just as you see her."

"Let me see."

Juan and Luis pulled Garcia up to a sitting position. It was then that they saw the blood matted in a wound on the back of his head. "What is this?"

Garcia reached up and gently probed with his fingers. He grimaced with pain. "I cannot remember. Though I am thinking it was the old woman." Despite the severity of his wound, he smiled. "She was well-known for her rock-throwing capabilities."

"What can you remember?

"Nothing until I woke up here late into the night. Help me stand."

Luis placed his large arms underneath Garcia's and lifted him. "Easy. Do not move too quickly."

The two men steadied Garcia and watched as he stood and looked toward the cooking pot. "Have you looked in the pot?"

"*Sí.* We saw nothing but bones."

"Lope and Jorge."

Juan and Luis looked at each other and back to Garcia. "The old woman did all this?"

Garcia nodded. "I watched her dismember both bodies and throw each piece into the boiling water. It has boiled all night." Garcia felt himself become faint at the memory. "Let us sit for a moment."

The three of them left the old woman and the pot of bones and sat beneath a nearby tree, where rays from the rising sun filtered down through the leaves.

Falteringly, Garcia spoke. "What killed the old woman?"

"It's hard to say. We found her lying near you as if she were sleeping. Perhaps a heart attack, stroke. Who knows?"

"What are we to do?"

"It is imperative that Capitan Torres investigate what has happened." Juan's face was grim. His well-thought-out plan to cultivate the piano teacher into a sub-agent had been usurped by a crazy old woman and two Nazi sympathizers.

He looked at Garcia and Luis, his face hard, his eyes dangerous as they darted around the barnyard, from the cooking pot to the dead woman. His voice lowered. "Of course, it is not necessary to inform him right away."

Turning to Garcia, he lowered his voice. "My friend, we must decide what we are to do about the Germans. But, first, you need care and rest."

"I...I know that I do. Yet, I..." He turned and looked at the Albeniz sister lying peacefully on the ground, her hands almost in prayer.

Incredibly, a smile creased the worn face as if her last thought was pleasant. "I do not want to leave the woman exposed. Animals, you know."

"I understand." He quickly nodded to Luis. "We'll move her to the cottage."

The woman's body weighed little. How she had hurled rocks with such force was a mystery. How she had dragged the dead bodies of Lope and Jorge to the barnyard was inexplicable.

Without speaking, Juan and Luis left her body in the cottage where she would be safe from prowling animals.

"I am indebted to you." Garcia hung his head, despair unlike anything he had ever known overcame him. First Blanka, now her sister. And, of course, Pedro, the wondrous donkey.

"Let us go."

Luis lifted Garcia to the top of his mule. "You are a lucky man, Señor Quinones."

"Lucky? I don't understand."

"The singing. It was your singing we heard in the mountains. It led us straight to you. We searched here earlier in the night, but there was no one. You were not at your cottage either. When we came through on our way back to the village, we heard music."

Saved by music. How appropriate.

Chapter Thirty-Seven

The mule carried Garcia Quinones through the trees and rocks of the Pyrenees. Alongside the mule, the spy and his sub-agent worked their way west toward the cottage. A brightening sun rose in the sky and crept closer to three o'clock and the Germans.

"We will have to involve the señorita. There is no other way." Juan pulled on the reins of the mule to hurry him along. "We will need her help. It is hopeful that she can sooth these wounds. Bathe him."

"How can he possibly pass the document pouch to the Germans? He can hardly walk."

Juan breathed deeply and looked to the sky, his words philosophical, his demeanor sober. "Who knows what this man can do? If he can sing to a woman when he has seen her mutilate two men and cook them, he is capable of many things."

Juan smiled and winked at Luis. "Our piano friend lives with the help of the gods. He will not falter."

They plodded on.

"There is something I have not told you." Luis cleared his throat.

"And that is?"

"I have learned from Tomas, Señora Lanzarote's yardman, that the Judge thinks his wife has a lover. The yardman thinks Garcia is the prime suspect, but he can't be sure."

Juan shook his head. "Whether it is true or not, Judge Lanzarote has a reputation for being an impatient, harsh man in his court. I'm not so sure he would be lenient with someone he thought was making love to his wife." Juan reminded himself to talk with Felipe; the mission was far more important than his personal concerns.

"Our troubles mount, Luis. We must keep a close eye on our piano friend."

Immediately, Juan's mind began to solve the problem of the Judge. He would speak to him right away. After all, he had been in Juan's clandestine life for years.

Juan and Luis' eyes swept the cottage and the barnyard where goats frolicked and bleated noisily. There was no sign of the señorita, but that was not unusual. Garcia had warned her to stay inside the cottage and she had complied.

The mule was led into the barn where Garcia slid off her back. "I am in need of water."

"Come to the cottage."

"Jordana will see you."

"So she will. We must tend your wounds. Then, you must sleep." Juan spoke in a manner that solidified his role as spymaster, his command of Garcia, his crusade for a successful mission.

Haltingly, with the aid of Juan and Luis, Garcia stumbled toward the cottage. At the door, he cried out. "Jordana, I am here. I have two companions with me. Do not be afraid."

Inside, the cottage was empty. There was no sign of her.

"Jordana," Garcia called. After waiting a few moments, he looked toward the corner of the cottage and the piano. "Are you here?"

Only the sound of the goats' bleating filled the morning.

Garcia looked at Luis and nodded toward the piano. Luis understood immediately and walked quietly to the corner of the cottage and leaned his tall body over the piano.

There, huddled in a ball in the small space behind the piano, was the young señorita. Her large dark eyes looked at him with a bewildered uncertainty. Afraid to move, she merely stared at him.

Luis smiled. "Do not be alarmed. We are friends of Garcia."

Still, the frightened young woman sat unmoving.

Luis turned to Garcia, who sat in a wooden chair by the small table. "Come, señor. Talk to your señorita."

Garcia grimaced as he pulled himself from a sitting position and walked to the edge of the piano, his lean frame bending forward to see Jordana's hiding place. "*No se preocupe, mi amor. Estoy aqui,*" he said soothingly. Do not worry, my love. I am here.

Haltingly, Jordana stood, her eyes darting around the cottage in apprehension. She saw Luis and Juan behind Garcia. "Who are they?"

Garcia looked back at Juan and Luis. Neither sent him a warning.

"They are my compatriots."

"Compatriots? I don't understand."

Garcia sighed heavily and turned toward Juan and Luis. "The large man is Luis. You should know him from the village. The other man is Juan. He is not from Brasalia but visits here on a...a..."

"I am here as an envoy for Britain, señorita. It is my duty to conduct certain...certain tasks. I have enlisted the aid of Luis and Garcia. You need not fear."

Jordana absorbed this. His voice, steadfast and resolute, emanated a trustworthiness that calmed her.

She looked at Garcia as if she recognized him for the first time. "You do not look well."

He smiled at her. "That is why I'm here." He turned and showed her the back of his head. "Do you think perhaps you can put my head back together?"

Jordana paled at the sight of the wound, of the hair matted with blood. She came from behind the piano and pulled Garcia to a chair. "Sit," she said.

The three men looked at each other; they were under the command of a woman. They watched Jordana heat water, gather rags and prepare soup, all the while muttering to herself about the irresponsibilities of men.

The young señorita found scissors and cut away the dried blood from Garcia's head. She removed Garcia's shirt and bathed him where bruises and swelling wrapped around his wrists. When he was almost naked, she pulled him to the bed, but not before filling him with hot soup and sassafras tea.

And there he slept. He slept with no dreams, no anxieties, no movement. It was as though the gods had proclaimed him theirs while they healed his body and soothed his mind.

In the barn, Juan read his watch. "Five hours," he mused. "Five short hours. If we let him sleep until two o'clock, that will give us one hour until the Germans arrive."

"Can he do it?"

It was a long moment before Juan answered. He smoked his cigarette almost viciously, pulling on it with his lips hard and tight. He blew smoke up into the air with such force that it lingered high above them. He paced the barn floor in anxious circles while his mind turned over every detail of the meeting with the Germans.

"Yes, he can do it."

At two o'clock, they returned to the cottage where the sleeping Garcia lay unmoving, one arm thrown over his chest, the other wrapped around Jordana. She was awake and looked at them with watchful eyes.

"It is time."

She nodded and eased her body from Garcia's grasp. He stirred slightly.

"Garcia."

Groggy-eyed, Garcia raised his head. "Piano. I must play."

Without speaking, they watched him leave the bed and remove the woolen blanket from the piano. He seated himself, leaned forward and placed his hands on the keys. Then, ever so slowly, he moved the middle finger of his right hand and repeatedly tapped the middle C key. From the grand Bösendorfer piano came a glorious sound. A blending of notes not unlike the ringing of crystal bells, music so like singing angels that tears began to fill Garcia's eyes. Behind him, Jordana gazed at him in wonder. Juan and Luis had been holding their breath as the notes lifted above them and hung there. When Garcia finished and his hands were still, Juan stared at him. *What a shame*, he thought, *to share such beautiful music with the Germans.*

Chapter Thirty-Eight

The pianist dressed in a freshly washed and starched shirt and a jacket made of light wool, fashioned with wide lapels and heavy shoulder padding, giving him an uncommon look for a small village in Spain, being more suited to Paris or London. He was somber as he looked at himself in the antique oval mirror that hung above the piano. *Who are you*? he asked himself, as he studied the serious set of his mouth and the steeled line of his jaw. He heard himself answer, the words from another place, not the heart of the pianist. "I am a spy."

Garcia stepped outside the cottage and felt the warmth of the sun on his face. He placed his brushed suede hat on his head and began walking down the road to Brasalia, with Juan and Luis on either side. Jordana had combed his hair to fall over the wound at the back of his head. The cuffs of his shirt hid the bruises around his wrists. Bandages wrapped his right arm near his shoulder where only hours ago a bullet had pierced his body.

"You have the document pouch, of course." Juan's words were formal.

Garcia patted his jacket. "Here."

"Are you ready?"

A cynical laugh. "Do not worry. I am ready. As you commanded, I have willed myself to believe these lies. Along with the boy, I found a spy's parachute and a top secret document pouch. It is my duty to turn them over to the authorities."

Garcia took a deep breath. "What of Señora Lanzarote? I fear she will lock the doors of the hacienda and there will be no recital. She detests the Germans."

Juan had no idea if Rosina would open her doors to Garcia or the Germans. When he left her, she was distraught. She had consumed too much whiskey and cursed the Germans late into the night. He must depend on her sense of duty.

"Do not worry about Señora Lanzarote. We will be nearby. We will wait for you to finish the recital. Most likely, they will question the boy. Perhaps even search your cottage for anything that might weaken the legitimacy of your story."

"Search my cottage? What of Jordana?"

"She will be safe. She is to hide in the mountains until she hears from us. And, yes, the Germans will want to ensure you did not manufacture this information you have found."

"The Germans are thorough, no?"

Juan stopped on the road and touched Garcia on the shoulder.

"My friend, the Germans are the most formidable enemy you will ever meet." The spy paused and looked deep into the eyes of Garcia Quinones. "Remember what you've been taught."

After crossing a small bridge, the two men left Garcia and proceeded to the high ridge that ran east and west across the foothills.

"It occurs to me I did not wish him godspeed," said Juan as he lit a cigarette. He squelched his match and blew smoke into the mountain air. "He will need it."

The village square seemed almost deserted when Garcia approached Alia Street. He turned when he heard loud voices coming from the front of the police station. There stood Capitan Torres, his face red, as he shouted at a woman who stood in apparent agitation in front of him. It took only a moment for him to realize the woman was Señora Rios. As he came closer, it was quite clear that a heated discussion was taking place regarding the missing Jordana.

"What kind of *policia* are you?" she spat. "You have not found my daughter. I will contact the authorities in Barcelona and they will do what you have not done. They will find her!" Señora Rios turned on her heel and puffed her way toward the market. Garcia watched as the capitan shrugged and shook his head.

"Capitan Torres, I see you have suffered an indignity at the hands of Señora Rios." Garcia smiled at the bewildered man.

"*Sí*, I cannot understand her constant badgering. I am working day and night. First her missing daughter, then the murder of Señora Albeniz. I am losing my mind, Señor Quinones. She has fallen off the face of the earth. Her mother wants me to search every house in Brasalia. I have searched dozens so far, but *every* house?"

Garcia's eyes widened. "Every house?"

"Every house. The señora suspects someone is hiding her so the poor girl will not have to marry the old man in Madrid."

Every house? Garcia slumped. "That will be a big job for you, eh?"

The capitan lifted his hands helplessly. "This is too much for one man."

"I understand," said Garcia. He saw the fatigue in the policeman's face and wished he did not have to tell him of Señora Inez Albeniz. Reluctantly, he leaned toward the dismayed Torres, "I am afraid I have more work for you, Capitan."

"More work? What more work?"

"The body of Inez Albeniz lies in her cottage. It seems that she has suffered a heart attack or stroke."

"Yi! How did this happen?" The short man threw his arms up in frustration. He stomped the ground with his right boot, like a bull preparing to charge. "*Condesation!*"

"I am sorry." He tarried only a moment before leaving the frazzled capitan and walking across the square to Señora Lanzarote's house. What about the bones of Lope and Jorge? Surely, the capitan will find them and collapse with the frustration of so many dead bodies.

At exactly 2:50, a timid Garcia knocked on the large wooden door. The polished door swung open and Señora Rosina Lanzarote smiled at him. She stepped back and swung her arm in greeting. The color of her dress was emerald green, fitted, a narrow belt at her waist. Wide lapels of the dress folded back and revealed the swell of her breasts, where smooth skin spoke of unending softness.

"Señora." Relieved, Garcia smiled broadly.

"Ah, Señor Quinones, I have been waiting for you. Come." She led him into the music room, a room soon to be filled with Germans.

He tried to determine if she fretted over their pending arrival. Her face was serene, controlled. It was clear she was ready for what was to come.

The buffet in the piano room was arranged with refreshments. Wine and wine glasses of fine crystal sat in a neat row along with whiskey in a myriad of beautifully shaped bottles. Garcia wondered why such finery had been provided for the Germans. "Nice," he lied.

"You are prepared for the recital?"

"Of course."

"I am thinking this will be the first time I have heard you play." Her large dark eyes were luminous, engaging him with their warmth, a thing women did so well. Did the señora know he had not played publicly in years? Did she know he prayed to the gods that he would perform to the satisfaction of Herr Himmler and his mistress?

"The first time?" His eyes fell to the floor and, oddly, began to count the stones leading to the piano. For some reason, he was uncomfortable. He did not want to fail. He did not want to fail the señora, Juan, Jordana, the Allies. He felt himself weaken. "A glass of wine would be nice, Señora Lanzarote."

"Please, call me Rosina."

"Rosina." He watched her back as she poured his wine. Her hair swept up like angel wings, a large ivory comb catching it close to her head.

"The Judge?"

She turned quickly, holding the wine glass out for him. "What of the Judge?"

Garcia sipped his wine. "He is well?"

He saw her eyes sweep around the room and return to him with candor. "As far as I know. I have not talked with him for a while."

In his nervousness, he held the glass tightly, steadying his hand and stilling the bile he felt in his stomach. He looked down to see if the document pouch caused any kind of noticeable bulge in his jacket and was relieved it did not.

Nodding his head toward the entry door, he smiled slightly, "Almost time."

"Yes," she said, with a calmness that surprised him.

"Maybe they will be late."

Laughter rose from the beautiful lips. "Or, not come at all."

"Ah, the miracle of miracles."

They laughed together, only to have their smiles falter as they turned and saw Judge Felipe Lanzarote standing in the doorway, a pistol as black as the devil's heart pointed directly at the piano teacher.

"Señor Quinones, I presume." The judge's words were laden with bitterness, the curve of his lips an ugly line, as if he had just bitten the head from a snake.

Rosina did not move. From within, she found her voice, almost windless. "Felipe, it is not necessary to greet us with a pistol."

Felipe's haggard face, a two-day old beard darkening the lower half, scowled at them. A meticulously neat man, his clothes were rumpled, his cape askew around his shoulders, his hair disheveled.

"Madam, I would not consider my arrival as a greeting." He teetered forward slightly as though fatigued. It was not fatigue – it was whiskey. So much of it, he tilted to one side, his body in a slow circuitous movement. The pistol in his hand wavered slightly, a precarious movement from the perspective of anyone in its line of fire.

A contemptuous smile. "Are you or are you not going to introduce me to your handsome young friend?"

Rosina raised her chin. "Of course. But, not until you put the pistol away." Unwavering, she held his gaze.

"How can I kill your lover if I do not have a pistol?"

Kill her lover? Garcia winced. At once he saw an image of the cemetery on the hill above the village. He would be buried alongside all the other lovers who had, over the ages, been murdered because of their desire to love a beautiful woman. Tomas had been correct in his prediction. Tomas' words...*if only you were not so handsome* ... swept into his head.

"My lover?" Her voice softened. "You are my only lover, Felipe."

Then, with an incredible tenderness. "*Usted es mi solamente amor, mi querido.*" *You are my only love, my darling*. She moved closer to Felipe and reached out her hand. "Come. Sit with me."

He was immovable. "You," he said, and pointed the gun at Garcia. "You are Señor Garcia Quinones, formerly of Brussels, Paris and London?"

He paused and narrowed his suspicious eyes. "The renowned pianist who captivates the world with his music?"

Garcia felt the wound in his arm throb; his stomach twist. "Are you a music aficionado, Judge Lanzarote?"

His smile was forced, but necessary.

"You must be if you know that I am Garcia Quinones... formerly of Brussels, Paris and London."

"I know who you are! You are my wife's lover!"

Garcia sipped his wine and contemplated the man who stood before him. "Señor Lanzarote, while I find your wife beautiful as well as desirable, I only teach her piano. It is what I do... teach piano."

From the couch across the room, Rosina spoke. "Felipe, I want you to come and sit with me."

Felipe looked at his wife and then back to Garcia, uncertain what to do.

Garcia leaned against the buffet and held Felipe's stare.

The Judge's face softened slightly as he turned to Rosina. "I cannot live without you, Rosina."

"I do not want you to live without me, Felipe."

Felipe lowered the pistol and, with a slight waver, walked to the couch. When he sat beside Rosina, she picked up his hand and held it. He was trembling. He leaned toward his wife and in a hoarse whisper spoke into her ear. "I am so lost."

Rosina placed her arms around her husband. "I am here, my darling."

From across the room, Garcia watched anxiously as Rosina soothed her husband. The Germans would arrive momentarily and the charade would begin. Yet, the Judge held a pistol and had consumed too much whiskey. Garcia finished his glass of wine and walked over to the couch and placed his hand on Felipe's shoulder. "Señor, you must prepare yourself for the Germans."

Felipe looked up and nodded. "Of course. Do you think I would miss a duping of the Germans? The bastards." Unsteady, the Judge stood and placed his pistol beneath his cape.

Rosina took his arm. "I will pour you some coffee. You will feel better. Will you comb your hair?"

Felipe smiled. "Thank you, my love." Then, he turned to Garcia. "My apologies, Señor Quinones. I hope I did not offend you." He smiled sheepishly, "You know, the pistol."

"Not at all. I am sorry if I have caused you some...unrest."

Felipe's expression became somber, teetering on the edge of a feigned sobriety. "My friend, we must discuss other things. Juan has sent me here to be of assistance. Though I am plied with too much whiskey, I am at your service."

"My gratitude."

"Rosina, please hurry with the coffee."

Rosina rushed into the room and placed the cup in Felipe's hands. "Drink, my darling. We have little time." She held a comb and began to comb his hair.

They heard the automobile long before it reached the town square. Garcia eased closer to the window and pulled back a corner of the draperies.

"It begins," he said softly to himself. He watched the long hood of the cream-colored Packard round the corner of the police station and stop in the middle of the square. Behind, a jeep with German soldiers slowed to a stop.

The flags above the erect headlights waved the insignia of the Third Reich and announced the arrival of the Reichsfuhrer. Garcia counted a total of five soldiers, including the driver.

In the back seat of the lead car, a woman wearing a bright red hat and the man beside her in his inglorious, contemptible military regalia, peered out into the square. The man's self-importance was flagrant as he stepped out of the gleaming car and onto the dusty earth of the square.

The woman followed her companion and they both stood and looked around the square. She was not overly attractive, her hips somewhat wide. She was short, the calves of her legs thick, the opaqueness of her stocking accenting their stocky.

She pulled the netting from her hat away from her face. Her demeanor held a practiced aloofness as she placed her hand through the proffered arm of the Reichsfuhrer.

As he walked toward the yellow stone house, Herr Himmler thrust out his chest, posing for an imaginary photograph. He lifted his feet in a prance and climbed the steps, slowly, one at a time.

In the quiet of the room, Garcia drank the last of his wine and waited for a knock at the door. He looked at Rosina, who stood pensively near the entrance. He then glanced at a somewhat sobered Felipe and winked. "Make them wait."

On the third knock, the señora opened the door slowly. She, too, could be pretentious. She stood smiling, her chin lifted in resolute calm. "Good afternoon."

"Ah, as promised Señora Lanzarote, we have returned for a glorious recital." With a tight smile, Herr Himmler, leaned forward. "May we come in?" A planned courtesy, of course, to impress his mistress.

"You may."

The Germans entered the house, none taking the time to wipe their feet on the rug the housemaid had so diligently placed at the doorway.

"May I present Hedwig Potthast? You may call her Hedwig."

The woman in the red hat moved forward with her hand extended.

"It is my pleasure to meet you, Señora Lanzarote."

"Hedwig. Herr Himmler. My husband, Judge Felipe Lanzarote of the Courts of Spain."

"Ah, what a pleasure, Herr Lanzarote. I am aware of your prominence in the courts of Spain as well as your friendship with the General."

Felipe bowed slightly, but did not offer his hand.

From across the room, Garcia watched the procession of Germans enter the house. Ridiculously, he again counted the stones, fourteen stones to where they stood, and then raised his eyes to see the man with the spectacles watching him with interest. Hedwig Potthast watched him also, a tilted angle to her head, scrutinizing him surreptitiously from beneath the rim of her hat, in an almost flirtatious way.

Garcia waited and watched the red of her hat and the red of her dress move toward him with a peculiar gait. She was unbalanced; her large hips and thighs out of proportion with her slim shoulders and head, giving her the appearance that, at the last moment of birth, her upper half was formed in a size much too small for the rest of her. A genetic faux pas. It was laughable that Heinrich Himmler would allow a genetic faux pas in his mistress.

She was charming. "Ah, we meet again, Señor Quinones. It has been a long time, has it not?" She stood close to him as she talked, a little too close. He could smell her perfume, a French perfume. Of course, it was French; everything in France now belonged to the Germans, including its legendary perfumes.

Her hand, puffy with short fingers, reached out and touched his arm. "My dear Señor Quinones, how long I have waited to hear you play again." She moved even closer. He felt her breath on his face as she laughed; a laugh so shrill, his ears began to ring. She touched him again.

She continued on without a response from him, asking questions but never waiting for a reply. Finally, as if checking herself, she paused abruptly. "What do you plan to play for me?"

Lipstick, *claret* like her hat, smeared her teeth. He moved his gaze from the colored lips to the wide eyes. "Beethoven, of course."

"Ah, my favorite German composer, Señor Quinones." Her gushing caused an anxiety within him and he eased away from the overpowering perfume and the red lips.

At that moment, Himmler joined the conversation from a few feet away.

"Did I hear you say Beethoven?" He sashayed toward them holding a glass of wine. The light from the overhead chandelier glistened on the brass of his shoulder boards and reflected in glasses that hid his somewhat small, insignificant eyes.

Garcia stiffened. Rosina touched his arm. "German composer? What about Bach?" she asked with feigned interest.

Both Himmler and his mistress responded excitedly. "*Nicht konnen wir Bach nicht auslassen!*"

"No, we cannot leave out Bach!" repeated Himmler's mistress.

Himmler raised his glass, "To German composers."

Hedwig promptly lifted her glass. "To German composers."

Garcia held his glass close to his chest and held Himmler's gaze. He saw contempt in his eyes, a supremacy that fortified his belief that one day soon he would have the world filled entirely with a supreme race. At that moment, he felt the depth of his hatred for the German, he felt it run the length of his body and consume his heart. He would play for the Germans at this fantasy recital. But, it would be the last time.

Never taking his eyes from Himmler's, Garcia raised his glass. "To all the brilliant composers of the world."

Rosina also lifted her glass. "To beautiful music everywhere."

"To the extraordinary pianists in the world," followed Felipe, looking at a subdued Garcia.

An uncomfortable silence followed. Hedwig refilled her wine glass. Himmler wiped his mustache with his handkerchief. Rosina and Garcia stood unmoving while the room settled into a superficial peace.

Felipe, still somewhat hazed with whiskey, cocked his head slightly and addressed Himmler. "The Allies have had many recent successes in this war, eh?"

Himmler looked at Felipe from behind his round spectacles. His face, with its weak chin, hardened before Felipe's eyes, the muscles in his cheeks sucking in and out in an obvious attempt at self-control.

"You are a war strategist, Herr Lanzarote?"

Felipe smiled warmly. He was a big man, tall, wide-shouldered, with an imposing deep voice. A perfect man to sit in a courtroom and wield his power. He was not intimidated.

His black eyes almost twinkled as he studied Himmler. "A realist, Reichsfuhrer." He watched as Himmler's face reddened.

"And a lover of freedom." Felipe's voice lowered as he leaned into Himmler, his lips a hard line, curled at the edges with loathing. "My grandmother was a Jew."

From across the room, "Shall we begin the recital?" Hedwig had taken a chair near the piano, close to Garcia, her thick legs crossed at the ankles. The red in her cheeks matched the red in her dress.

Himmler walked to her side and stood stiffly, one hand resting on the holstered pistol on his hip.

"Do begin, Herr Quinones."

Rosina smiled hesitantly at Garcia. "Señor Quinones, we anticipate your recital with much joy." Her breathing was shallow. Pink splotches lined her neck where a single strand of pearls hung in perfect order. She had had enough of the Germans.

Garcia's tall, lean frame leaned on the edge of the piano, a perfect picture of practiced ease. He smiled at Hedwig Potthast and settled himself at the bench. "It gives me great pleasure to play for you."

The ivory keys lay in hushed anticipation, waiting for the majestic hands of the pianist. He straightened his back and placed his hands on the keyboard. He hesitated and allowed his mind to gather the notes of Beethoven's *Pathétique in C Minor – Grave-Allegro molto e con brio-Grave-Allegro molto e con-brio.*

The little finger of his right hand twitched slightly as he moved it to the middle C. He paused, then placed his index finger on G. He drew a breath before his thumb gently rubbed the E flat, warming the ivory. Farther down the keyboard, an octave lower, his left hand rested and then formed the C minor four-note chord. He began with forte, loud and aggressive, then slowed the notes that followed to Piano, a quiet, seductive movement.

At last, the notes lifted into the room. Alluring notes, notes that could cajole the heart of a dead man to rise again and dance to its melody, swept around the room.

On he played, *adagio sostenuto*, tender and slow, a melting of melodies that flowed together to send their beauty soaring into the heavens. It was then, in a place all alone, the pianist, whose slim and delicate hands found solace as he played, was reborn, sent into the universe to recall his soul and mend his heart. Time stood still and then, delicately, as if the piano keys were the heart of a newborn baby, he struck the last notes.

The loud clapping of Hedwig Potthast pierced the room like flying bullets. "Bravo!" she cried. "Bravo!"

Still standing, Heinrich Himmler barely moved his hands as he stoically applauded.

Garcia turned around on the piano bench and smiled as he faced the exuberant Hedwig. Across the room, Rosina looked in wonder at her piano teacher. Next to her, Felipe nodded his approval. Garcia saw he held Rosina's hand.

"More. You must play more." Himmler's mistress looked up at Germany's Reichsfuhrer. "He must play more. Tell him," she commanded.

"An encore, please," said Himmler, coldly.

Imperceptibly, Garcia nodded and turned around on the bench and again placed his hands on the keys. Claude Debussy's *Clair de Lune* began with a lilting C note. Before the first chord could be completed, he heard the Reichsfuhrer's biting words.

"I don't believe, Herr Quinones, that Debussy is a German composer." He looked through his spectacles as if examining a body for autopsy, his eyes so penetrating that Garcia shivered involuntarily. He then turned slowly from the keyboard.

"Debussy? He was a brilliant French composer, Herr Himmler."

Himmler, rubbed the leather of his holster, pressed his lips together for an agonizing moment. "I detest the French."

Garcia turned back to the piano and paused. He lowered his head, his breath shallow. He felt perspiration above his lips while a peculiar coldness crept over his body. As he looked down, his eye caught the edge of something red on his white shirt. It was a long moment before he realized it was his own blood. Casually, he reached up and pulled his jacket together, buttoning the middle button.

The grating voice of Fraulein Potthast jolted Garcia. "More," she cried and again clapped loudly in the quiet room.

Garcia raised his hands and placed them on the keys of the piano. Delicately, his fingers hardly touching the keys, the notes of Beethoven's Piano Sonata No. 23 F minor, Op. 57 "*Appassionata*" floated out into the room, pensively at first; then, a romantic, almost feminine melody, smooth and silky, captivated everyone in the room.

Himmler smiled smugly. He raised his chin and nodded his approval of Beethoven. He removed his hand from his holstered pistol and placed it on Hedwig's shoulder. She looked from the hands of Garcia to Himmler and smiled.

The last note fell softly, an appropriate ending to Garcia Quinones' recital. He stood from the piano and faced the room and bowed slightly. "Your applause humbles me."

He looked at Himmler who still clapped. His eyes then traveled to the pistol whose looming blackness continued to intimidate him.

It was time. He must approach the Reichsfuhrer privately and inform him of the secret pouch. Fear washed his body like a giant ocean wave. He teetered somewhat as he stepped forward.

"Herr Himmler, it pleases me to play for you."

Himmler replied dispassionately, as was his nature. "The music of a German composer is always pleasing to listen to."

With difficulty, Garcia moved closer to the German and lowered his voice. "I would like to have a private word with you, Herr Himmler."

Himmler seemed confused. "A private word with me? Of what nature?" He turned slightly as if dismissing Garcia.

"Of dire importance," Garcia lied.

"And what would a pianist consider of dire importance?"

Garcia smiled slightly, a conspiratorial smile that promised Himmler he would not be disappointed. He moved even closer, touching the cuff of Himmler's sleeve. Himmler flinched.

"May we retire to another room for a moment?" Garcia asked.

Himmler stared blankly at him. A commoner was addressing royalty and Himmler's need to withdraw from the conversation was tantamount. He stepped backward.

"Your familiarity offends me, Herr Quinones."

For a moment, Garcia was taken aback.

"My apologies, but it is my desire to give to you top secret information that substantiates my request to confer with you privately, Herr Himmler."

There. He said it. The lie was between them. Upon hearing the words *top secret*, Garcia saw an infinitesimal widening of the pupils in Himmler's eyes.

"Top secret information? How is that possible?"

"It is so."

Himmler looked away from Garcia in contemplation. Without looking at him, he said. "Let us hope your knowledge of top secret information is as expert as your knowledge of German composers."

He skulked away toward the hallway and into an adjoining room. Garcia followed, breathing deeply, putting oxygen into his blood. He must think clearly.

Upon entering the room, Himmler turned and crossed his arms upon his chest." Well? Do not keep me waiting."

"Of course," Garcia stammered. He reached inside his jacket and removed the leather pouch. *Classified Top Secret – Not to Be Opened by Unauthorized Personnel.*

Himmler extended his hand, palm up. Garcia dutifully placed the pouch in the waiting hand.

"What have we here, Herr Quinones?"

"I do not know."

"Then, what makes you say it is of dire importance?"

Garcia pointed to the printed words on the pouch. "Classified Top Secret."

Himmler raised his eyebrows. "Have you read the contents?"

"No."

Himmler looked at Garcia over the rim of his spectacles. "Where did you get this?"

"I found it. Along with someone else."

"Who?"

"A boy."

"What boy? "

Garcia hesitated. "A boy I visit weekly to give piano lessons. He's twelve. We take walks along the mountain paths."

"You both found it? Together, while walking?"

"Yes. Well…" he stammered, "along with his dog."

Himmler's eyes slitted, "You are telling me you, a twelve year old boy and his dog found a top secret document pouch?"

"Yes. On a path in the mountains near his house."

"How could it be found in the mountains on a walking path?"

More lies. Garcia slowed his breath to an even, calm rhythm. He braced himself.

"Have you not heard of the spy?" Garcia pretended incredulity.

The cold, deliberate sigh that left Heinrich Himmler fell upon Garcia with icy loathing. The German continued to glare at him from behind his spectacles until Garcia felt he could not breathe.

From the hallway, Hedwig Potthast called for Himmler. "Heinrich, I have prepared a plate of refreshments for you." The heels of her shoes clunked their way toward the two men.

"*Nicht jetzt, Hedwig. Lassen Sie uns!*"

Though Garcia did not understand German, he knew Himmler had told his mistress to stay away.

Himmler clipped his words when he spoke. "I must confess, I have not heard of the spy." His lips twisted up in a conciliatory smile. "Do tell me."

Garcia had an urge to laugh at the German and his unconvincing effort to appear unaffected by the secret pouch.

Abruptly, the Reichsfuhrer waved his hand. "Nicht, do not tell me. Leave me while I open the pouch."

"As you wi…," said Garcia.

"Go!"

In the music room, Hedwig and Rosina clustered around the buffet, Hedwig's chatter monopolizing the conversation. From across the room, Felipe eyed Garcia and lifted his eyebrows in question. Garcia casually walked to where he stood by the large window that faced the courtyard. Without speaking, they both watched the German soldiers, who smoked incessantly and kept a nervous eye on the entrance of the house.

"I was unaware of your close relationship with the Reichsfuhrer." A smile played at the corners of Felipe's mouth, laden with sarcasm.

Garcia's voice was low when he leaned in slightly to Felipe. "I would not describe my relationship with Himmler as close."

Felipe tilted his head toward the hallway. "The back room?"

It was Garcia's turn to smile. "I was settling a gambling debt."

"Your humor is refreshing. Let's hope it serves you well."

Garcia laughed quietly. His nerves were brittle as he glanced in the direction of the hallway. "Perhaps."

Felipe sipped his wine while observing Garcia. "You look pale, señor. Problems?"

"Why do you ask?"

"Simple. There is blood covering your shirt beneath your jacket." His tone was matter-of-fact.

For a long moment, without moving, Garcia continued to watch the Germans milling about the courtyard. Slowly, he unbuttoned his jacket, pulled it open slightly and looked at his shirt. The blood was bright red, creeping through the fibers of his shirt like a leaking pen. He almost laughed; the stain was shaped like a map of Germany.

Garcia turned to look at the Judge. He noticed his eyes held an alertness that seemed to absorb his surroundings with amazing clarity. He also saw a sensitivity that belied his gruffness.

Felipe returned his stare and whispered, "I think you are in need of my assistance."

"So I am."

"*Gekommen, Hedwig! Wir mussen gehen!*" The Reichsfuhrer stormed through Rosina's music room, Hedwig following close behind, her red hat flopping sideways. Himmler's face flushed as he abruptly turned from the heavy wooden door at the entryway and looked at his hostess.

He bowed slightly. "My apologies. I must return to Headquarters."

The Germans left in a fury, their automobile engines roaring across the mountains, toward Barcelona and over the border into France.

Rosina was the first to speak. "I'm not sure what has just happened."

Felipe walked to his wife's side and placed his arm around her shoulders. "It was your canapés, my love. Again, you put too much salt in them."

Garcia laughed with relief. "Your canapés were perfect, I'm sure."

"Your humor goads me, Felipe. I shall take them outside for Tomas."

When they were alone, the two men eyed one another. The piano teacher felt relieved. The Judge, however, felt a heavy premonition. As a judge, he relied on his intuition. And, his intuition was telling him the piano teacher's life was in peril. Felipe narrowed his eyes at Garcia, a look he gave his court when their only way out was the truth.

"You must acknowledge your vulnerability, señor."

Garcia was quick to respond. "Exactly what do you perceive as my vulnerability?"

"Do not think I am ignorant." The Judge was impatient.

Garcia studied him with a discerning eye. "I cannot deny that my life is in danger."

He closed his eyes and slowly crumbled to the floor.

PART II

Chapter Thirty-Nine

In the dark of the night, while Garcia slept in a fitful sleep, Juan waited in the dark of the barn. Should he have told him? If he had, would it have made a difference?

He heard the engine of the car, an ominous rumble, as it crossed over the small bridge leading to the cottage. He knew they would come. The car lights dimmed as it proceeded slowly up the incline to the cottage. From a quarter of a kilometer away, it stopped, its motor stilled and its occupants waiting.

Juan's hiding place in the top of the barn was cramped. He pushed himself closer into the wall that faced the barnyard and the lane to the cottage. Below him, the goats slept peacefully, with an occasional soft bleat. They were all there except Tia. She had left the barn earlier, perhaps seeking a place to give birth. He peered through the crack in the barn siding and watched for any movement. From the mountains, he heard the call of an owl. *Luis*. He knew Jordana was with him. They had planned it that way.

The moon was barely visible, already inching its way to the western curvature of the earth. The perpetual mountain wind sang haunting songs through the trees and up to the higher peaks. Still, they waited.

Only hours before, while the wound in his arm was bandaged, Garcia told him.

"They have the documents, Juan. Our mission is complete." He smiled weakly as he reached out and touched Juan's arm.

"Himmler's face. So confused. A twelve year old boy and a dog? Impossible!" Both men laughed.

"Well done."

"Only with your instruction, my friend."

"What now?"

"Need you ask? I shall sleep for days, make passionate love to Jordana and play the piano. My goats! I shall take my precious goats to the mountains where they can enjoy the abundant brush."

Garcia paused. "And what about you? Where will you go, what will you do?"

"The war is not over. I will return to my headquarters and begin the next phase of the operation." He looked past Garcia, a far-away look. "There will always be a need for spies."

"Do not forget me."

"Impossible. Now, you must rest. I will see you tomorrow before I go."

Lies. All lies.

Movement on the roadway alerted Juan.

They are here. Two of them. Walking slowly. A third is driving the car behind them.

It took them six minutes to reach the barnyard. There, they stood silently, carefully scanning the area. Only one had a sidearm in his hand, a 9 mm. The others had their hands in their coats to ward off the cold night air.

A shiver ran down Juan's spine. He had seen men like these; cold, calculating men who followed orders without question, without conscience.

They were Gestapo; Spain was swarming with them.

The agents approached the cottage. Two remained outside while the other opened the cottage door and stepped in.

Garcia thought he was dreaming. Through a fog he saw a bright light. Was he dying? Was this the light one followed when swept up to heaven? *I don't want to leave Jordana.*

His mind struggled to comprehend the reason for the light. What else could it be? Shouldn't there be a tunnel to travel through, where, at the end, the bright light turns into heaven?

He forced himself to turn over, fighting the light and his exit from earth. It was then that he felt a cold, hard object press his temple, softly at first, but then a constant pressure that turned into pain.

"Who is there?" He spoke before he opened his eyes. Then, with rising fear, his lids opened. The face he saw was pale, a winter white, lined with a vertical frown between his eyebrows.

"What do you want of me?"

The voice of the intruder, quiet and calm, was so soft Garcia had trouble understanding his thick German accent. "I want nothing from you other than cooperation. I want you to get up and walk out of here with me." He turned his flashlight away from Garcia's face.

"Who are you?"

"Shut up. We're going to France. Come." He pulled the barrel of the pistol from Garcia's temple and waved it toward the door. "Now."

Garcia stared at the pistol, confusion setting in. Where was Jordana? "France? You are taking me to France?"

The pistol turned back to Garcia. "France."

Garcia rose from his bed with difficulty, sitting on the edge to steady himself. *France. He was going to France. But why*?

The man reached out and grasped Garcia's arm gruffly. "You must hurry. It is near daylight."

Quietly, Garcia dressed, all the while watching the man in the long coat who waited near the door and occasionally glanced outside. He saw two shadows cross the window to the left of the door. *So, there are two more.*

The door opened and one of the men came inside and spoke in German to the man with the pistol. *"Die Strabe ist frei. Sie warten uns am Rand."*

"Gut," he nodded. *"Zeit zu gehen."*

They were taking him. Both of them walked purposefully toward him; they knew exactly what they wanted to do. Garcia never saw the needle but he felt it. They had injected him in his wounded arm and he felt his body weaken and become slack.

Outside the cottage, the two men lifted Garcia and placed him in the back of the car while the third man settled himself into the driver's seat. Before getting in, one of the men turned and looked at the barn.

He had heard something and remained still while he listened, his eyes scanning the barnyard. He jumped in alarm when two goats came running out of the barn bleating loudly. "*Bumsen!*" he cried, while pulling his pistol.

"*Ziegen! Ziegen!*" He laughed and raised his pistol. Two shots rang out and the goats fell to the ground. At the noise, three more scurried from the barn where they, too, were shot in succession. The laughter of the three men rang throughout the barnyard and down the lane where they turned and headed for the border.

Garcia lay in the back seat, conscious, but curiously unmoving. *My goats. They murdered my precious goats.*

Juan stared at the dead goats for a long while from his hiding place. Senseless. He eased his body from the top of the barn and stood looking at the small, innocent bodies of the goats.

Why does this anger me so? Slowly, he pulled his gun and checked the cartridges. He knew it was fully loaded, but he wanted to see the bullets. He wanted to feel the metal of his gun. He rubbed the short barrel until it warmed. He then aimed his weapon where the Germans had stood and pretended to shoot each one of them. Twice. Then, he reloaded his pistol and shot them again. The dirt kicked in the air as the bullets found empty targets. At last, panting from hatred, he holstered his gun and wept.

The sun began to ease over the tops of the mountains as Juan lit a cigarette and watched the empty road. He calculated it would take the Germans an hour to get to the border. From there, they would travel eighty-five kilometers to Perpignan, France, where a Gestapo outpost had been established by the Germans earlier in the war. His sources were amazingly accurate.

From behind, he heard the approach of Luis. "They are gone."

"So they are. We have lots of work to do."

"I see." Luis studied the five dead goats and shook his head. "Monsters, no?"

"Indeed."

"What of Jordana?"

"Safe."

"Does she know?"

"She suspects."

"What do you think she will do now?"

Juan deliberated as he lit another cigarette. "I'm not sure." Jordana knew too much. She knew Garcia had aided the Allies. Whether or not she knew Garcia had passed intelligence to the Germans was unclear. She might have deduced on her own what the mission entailed and maybe not. How much she had heard and understood was unknown.

"We cannot jeopardize the mission. So far, she has been close by. When she learns they have taken Garcia, she may falter."

Juan sighed heavily. He could not let five dead goats and a young señorita thwart his mission. Slowly, he felt the coldness enter his blood, a blackness consume his heart. The fate of the Allies and thousands of lives were at stake.

Garcia slept through the border crossing. He vaguely remembered the Germans showing papers to the guards, exchanging information and waving at them as they crossed into France. He wanted to sit up, but the nausea he felt would not allow him to move. Perspiration soaked his clothing and he began to smell an odor, finally realizing it was his own urine. He weakly rolled down his window for fresh air.

The Germans did not speak. They smoked their cigarettes one after the other, flipping them out the windows of the car as they sped past the rocks and trees of the great Pyrenees. In the soft light of the car, Garcia saw their fearsome silhouettes. *These men are killers*, he thought.

It was well into morning when they reached the pinnacle of the Pyrenees. From there, they saw the wide expanse of France, valleys with pastures set in manicured squares, where cows grazed and swished their tails and their udders filled with milk. The scene was an illusion; brutal armies fought to the north where the cows were replaced with tanks and blood flowed like a pasture of red.

"Slow down," said the German in the front seat. "There is a cow in the road."

"Are you going to shoot it?" the driver laughed.

"Shut up and do as I say."

The car slowed and eventually stopped as the cow meandered across the road from a small pasture on their right. At the last moment, a head popped up from behind the fence row and a farmer waved to them.

"Good morning," he called and began walking toward the car as his cow stalled on the road.

"She is a slow one today. It will be just a moment." He looked into the car, glancing at everyone. "Heading for Perpignan?"

"Yes," said the driver. "How much farther?"

"Only fifteen kilometers."

Garcia opened his eyes and watched the farmer with interest. His accent was Spanish not French. Probably one of the many Spanish who fled Spain during the Civil War and took refuge in France. The man returned Garcia's stare and seemed to recognize that Garcia was also Spanish. He said nothing as he glanced at his wayward cow.

"There she goes, the little darling. Thank you for waiting." He moved back from the roadway to allow the car to pass. His eyes turned back to Garcia and watched him until the car was out of sight.

Garcia pushed his body forward. His throat was dry and his words a raspy struggle. "You have taken me illegally," said Garcia. "You have no authority to remove me from Spain. I demand you turn around and return to Spain."

The man to his right turned to him and slapped him hard. "Shut up!"

Garcia tasted blood on his lip. Weakly, he squared his body in the seat and lifted his face to feel the wind from the open window. He thought of Himmler's words...*let us hope your knowledge of top-secret information is as expert as your knowledge of German composers.*

Chapter Forty

Blackeye was only a speck when Juan first sighted him strolling along the wharf at the Port of Barcelona, the wide legs of his cream-colored linen suit and the red scarf around his neck flapping in the Mediterranean breeze. His wide-brimmed Panama hat shaded his face and belied the fact his eyes were sweeping the wharf with a practiced acuity.

The fact that he was one of the most sagacious spies in His Majesty's Secret Service was hidden in his flamboyant style. No one would ever suspect he had a mind like a camera's eye, remembering everything he saw and everything he heard. After all, he was too handsome, drank too much, made love too often. He was known simply as a man about town, carousing in the homes of wealthy Spaniards who sympathized with the Germans. Little did they know he could slit a throat in three seconds without getting a drop of blood on his crisp, white jacket.

Juan looked away, not acknowledging Blackeye's approach. Nor did Blackeye acknowledge him. They both leaned against the railing on the wharf, five meters separating them. When Juan lit a cigarette, Blackeye knew it was safe to begin a conversation.

Juan eased a few steps closer to the man in the cream suit and looked out over the harbor. "Can you dress a little more dashing, my friend?"

Blackeye laughed. "The women could not bear it. They would collapse and fall to the ground, with their legs open."

Juan couldn't help but smile. Blackeye was always about women, a good cover for a very serious, calculating man. "Things are heating up, you know."

"So I've heard. Should we go in?" Blackeye saw the tension in the cords of Juan's neck muscles and knew immediately he was in the throes of a decision.

"Don't have a choice. We've been called in as of midnight last night."

"Got the same order. The pianist? Is he expendable?"

"He is expendable." Juan's cigarette was short and smoldering in his fingers. He tossed it out into the water.

"I sense you don't want that."

"You are correct. Nor, do I want to jeopardize the Allied invasion."

A shrill horn from a tugboat sounded, sending fluttering sea gulls into the air. Flags on the tall wooden posts snapped loudly as the sea wind gusted from the east.

"Whatever we do, it must be done quickly."

Juan sighed. "They crossed into France around nine thirty. Not far from the outpost."

"Do you know who's there?"

"Sources tell us Muller is on his way from Berlin."

"Gestapo? Why Gestapo? Doesn't make sense."

"Direct orders from Himmler from what I understand."

"He'll never survive Muller."

"I agree."

Heinrich Muller, who enjoyed a reputation as Gestapo chief, was a small man with laser eyes and thin lips. His ruthlessness was legendary. It was, however, out of ambition, not devotion to Hitler that he carried out his mission to arrest and interrogate without mercy.

Juan watched a pelican sail to a dock post and open his mouth while a young boy threw in a small fish. "Muller can't leave Berlin until Monday. That gives us about forty-eight hours, maybe a few more."

"Time for what?"

"Quinones must stay in place in order to be interrogated. If he holds up, the interrogation will hopefully convince the Germans the information on the Allied landing is legitimate. Problem is, once the interrogation is completed, they will kill him."

The two watched the boats in the harbor. The cries of the fishmongers swept up and down the wharf. *Mussels. Clams. Big fat snapper.*

Blackeye turned toward Juan, a frown creasing his handsome face. "I see you're reluctant for things to take their course. What of the pianist?"

Juan turned toward the railing and rested his arms. The stiff harbor breeze blew the brim of his hat upward, the salty air dousing his lips and tongue.

"I cannot give you a simple answer." Deep in thought, he watched the clouds move in from the west, over the waters of the sea to cover the sun. He peered far out in the harbor where the comings and goings of the boats, large and small, ploughed through the choppy water in organized tandem.

Finally, Juan said, "Ah, the pianist." What of the night he had stood outside Garcia's cottage and listened to him play? His heart had swelled, his eyes had filled with tears as he listened to the music drift out into the night air. He had felt the lilting notes, one by one, lift him away from war and death, away from the evils of Hitler, away from the fear that gripped him like a vise his every waking moment. How, then, could he abandon a man whose music could make the world seem beautiful again? If he let Garcia die, he would destroy his own soul.

"I cannot let the Germans kill him."

Blackeye nodded slowly. "I see, but how can you prevent it?"

"Simple. We will do what we do best."

Blackeye laughed. "And, in your opinion, what is that?"

"Lie. We are brilliant liars, you and I." A sly grin spread across Juan's face. "Are we not?"

Blackeye gave Juan a puzzled look, cautious, as he adjusted his Panama. His expression did not go unnoticed by Juan.

The two men separated, one at once losing himself in the crowds and disappearing in seconds; the other smiling rakishly at those he passed before beginning to whistle a jaunty tune and heading for the German Embassy.

Chapter Forty-One

At precisely 11:00 o'clock, Judge Felipe Lanzarote, looking important in his black cape and hat, arrived at the apartments on Madrid Avenue. His walk was hurried. His Majesty's Secret Service had summoned him.

Felipe found Juan and Iliana drinking coffee on the terrace. "Iliana, coffee, please." He whisked past her and grasped Juan's arm. "The pianist has been abducted?"

"Wait until Iliana returns. Then, we must talk alone."

"Of course." Felipe sat in a chair across from Juan, a look of anticipation on his face. He was not the dark Catalonian as was Juan. Instead, his skin was lighter, his hair more brown than black. He had the same black eyes as his sister and, at the moment, they stared at the spy soldier and waited.

In moments, Iliana returned with coffee. After serving Felipe, she smiled at them both. "I will leave you two to your spy talk." She turned and looked at Juan, a forlorn look that said she knew he would be leaving her again.

Juan watched her leave the terrace through the wide French doors that opened to the library. He did not turn his eyes away until he could see her no more, almost calling out to her and saying *I do not want to leave you.*

Finally, he turned to Felipe.

"Garcia briefed me after the Germans left the village, but I'd like you to tell me what you observed." He lit another cigarette, settled back into his chair and at once became the soldier spy.

Felipe nodded and knitted his brows together.

"One thing was very clear to me — Himmler was very affected by the contents of the document pouch. He came storming out of the back room, looking grim. Highly agitated, of course. And, left so fast he just about left one of his soldiers."

"What did he say, if anything?"

"He offered a very curt apology to Rosina and simply left."

Juan watched two squirrels, skittish and indecisive, run back and forth across a tree limb.

"Garcia is being held captive at the Gestapo outpost in Perpignan. We expect Heinrich Muller to arrive from Berlin on Tuesday morning to interrogate him. Himmler's request."

"Gestapo Muller?"

"Yes. The one and only."

"It seems the Germans have given the documents extreme priority."

"Rightfully so. If they deem them to be authentic, they will divert their armies to Pas de Calais and away from the actual Allied landing. This is their only chance to turn the war in their favor."

"How do you think Garcia will fair?"

"What does it matter? They will kill him regardless."

Felipe looked hard at Juan.

"I'm beginning to see why I'm here. It does not please you that they will kill Garcia Quinones."

Juan shook his head.

"No, it does not please me at all."

His eyes wandered across the gardens and into the morning sky where he thought he heard the notes of a piano. Puzzled, he turned back to Felipe, his cunning eyes alert and unforgiving.

"You and I are going to prevent his unnecessary death."

Felipe's smile was conspiratorial. "Of course we are. Just tell me how." He sipped his coffee and sat back, waiting for the master spy to begin.

"Since we have no one on the inside, there is no way we can know precisely when the interrogation is complete. Nor know the optimum time to execute a rescue. I'm thinking our only hope is a legal request by the Spanish government to the Germans to release Garcia."

"Will they do this?" Felipe was aghast. Since when did the Germans bother about legalities?

"Perhaps...if we put pressure on them."

"You? Me? What leverage do we have? None!"

"Ah, Felipe. You disappoint me. Where is your imagination?"

"For the life of me, Juan, I cannot imagine going through the courts to release Garcia from the Germans. First of all, there is no time."

"Again, your lack of imagination disappoints me."

Felipe's eyes darted back and forth in confusion. "Humor me, Juan. I defer to your brilliant creativity."

Juan ignored Felipe's sarcasm. "Generalissimo Francisco Franco, dictator of Spain. Is he not an old friend of the Lanzarote family? Bound by years of Spanish brotherhood?"

Felipe was incredulous. "My friend, you forget I did not support Franco in the Civil War. "

"But you are still a judge in the most powerful court in Spain. Were you not in Franco's favor, you would be selling fish at the wharf."

Felipe narrowed his eyes. "Señor, your imagination is truly laughable. It is not like I could just pick up the telephone and ask the General for a favor."

Juan lifted his hands. "Why not?"

The two remained silent, each one vacillating between the complete absurdity and the extraordinary brilliance of befriending Franco.

Felipe was the first to break the silence, preceded by a huff of frustrated air. His voice was just above a whisper..

"So, it is a matter of calling the General, perhaps conversing socially at first and then what?" He leaned over the table and lifted his eyebrows.

"Here is what I propose." Juan paused and stubbed out his cigarette. "As Supreme Judge of the Catalonian region of Spain, you issue an arrest warrant for Garcia Quinones for the murder of Lope and Jorge, as well as that of Inez Albeniz.

"You then contact Franco and tell him the Germans have illegally taken Garcia into France for interrogation. Tell him you have no idea what the interrogation is about; but, once Garcia is interrogated by the Germans, they must return him to Spain. No need to tell him about the arrest warrant and extradition documents. We will need those later."

Juan pulled a cigarette from his case but did not light it.

"Tell him time is crucial. Tell him he must call on his German friend, Heinrich Himmler, to intercede with the interrogation of Quinones. And that once Quinones is interrogated, he must be returned to Spain immediately."

Felipe leaned back into his chair and stared at Juan. Laughter rumbled up from his chest.

"Let me get this straight. You expect the German war machine to listen to Generalissimo Francisco Franco of Spain? Furthermore, why should either Germany or Spain care about Garcia Quinones?"

Juan tapped his unlit cigarette on the table and was quiet for a long moment. Finally, he nodded.

"Good questions, Felipe. Here are my thoughts. Franco is an egotistical man. How dare the Germans abduct one of Spain's finest citizens, the great Garcia Quinones, virtuoso pianist who studied in Brussels and Paris, who once performed for our king? How could he abduct one of Spain's greatest cultural assets?

"Himmler, being the murderer he is, would delight in having Garcia killed by the Gestapo. He would, however, capitulate to Franco if he thought there would be something in it for him."

Felipe crossed his legs and played with a thread that hung from the tablecloth. Nervously, he reached up and pinched the edges of his mustache.

"What is it that Franco would give to Himmler?"

"That is up to Franco and Himmler. It is, however, up to you to suggest to Franco to make some sort of concession to Himmler."

Felipe gave an exasperated sigh.

"You are hurting my brain, Juan. Franco will laugh in my face. And, whatever could I suggest as a concession?"

Juan smiled his lazy smile. "You could suggest Franco offer to deposit 150,000£ into Himmler's Swiss account."

"Impossible."

"Of course, he will. If you deem it necessary, mention that 150,000£ will also go to his own Swiss account."

Felipe shook his head in denial. "And who has 300,000£ to give away to Himmler and Franco?"

"Your imagination again, Felipe," he chided. "Surely, you have underestimated His Majesty's Secret Service."

A dawning light crossed Felipe's eyes. "Of course, how could I be so stupid?"

Felipe stood quickly.

"I have many documents that must be readied for Garcia's arrest as well as his extradition, all for the border guards. The call to Franco will be the most difficult. I'll be in my chambers if there is more to discuss."

He walked toward the French doors, but turned and raised his hand, pointing his finger at Juan. Smiling, he said, "You, my friend, are to be commended for your extraordinary imagination. Let us hope it does not get us killed."

Juan sat for a long time beneath the trees that leaned over the terrace. He'd neglected to tell Felipe the rest of his plan, a flaw in his character, he supposed.

From the French doors, Iliana called to him. "I have soup for you."

Juan looked across the terrace at the beauty who had bathed him and smiled. "Is that all you have for me?"

Illiana undressed while across the room, naked himself, Juan watched. His breathing was slow, his half-closed eyes wandering the length of her. There was something about making love in the middle of the day that was somehow forbidden, as if the light would reveal more than ardent desire, would reveal in the lightly shadowed room a hidden truth in a lover's eyes, perhaps an unveiling of past indiscretions or even an unrequited love. Forbidden or not, he felt he had spent too many dark nights alone to relinquish an afternoon of fervent yearning, especially for someone who desired him as much as he desired her. He had always been a tender lover, perhaps compensating for the harsh cruelties in his secret life. Now, as his eyes lingered on Illiana, he knew his tenderness would not be enough for her.

His heart beat quickly as she walked toward him, that mystic smile on her lips. She lay on top of him and kissed him hard. He knew from her kiss she would be demanding, would pull his hair, bite his shoulders and then, with breathless moans, plead with him to enter her.

Afterwards, she would cry uncontrollably. All because he was leaving her again.

Juan lit a cigarette and turned on his side. Illiana's eyes were closed, her hair in a mad tangle around her head, her cheeks flushed. Across her forehead, a dampness glimmered in the low light of early evening. He saw her mouth turn upward into a smile.

"Are you watching me?"

"Yes."

"Why do you do that?"

"I want to always remember you."

She turned and opened her eyes. The sadness he saw caused a catch in his breath. A question. *How can you leave me?*

Her lips trembled, her voice a hoarse whisper. "You must come back."

His fingers pushed the wild hair away from her face, then brushed her lips. "I'll be back. I'll always be back."

Chapter Forty-Two

Felipe stared at the telephone that sat on the right of his large, paper-filled desk where he also rested his long legs, the sun glinting off the sheen of his polished shoes. He closed his eyes and leaned back. His Excellency Generalissimo Francisco Franco, Head of State of Spain, had long been a part of his life. They were the same age, same schools, both Catholics. Politically, they were miles apart: Franco was a dictator, a military general, who controlled every aspect of Spain and its people.

True, Felipe had not supported Franco in the Civil War. Yet, it seemed he was still in the good graces of the dictator. They had seen each other at various cultural events over the years. The General would seek him out and chat of times past, always smiling at Rosina who stood at his side. He was an affable man whose charm hid a cunning and manipulative mind; his smile, however, never hid the shrewdness in his eyes.

Taking a deep breath, Felipe picked up the telephone and called the number of Franco's residence in El Pardo in Madrid, a number he had had for at least twenty years.

After only a few rings, a woman's voice answered. "The residence of Francisco Franco."

"Good evening, señora. My name is Felipe Lanzarote. I am calling for the General."

A pause. "One moment, please."

While he waited, Felipe wiped his brow and noticed how fast his heart was beating and the dryness in his mouth, sure signs of anxiety. He was startled when he heard the voice on the other end.

"Ah, Felipe. It is impossible that we have not spoken for such a long time." His voice was familiar, the somewhat nasal sound slightly effeminate.

"My apologies, General. It baffles me that we cannot talk more often. But, regardless, our friendship never wanes."

"My Rosina? How is the most beautiful señora in Spain? Oh, what I'd give to see her."

"Well. Rosina is very well. And, yes, she is as lovely as always. Asks about you frequently."

"That is good to hear. Tell her I shall come to Barcelona before the year is out and we shall dance the rumba."

Felipe laughed. "I cannot tell her that, General. She will pester me every day to have you visit."

A pause in the conversation allowed Felipe to swallow a large amount of whiskey.

"And, what do I owe the pleasure of this telephone call, Felipe?"

"My General, I have a situation that needs your guidance. A situation involving one of Spain's most beloved citizens."

"Oh? Tell me."

"Garcia Quinones, the—"

"Garcia Quinones, the pianist?"

"Yes, that is so. It seems the Germans have abducted Señor Quinones for unknown reasons. They kidnapped him two nights ago in the village of Brasalia and took him across the border into France."

"*Esos alemanes de mierda*! cried Franco. "The Germans. Those bastards have no morals."

"Yes, I am sad to say one of Spain's most hallowed artists has been stolen from the people of Spain."

Franco's voice was grim. "What else do you know of this abduction, Felipe?"

"I am told it is the Gestapo who made the raid."

"The Gestapo? What would the Gestapo want of Quinones?

"I do not know the answer to that question, General. All I know is that something must be done to ensure his safe return. And you, Your Excellency, are the only one with power to do so."

Felipe's hand trembled as he picked up his almost empty glass and waited.

On the other end of the telephone, there was quiet. Felipe waited a few more moments. Finally, he heard Franco clear his throat.

"I agree with you, Felipe, that the most beloved pianist in all of Spain must be returned. However, I am at a loss as to how to go about it. What do you suggest? Through the courts of Spain? The international courts?"

Felipe breathed heavily.

"General, I feel that Señor Quinones' life is in immediate danger if we do not act quickly. I am thinking a call must be made to the German embassy to have Quinones returned."

He paused. "Or, General, since you are the Head of State, it would hasten matters if you called Berlin and perhaps discussed the situation with...with say...Heinrich Himmler. I'm sure he could take action. And, of course, in time."

Again, the ominous void of sound on the other end of the telephone.

"I see," mused Franco. "Himmler. That is certainly an option. I am thinking the German would do what I ask, but only if I was able to repay him in some way. You know, Felipe, it is a time of war and we must negotiate for what we want. That is the way of the world."

Felipe knew exactly how to respond. "General, you are brilliant. Yes! A reward of some kind for Himmler's cooperation in this matter. After all, Señor Quinones is a national treasure."

"Ah, yes, a national treasure."

Felipe hesitated. "General, I am but a proud Spanish citizen, only interested in our glorious country and all its priceless treasures, whether tangible or intangible. It is my heartfelt opinion that we should compensate Herr Himmler. I am willing to use my personal funds in this matter. Say 150,000£ as a deposit to his Swiss account."

Franco responded immediately. "A generous amount, Felipe. Your countryman obviously means a great deal to you."

"Thank you, Generalissimo. It is my pleasure to preserve our cultural arts." Felipe poured another whiskey and sipped it slowly. "Your opinion, please. Do you feel your call to Himmler will be successful and do you think 150,000£ is a sufficient amount?"

"Who knows how the German will respond to my request, Felipe? He is a cunning man, not prone to leniency for anyone. I am curious, though, as to why Quinones has been abducted."

"I understand."

Franco became the all-powerful dictator of Spain.

"I shall call him. He is presently in Berlin at German Headquarters. Interestingly, I understand he recently visited Barcelona."

"So I understand."

"Call me later this evening, Felipe. We'll discuss my findings. And, you say 150,000£?"

"Yes, General."

Silence again. "Felipe?"

"Yes."

"Shall I give you my Swiss account number now or shall you call my office?"

After quiet contemplation, Generalissimo Francisco Franco picked up the telephone and dialed German Headquarters in Berlin, a special number, a direct line Himmler had given him during the Civil War. The two men had talked frequently of the Nazi invasions, Himmler imploring him to provide war materials as well as soldiers. He did both.

When Himmler had ordered a list of the names of six thousand Jews in Spain for the Nazi's Final Solution, Franco complied, though he had no intention of handing over the Jews to the Germans. Instead, he kept open borders for the Jewish refugees from France. So far, forty thousand Jews had found safe haven in Spain. Franco was a diplomat. He said yes, but he did exactly what he wanted to do.

Franco was just about to hang up, when he heard the German answer. "Reichsfuhrer."

"Greetings, Herr Himmler. Franco."

"Yes, General Franco." Himmler was his usual stoic self.

"I am calling regarding my concern for one of Spain's most revered citizens, Garcia Quinones. It is my understanding he was abducted from his home in Brasalia by some of your people."

How did Franco know who abducted the Spaniard? Himmler mused. Perhaps Quinones was not the only one who knew of the document pouch. Perhaps someone observed his abduction. Nonetheless, he could not deceive Franco; Franco had as many clandestine forces as did Germany. Not much happened in Spain that Franco did not control.

"That is a possibility, General. I shall investigate the circumstances."

His Excellency Generalissimo Francisco Franco's voice hardened. "There is nothing to investigate, Heinrich. The truth of the matter is that the Gestapo has Quinones in their captivity in France, for what purposes I do not know. It is my wish that he be released to the Spanish authorities immediately and guaranteed a safe return. By you."

Himmler smiled, but did not miss the other man's resolve. Interesting that the dictator is so intent on the return of Quinones. What would be the reason?

"Your demands are well spoken, Franco. Of course I shall look into the matter, if, indeed, he is in our possession. However, it is also my desire to understand the circumstances regarding his alleged abduction by...by whomever."

"Your pussy-footing amazes me, Heinrich. Perhaps it would help you to know that a reward has been offered for his safe return."

Himmler did not hesitate. "My dear Franco, it is my utmost desire to ensure the safe return of Quinones and now that I have the resources to do so, I shall begin immediately."

"Where is Quinones at the moment?"

"He is being held at a Gestapo outpost in France, near the border."

"So, you are well aware of Quinones and the fact that he's been abducted by the Gestapo," said Franco sarcastically. "And for what reason are you holding him? He is a citizen of Spain who is uninvolved in your war."

Himmler tread carefully. "It was thought that Quinones may have information that would help us in an investigation involving the French Resistance. You know, Quinones lived in France some years ago."

Franco laughed. "So he did, but I guarantee you he was not involved in any underground activities." Franco paused. "So you are holding him simply for interrogation?"

"That is correct."

Franco's words were firm. "You may question Quinones, but I want his immediate release afterwards. When do you plan to interrogate him?"

"The interrogator is on his way from Berlin as we speak. I would estimate Quinones' release by noon Tuesday."

"Very well. I shall be waiting for your call."

Himmler enjoyed his next few words. "Franco, I will put my assistant on the line who will give you my Swiss account number. How much may I tell him you are depositing?"

Franco's mouth was set in a grim line. How he hated the Germans. "150,000£."

As promised, Franco telephoned Felipe Lanzarote. "Himmler has agreed to release Quinones by noon on Tuesday. He has given me the account number of his bank. If I were you, I would transfer the funds as soon as possible. The German bastard will do nothing until that is done."

"Thank you, General. I will be in touch."

Felipe closed and locked his chamber doors and left for Madrid Avenue, where he knew Juan waited for him.

Chapter Forty-Three

Garcia vomited for the second time; his body trembled uncontrollably. When he arrived at the Gestapo outpost in Perpignan, he was placed in a small locked room in the rear of the building. The cold was unmerciful, his inability to get warm wreaking havoc on his hands and feet. He tried curling into a ball on the small mattress to retain what little body heat he could generate. If only they would give him a blanket.

There were three of them. Large, grim men who spoke little, who smoked incessantly and who eyed him with cold, menacing stares. It seemed they were waiting. Waiting for what? *They are going to kill me.* He accepted the fact he would die. How could he not? They left him like an animal with no food or water and did nothing for him as his body weakened and begged for warmth.

He estimated he had been in the room for twenty-four hours. He looked up when the door opened and one of the men walked toward him and spoke to him in a thick German accent.

"You are hungry?"

Garcia stared. "Very hungry. And thirsty. And cold."

The German nodded. "We do not feed our prisoners."

"I am a prisoner? For what reason?"

He laughed. "Of course, you are a prisoner. You cannot leave, can you?"

"Why do you not feed your prisoners?"

He laughed again, this time more heartily, throwing his head back. "Why feed a man who is going to die?"

Garcia studied the man's face and looked for some sign of humanity.

"Does it give you pleasure to see a man in pain and hungry and thirsty, señor?"

"Why do I care? And, yes, it does give me pleasure."

Garcia held his stare. "Do you have a mother and a father or were you just lifted from the bowels of hell?"

The man did not move, but continued to stare. He lifted his chin in defiance. "I born in small village near Munich, not hell as you say." He hesitated. "I have mother and father."

A glint of humanity. "Where are they?"

"Buried in small graveyard near our village. War, you know."

Garcia nodded slowly. "If your mother were here, would she give me water? Food?"

The German's eyes narrowed as he contemplated Garcia's question with a studied thoughtfulness. There was a slight softening around his mouth and eyes. He would not say anything unkind about his mother. "If she knew you were spy, maybe not?"

Garcia persisted. "What if she didn't know who I was? A stranger? Along the road?"

"These questions are not necessary."

"Your mother? Would she feed me?" he asked again.

Garcia felt the German's uneasiness as he backed toward the door. He said nothing as he left the room.

Juan waited in the dark outside the apartments on Madrid Avenue. He had spent the day conferring with Blackeye as well as Luis, who had traveled from Brasalia. Early that morning, Luis took Jordana to the home of Señora Rosina Lanzarote who would harbor the young woman until they returned.

The three men agreed they had no choice. They must go over the border into France where they knew Garcia was held captive. Timing was crucial; they did not want to rescue a dead man.

Juan saw the headlights of Felipe's automobile turn onto Madrid Avenue and park in front of the apartments. There was no sign of anyone on the street who may be watching the Judge's comings and goings, only a spy from His Majesty's Secret Service.

He whistled as Felipe pulled his key to open the door. "Felipe, wait for me." Juan walked briskly across the street and up the steps.

"You surely have a whiskey for your old friend."

Felipe smiled as he pushed open the door for Juan. "Always."

Inside the large living room, Iliana poured their whiskey. She poured herself wine, a rich purple that matched the skirt she wore. She sat on the long white couch that faced the fireplace and turned her exquisite face toward Juan.

"Did you find what you were looking for?"

Juan nodded. "Yes. And more."

Iliana raised her eyebrows. "More?"

He didn't comment further and Iliana knew not to persist.

The room was quiet until Iliana stood.

"I am finishing dinner for us. I shall be in the kitchen." Her lithe body passed Juan, who smelled the fragrance of her perfume and felt his heart skip a beat. Yes, he was deeply in love with Iliana Lanzarote.

The two occupants of the room turned toward each other, the plan to rescue Garcia foremost on their minds.

"Franco?"

"Cooperative. Totally aghast at the kidnapping of Garcia. Quite willing to do what he could to ensure his safe return. He called Himmler who, after some coercion, agreed to intervene. At a price, of course."

"What was promised?"

Felipe rolled his eyes. "150,000£ to Himmler; 150,000£ to Franco."

"Timing."

"Himmler said they would release Garcia by noon on Tuesday."

"Alive?"

Felipe looked at Juan with surprise. "I am certain the Germans would not kill him after Franco's discussion with Himmler?"

"You are?"

Stammering slightly, Felipe hesitated. "What are your thoughts?"

"I think we should be prepared for anything. Are the extradition documents prepared?"

"All in order. What else?"

Juan smiled at Felipe. "What makes you think there is anything else?"

"There is always something you haven't told me, my friend. Don't forget – I have known you a long time."

Juan picked up his glass. "You're right. There is one more thing. I need three uniforms of the Spanish Guardia."

A wry look crossed the face of Felipe Lanzarote. "Your brilliant imagination again, señor?"

"Of course."

"Have you told me everything?"

Time went by as the spy emptied his glass of whiskey and studied the fire. His mind traveled to London, to the Secret Intelligence Service where he had first begun his life as His Majesty's soldier, where he had murdered a German agent as he walked the streets of London during the first year of the war. He turned back to Felipe.

"Be ready at midnight. We cross the border into France, to Perpignan and the Gestapo." The fire blazed in front of them, a hot wave of fragrant wood smoke permeating the room.

"And, hopefully, the pianist," he said quietly.

Chapter Forty-Four

It was near midnight when they converged on Madrid Avenue, all from different directions, down the narrow streets running along the wharf, across the square where political speeches were held, and through the trees that surrounded the Judge's lavish apartments.

They moved under a cloudy night sky where the Port of Barcelona lay in rest only four blocks east. Their steps were cautious, acutely aware that Germany's Gestapo had infiltrated all of Spain, mostly in the northern region, near the border, watching the comings and goings of everyone. It was clear the Germans were on high alert. After all, the Allies were coming.

Juan pressed his body against the cold stone fence across from Felipe's apartments and waited. He felt the night dew clinging to his clothes. He breathed the damp air, laden with the fragrance of the lilacs that bloomed along the avenue.

In the night, the pupils of his eyes widened and allowed him to determine what lay in the deepest shadows. It was a practiced skill, honed when he slipped into Paris the night France fell. He saw movement near a tree on the apartment grounds. Then, in a few moments, the call of an owl. Luis.

Blackeye, as was his style, openly sauntered down the middle of the street, whistling a tune from a current American play by Rogers and Hammerstein, *Oklahoma*.

A black Mercedes 770 W150, Felipe's love second only to Rosina, was parked in front of the apartments, its whale-like front fenders gleaming from a nearby street light. Like the breasts of an obese woman, the two headlights set ominously on either side of the chrome grill, flanked by wide running boards. Felipe Lanzarote knew high-ranking Nazi officials, including Hitler and Goering, owned a 770, a diesel limousine that maintained speeds of 90 kilometers or more without the slightest difficulty, but insisted on having one of his own.

Juan smiled. Felipe's Mercedes would be appreciated once they entered France.

Once Blackeye approached the apartments, Juan crossed the street. From his left, he saw Luis leave the wooded grounds and join them. The entry-way door opened and all three men slipped inside.

"Your timing is good," said Felipe. "Everything is ready." He pointed the way to the library where the three uniforms of the Spanish Guardia waited for them.

"You, Luis, have the largest size, of course. Juan and Blackeye, you have the other two. And, I, of course, will remain as I am – the most renowned judge in all of Spain." He laughed as he returned to the front room where he poured a whiskey for all of them, waiting anxiously for midnight and for their transition into members of the Spanish police.

Luis moved through the doorway, his looming body smartly attired in a police uniform of the Spanish Guardia. The holster that held his Browning HP 9mm pistol wrapped around his wide girth and proclaimed him a man of authority, willing to perform at a moment's notice. The thirteen-round semi-automatic could kill a man at fifty meters; Luis Neruda kept the hammer cocked.

He was followed by Blackeye, whose jaunty smile covered his handsome face. His weapon of choice was a Sauer 38H, an 8-round, semi-automatic made by the Nazis. He enjoyed the irony of the gun's origin and kept his weapon in immaculate condition, expressly for use on the Germans.

Juan entered the room, imposing in his uniform. Somehow, the dark man who wore it emanated a quiet strength, a message of power that embodied who he was: a killer of the enemy. His weapon was a military double-action revolver, a Webley Mk IV — specifically designed for use by the armed forces of the British Empire. A powerful gun, its most effective range at fifty meters. It could, however, reach a maximum range of one hundred and fifty meters, a range that empowered its user to stand firm in any situation. He knew the gun would serve him well on their mission to France.

Juan looked at his watch. A precise man, he demanded a highly-disciplined regime and ruled with an iron hand. Those who stood before him knew it and offered themselves into his leadership without the slightest hesitation. It was a matter of trust.

"We are ready." Juan paused and looked at Felipe. "Papers?"

"In my possession."

"Proceed and I'll join you momentarily."

The men quietly disbursed to the waiting Mercedes. From his vantage point, Juan looked up to the landing to see Iliana watching him. Their eyes met and he slowly ascended the stairway toward her.

Her eyes watched him with a solemn resolve. "It's time, my love?"

Without speaking, he reached out and held her, feeling her tremble in his arms.

"I'll be back. As always, I'll be back."

Chapter Forty-Five

Their plan was simple: Rescue Garcia Quinones.   Judge Felipe Lanzarote, accompanied by three of Spain's Guardia, local police who were trained by the military and who wore the insignia of the Spanish army, guided his limousine to the border crossing and stopped. The German border guards appeared nervous. It was obvious they were on high alert—the Allies were coming. The guards motioned for everyone to exit the car while they studied the official documents.

Six German guards stood near the Mercedes, one of whom took the lead. He puffed his chest toward the Spanish Guardia and barked his commands in poor Spanish.

The Spanish border guards stood nearby. They knew Judge Felipe Lanzarote by sight. They especially studied Luis, an imposing figure, whose semi-automatic pistol screamed a potent efficiency. His return stare countered with the ominous intention of a soldier born to kill.

Juan and Blackeye's years of working together had provided them with an uncanny ability to read each other's thoughts. They subtly moved into positions that enabled them to view both sets of guards. Hands were behind their backs, feet spread apart, their posture pronounced them professional soldiers.

The lead German lifted his eyes from the documents Felipe had given him. "Why does it take three soldiers to accompany you?"

Felipe nonchalantly crossed his arms. "One is the driver, one is the cook and the other sleeps with me."

The German looked at him for a long moment, then turned his eyes to Juan. Then, to Blackeye. And, finally, Luis.

"You are a funny man, Herr Lanzarote."

Felipe smiled engagingly. "Thank you. A little laughter in this war is welcome." He paused. "Any other questions?"

The German's eyes hardened. "Your humor offends me. I asked you a reasonable question. Surely, a man of your position is capable of a reasonable answer."

"That I am," replied Felipe, his voice becoming that of a prominent judge. "The man we will take prisoner is a dangerous man. We want his extradition to be successful, of course."

Behind Felipe and off to the side, Juan glanced at Luis and Blackeye. Their body language told him they were prepared for trouble.

The German slowly folded the documents and returned them to the large envelope. Again, he panned his gaze to Juan – almost as if he were contemplating something. At last, he handed the envelope to Felipe.

"I will be expecting your return by noon on Wednesday."

"Good evening," said Felipe and began walking toward the Mercedes.

The barrier arms raised and the Mercedes passed into France.

The road to Perpignan was narrow and hilly. The men sat in silence, each with their own thoughts. Juan pulled his Webley from his holster. Himmler may have accepted the 150,000£, but that didn't mean he would deliver on his promise to release Garcia. Juan's senses were heightened, as they always were when he faced the Germans.

Luis and Felipe relied on their own instincts. They, too, felt the danger that awaited them. And Blackeye? He sang a boisterous tune about a naked woman who ran the streets of Madrid looking for her lover. *And the lady bared her breasts, so her lover would confess, My lady, my lady, it is your breasts I caress.*

After two hours, they approached Perpignan and its few cottages. SIS information told them the German outpost was located one kilometer west from the outskirts of the small village, amongst trees and low lying brush in the foothills of the mountains.

"Pull to the side of the road, Luis, and run the car amongst the trees where it can't be seen from the road."

In moments, the car was hidden and its occupants out and walking the woods to the outpost.

"You lead, Luis. Your nose is much stronger than mine," said Juan. "We will scatter behind you."

Luis nodded. Stealthily, his gun in his hand, the Germans ahead of him, he watched the woods like a wild animal. Adrenalin pumped through his heart at an unheralded speed.

Juan followed and to his right, Blackeye skirted the trees, crouching as he moved in a serpentine pattern toward the outpost. To his left, Felipe cautiously moved toward the dim lights of the outpost.

The four men, each one a deadly shot, moved into position and settled into the cold night, watching the small building where Garcia Quinones slept fitfully and prayed for his life.

Chapter Forty-Six

Garcia heard the door to his prison open. Without moving, the silhouette of the large man stood in the doorway. He spoke without turning on the light.

"Food and water." The door closed and Garcia heard the footsteps fade.

He was afraid to move. The pain of his imprisonment had left him lethargic and unresponsive; his wounded arm and injury on the back of his head ached, a reminder of his close brush with death.

He stared at the door and counted the seconds. Gritting his teeth, he moved off the mattress and onto the floor. *I will rise*, he said to himself. He reached out and grasped the pipe that ran the length of the wall and pulled himself up.

He waited a moment to steady himself, then felt his way along the wall toward the door. The darkness had been depressing to him; he wanted light, glorious light – even if it did come from a lone light bulb hanging from the ceiling in his dismal cell.

When he neared the doorway, his hand found the string that controlled the light and pulled gently. His prison was illuminated, a grim reminder of where he was – a captive of the Germans. Not only the Germans, but the German secret police, who wielded their authority with a ruthlessness that belied the fact they were even human.

On the floor near the door, he saw a plate of food and a cup of water. The food was a simple piece of bread and sausage. German sausage, he wondered? For some reason, he smiled. He was in France eating sausage in a locked room with Germany's Gestapo on the other side of the door waiting to kill him. It was what they did best.

He quickly ate the bread and sausage and drank the water, then promptly belched. German or not, it was good sausage.

He turned his head and stared at his mattress. Something had changed. He had felt it when he lifted his body from the mattress and began to walk. While he watched the mattress, he concentrated on his breathing. It was deep, a slow rhythm that brought oxygen to his brain in prodigious amounts and caused within him a sense of growing resolve.

He curiously felt himself unattached from the circumstances around him, that in some way he had ended up in a meeting with the gods, the same gods who had rebuked him from the beginning. He heard them speak to him – so distinct and unambiguous. *You will not yield.*

Garcia lifted his chin and peered at the ceiling, wondering if he would find those gods watching him. Were they the same gods who flaunted the white parachute before him, who sent him the run-away señorita, who jeopardized his life with bullets and a rock-throwing maniac of a woman? He stilled. The same gods who aligned him with the master spy and demanded he become one, too?

Si, he said to himself, these are the same gods.

Garcia's eyes swept the room. *I will not go back to the mattress.* From his position at the doorway, he pulled the light string, sending the room into darkness once again. He moved into the corner behind the closed door and waited.

The faint light of morning came with a dimness that seemed hesitant, as though it was afraid to light the world and reveal the war, or the maggots that ravaged the bodies of dead soldiers and forever kept them from dancing again with a beautiful woman.

From their hiding places above the German outpost, the four Spaniards awaited the dawn. They watched the road from Perpignan where they knew the German, Heinrich Muller, sped toward the outpost, eager to perform his duties as an interrogator.

Luis crouched next to Juan and scanned the road below. To his left, Blackeye fiddled with the military insignia on his Spanish uniform. Felipe dozed behind them, his black cape covering his body.

Quietly, Luis reached out and touched Juan's arm and then held his finger to his lips. His eyes told Juan there was danger. He crouched to the ground and turned to the woods behind them. All of them heard the hammer click of a pistol and immediately pushed their bodies to the ground, their breathing quiet as they listened and waited.

The sound of soft chuckling came from the bushes about thirty meters behind them. "Ah, you Spanish imbeciles. You cannot protect your own asses much less those of your compatriots."

Through the bushes behind them, a short, stocky man with an unkempt mustache walked toward them, smiling. In the soft light of morning, his skin was dark, his nose long and narrow. A Frenchman.

"Juan, where are you?" he called. He pushed the brush aside and skirted around the trees toward the small clutch of Spaniards, holding his pistol, a Browning GP, a *Grande Puissance*. It was a powerful weapon and, at the moment, it was out of its holster, hammer cocked.

Juan replied, irritation in his voice. "Quiet, Marcel!"

"Ah, you are awake. I could have killed you, you know."

Marcel, a leader in the French Resistance since 'forty' when German tanks rolled into his country, returned his pistol to his holster. He grinned his Frenchman's smile. His favorite pastime was killing Germans. He had escaped the forced labor camps by fleeing to the south of France and into the mountains where he spent his time blowing up supply trains traveling from Germany and, of course, killing Germans.

Juan looked around him for others but saw no one. "Does nothing escape your nose for trouble, Marcel?" He reached out his hand to his old friend. He was a fierce freedom fighter, a patriot who spent his every waking moment in the pursuit of Germans, especially Nazis. "*Bienvenue, mon ami. Enfin vous etes revenu a la France.*"

"Thank you, Marcel. It is good to see you and to return to your country. I see it is impossible to arrive without your knowledge. *Si?*"

"True, my friend. I have been watching you since you crossed the border. I have information for you."

"Oh? Let me hear it."

"The German, Heinrich Muller, will pass here within the hour. His entourage includes a driver and four soldiers. Two automobiles. Weapons, of course."

"We are ready for them."

"What is your plan regarding your man, Quinones? How can the Resistance help you?"

Juan squatted to the ground. Blackeye and Felipe joined him while Luis watched the road.

Marcel nodded to Blackeye and Felipe and smiled. "The French are here – you need not worry." Both men grinned in return, then turned their attention to Juan.

"I am going to believe that Muller will do as instructed by his superiors – release Garcia after he has been interrogated. In Franco's conversation with Himmler, it was agreed Himmler would ensure Quinones' safe return to the Spanish courts. Of course, we are dealing with unknowns. Muller is far away from the watchful eyes of both Himmler and Franco. My understanding is that he is a pompous little son-of-a-bitch. Has his own agenda."

Juan hesitated. "We can expect trouble."

"*J'ai peur pour vous, mon ami.*"

"Do not be afraid for us." Juan's eyes held laughter. "After all, we have the French, no?"

Marcel nodded. "We are here."

Juan continued. "Once Muller has arrived at the outpost, we will give him thirty minutes to interrogate Quinones. After thirty minutes, we will arrive with our entourage."

He looked in the direction of Felipe and Blackeye. "The Spanish Guardia as well as the prominent Judge Felipe Lanzarote will present themselves to Muller with all the official documentation for Quinones' extradition back to Spain."

"And you expect Muller to hand him over?"

"Reluctantly, but yes. He will hand him over."

"And, if he doesn't?"

"We are pre…"

"Who is this Quinones that you would cross the border into the German's backyard?"

Juan raised his eyebrows. "Ah, there is actually something the Frenchman doesn't know?"

The wind lifted the boughs of nearby cedar trees and the sound of soft swishing moved through the small camp. Juan rose and looked across the low hills. "Quinones? He is a pianist."

"A pianist? You have risked your lives for a pianist?"

Juan turned around and stared at Marcel.

"Yes, a pianist." *Yes, a gentle pianist who herds goats and plays music that makes you weep. A pianist who became a patriot when all he wanted was his music and to live his quiet life in the mountains.*

Felipe watched Juan carefully; his friend's face had become steely. He turned to Marcel. "Actually, Marcel, we are rescuing one of MI6's most brilliant spies, one who also happens to be a pianist. His importance to the Allies is immeasurable."

Marcel looked from Felipe to Juan and back again. Finally, he smiled. "Maybe after he is rescued, he can play the piano for us."

The Spanish watched as Marcel disappeared into the woods, where they saw three Frenchmen fall in line behind him and fade into the brush.

From his vantage point on a rise near the camp, Luis saw the approach of two vehicles from the west. The lead vehicle, a black Mercedes, long and sleek, swerved around a curve with an obvious urgency, the flags of the Third Reich flapping furiously at the front of the vehicle.

Behind the Mercedes, a jeep with the Nazi swastika emblazoned on its side followed closely. Four German soldiers sat erect in their seats, the barrels of their rifles protruding in the air.

Juan heard the familiar call of an owl. He looked at his watch; eight twenty. All four men gathered on the low ridge above the outpost and waited. In only minutes, they would drive Felipe's Mercedes to the outpost and confront the Germans.

Chapter Forty-Seven

Heinrich Muller was born to wield authority, obvious in his pomposity, in the lifting of his pock-marked forty-four year-old face, graced with an Aryan nose that seemed to sniff the air around him. His mouth was almost non-existent, a thin straight line with little evidence of lips.

His heavy involvement in espionage and counter-espionage subjected him to a myriad of mysteries. That was why he was here. To solve a mystery.

He was a dangerous man.

His driver opened the door of the Mercedes and stood smartly while Muller alighted from the back seat, shiny black boots first, then gray breeches ending at the knee, the uniform of the Gestapo. His jacket, belted at the waist and across his right shoulder, was magnificent. He wore it splendidly. The armband, red with the black Swastika in a white circle on the band, pulled the eye as if it were a magnet. And, finally the stoic face. The visor of the German field cap veiled his eyes in a deep shadow; the better to see what he deemed worthy of his attention.

"What a dismal place," he said. He moved his head slowly from side to side like a rotating gun turret atop a German tank.

"Remind me to blow this place to bits once we return to Berlin," he said to no one in particular as he began his dispassionate walk to the door of the outpost.

The four soldiers who accompanied him took positions outside the small building while the driver returned to the Mercedes. They all watched as the door opened and Muller stepped inside.

The three plain-clothed Gestapo agents stared at their superior as he removed his cap. Muller smiled a smile that had nothing to do with happiness, but rather a conspiratorial sort of look that promised an interesting morning.

"My dear fellows," he began, almost pleasant, as if it were a morning of *kaffee und Geback*, coffee and pastries and frivolous chatter.

The Gestapo agents waited, slightly unnerved. Their superior had an abhorrent reputation.

"The prisoner?"

At once, the agent in charge nodded to Muller. "Yes, Herr Muller. In a locked room in the back."

"Well, get him."

The agent pulled his pistol from its holster and raced toward the hall that led to the back of the building.

Garcia had heard the arrival of several vehicles, their motors a drone of doom. He also heard voices, low and garbled. He knew he was to be interrogated; what he didn't know was by whom.

He listened to urgent footsteps coming down the hall and pushed himself farther into the corner. Without moving, he watched the rim of soft light at the bottom of his closed door.

His breathing was slow, controlled. He heard the footsteps stop and hesitate, then a stealthy push on the door. It was unlocked.

As the agent reached for the light string, Garcia lunged, his weight hitting him in the side and throwing him to the floor. It was then that he used all his strength to subdue the fallen agent and pull the pistol from his grasp.

"Señor, your life is in my hands, no?" His voice was but a whisper, his mouth almost touching the agent's ear. He smelled sausage on his breath. "I think I am going to kill you."

He felt the agent squirm beneath him and he tightened his grip around his neck. The German gasped, "If you kill me, the others will kill you." His thick German was quite understandable.

Garcia contemplated the German's words.

"Get up," he said, easing off the agent and standing above him. He pointed the gun squarely at his chest. "I may still kill you, señor."

The German obeyed and struggled to his feet. He stared at Garcia. It was the same agent who had brought him food and water. His eyes never left Garcia's. "So kill me," he said, an almost comic expression on his face.

What did the gods say? You will not yield to the Germans. Garcia raised the pistol and fired. The bullet struck the German in the stomach, a gut wound, the kind of wound that results in an agonizing death. The German's eyes held Garcia's until he fell to the floor.

Outside his prison, Garcia heard a stampede of footsteps move down the hall toward his prison. *You will not yield to the Germans.* He turned to fire into the doorway, only to be pummeled to the floor by two Gestapo agents, one of whom pushed the barrel of his Luger 9mm into the softness of his neck.

The man who once referred to Hitler as an "Austrian draft-dodger" paced in a slow, deliberate way, his heels clicking on each turn from one side of the room to the other. It seemed only his feet moved, leaving his legs and upper body stiff, as if too angry to participate in his pacing. His forehead glistened under the lights that hung from the ceiling. Occasionally, he reached up and patted it with a crisp, white handkerchief.

Across the room, sitting in a chair, Garcia Quinones watched the chief of Germany's Secret Police, a police that had no restrictions on what they did or to whom, with mounting trepidation. He turned his head to the right when Muller reached one side; to the left when he reached the other. It was like a tennis match, played in menacing slow motion.

"Garcia Quinones," said Muller. A few more paces. "Garcia Quinones," he said again, this time stopping and turning toward Garcia, his chin lifting.

His small eyes, brilliantly blue, drilled into Garcia's large brown eyes as if in a trance. His absence of lips seemed to clip his words as he spoke. "Have we met?"

Garcia jerked slightly, but his voice was strong. "We have not." He moved his eyes to the leather strap that hung from the German's belt.

Muller laughed. "But, I feel we...know each other. Do we not?" The German's face seemed pleased, as if suddenly discovering an old friend.

"How so?"

"I'm not quite sure. Perhaps through the symphony in Berlin." He almost squealed, "I *love* the symphony!"

"I have never played in Berlin." The leather strap swung as the Gestapo chief paced back and forth.

"But, you are a famous pianist, are you not? I would think you have played in all the great symphony halls of the world."

"I am a well-known pianist, yes. But, as I said, I have never played in Berlin." Garcia never blinked as he held the German's questioning stare.

"A pianist? Who studied in Brussels?"

"Yes."

Muller laughed again. "Of course. Brussels." He paused. "The symphony hall there is no longer standing, you know."

He took a step closer. "German bombs, you see."

As an afterthought: "Did you hear? Belgium surrendered in a day?"

Garcia continued staring into the killer eyes of Muller. "I heard."

Muller moved closer. As he looked up, Garcia could see the nose hairs protruding from his long nose, a small chip in his front tooth and large pores in his cheek area whose formations reminded Garcia of the constellations.

Abruptly, Muller clapped his hands together in front of Garcia's face. A loud noise, meant to be intimidating, making sure he had the pianist's full attention. "So, you discovered a document pouch containing secret information having to do with the Allied landing?"

Garcia was prepared – Juan had ensured it be so.

"I discovered a document pouch. I did not see the contents."

"Really? You saw the words '*Top Secret*' clearly stamped on the pouch, yet your curiosity did not provoke you into opening it?"

"That is correct."

"I find that interesting. Why, if I saw a document pouch with the words '*Top Secret*' written on it, I would open it immediately. I love mysteries." Again, an upward squeal on the word *love* accompanied by sly laughter.

Garcia did not reply.

The German wrinkled his brow.

"You are a mystery to me, Herr Quinones. It puzzles me that you have discovered a document pouch...obviously, a military document pouch, obviously top secret, yet you are not curious enough even to look at its contents. Perhaps you are not a curious man?"

Garcia shrugged. "I am curious about some things, not a military document pouch."

"I see. What are you curious about?"

"I am curious as to why I am here. In France. In this prison."

Muller nodded in understanding.

"So, it is your personal safety that you are curious about?"

"Of course. Wouldn't you be if someone abducted you by force in the middle of the night and took you across the border into another country?"

"By all means, that would definitely instill a curiosity in me."

Muller's eyebrows furrowed together. He shook his finger, punctuating his words.

"Please allow me, Herr Quinones, to be curious—why would you murder a Gestapo agent? It appears to me that if you felt you had been abducted for no apparent reason and, therefore, not guilty of any crime, then you would not have need for violence."

Garcia nodded his head slowly. *You will not yield to the Germans.* He gathered his thoughts. "I feared for my life."

"Feared for your life? I am amazed. Who would harm a virtuoso pianist, famous throughout Europe? You amuse me, Herr Quinones."

Garcia remained still. Calm, with a slow beating heart and quiet breaths.

Again, Heinrich Muller clapped his hands only inches from Garcia's face, sending his sensitive ears into painful spasms.

"So," he said. "You were walking in the mountains with this young boy and the two of you found a parachute and with the parachute you found the military top secret document pouch. Is that so?"

"That is so."

At the moment Muller's hand hit Garcia's face, the pianist closed his eyes. When he opened them, he saw the German smiling at him. He also felt blood trickle from his lips. When the hand came again, it held the leather strap. The blow left Garcia panting, gasping for air.

Muller sauntered to the end of the room and turned toward Garcia, his eyes slowly ran the length of his body and then moved to his hands. Garcia saw a smile enter the German's expression when his eyes found his fingers.

"Herr Quinones, what long fingers you have. A pianist's fingers, I suppose." He moved closer. He laughed as he spoke, as if he were going to tell a joke that was so funny he had trouble telling it. "We could not refer to you as a pianist if you had no fingers, now could we?" He waited; his penetrating blue eyes boring into Garcia's. His voice rose. "Could we?"

Garcia studied the man in front of him. *Your stupidity amazes me. Fingers, no finger; I am a pianist.* "What are you saying?"

The German shrugged his shoulders and reattached the leather strap to his belt. "You seem to lie as brilliantly as you play the piano."

"I have told no lies."

Muller's thin lips parted. "You seem unafraid, Herr Quinones. Perhaps it is an innocent man who is not afraid. Or, perhaps it is abundant courage. I do recognize courage, you know."

He remained quiet for a moment. "If I removed one of your fingers, could you still play the piano?" What a casual question – no different than '*If I closed the door, would you be too warm?*'

Garcia did not answer. Instead, he moved his eyes along the German's uniform. Looking for a knife, he supposed. His eyes traveled to the pathetic face of the man who stood waiting. How could the German know? Know the moment a finger touched a cool, ivory key – the hush that waited for the first note. The rhapsody that followed, capturing one's heart and soul until his breathing quieted like the hush of an autumn dawn.

"Is that question too difficult for you to answer?" The German raised his eyebrows. "Just imagine it – you're sitting at the piano and you place your hands on the keys. Oops! Where is my middle finger? Oops! Where is my thumb?"

The German laughed; behind him the Gestapo agents chuckled. They did not know their superior was such a funny man.

Garcia spoke. "I will always be a pianist."

"Oh? So it would not distress you if I removed a finger or two?"

Garcia felt a coldness wash over him. He looked down at his hands and studied his long, thin fingers. He looked up at the German. "I am wondering why you would cut off my fingers."

Again, hysterical laughter rushed past the thin lips of the German. "For the pleasure of it, Herr Quinones! For the pleasure of it!"

The Gestapo chief walked to the end of the room, his back to Garcia. When he turned, Garcia saw a knife in his hand. At once, his heart rate soared. He shifted in his chair, his eyes never leaving the knife.

Muller walked slowly toward Garcia and stopped. Casually, he cleaned his nails with the tip of the blade, all the while chatting. "So, you have told no lies. You and the boy found the document pouch. You turned it over to Herr Himmler. End of story."

Muller leaned forward slightly and returned the knife to its sheath. "Somehow I believe you, Herr Quinones. Not only that, but Adolf Hitler also believes you. The Fuhrer has already sent reinforcements to Pas de Calais where he believes the Allied invasion will take place. Of course, his decision is, by and large, based on the contents of the document pouch you and the boy discovered."

Garcia raised his eyebrows. He said nothing.

Muller began his pacing again, his hands behind his back in a studious stance.

"Of course, although we believe you have told the truth about the discovery of the document pouch and that its contents are authentic, we have to consider the murder of one of Germany's most loyal Gestapo agents, do we not?"

Garcia looked around the room. *You will not yield to the Germans.*

He half rose from his chair. "You cannot condemn a man who…"

The door to the building opened and Felipe Lanzarote, in all his Spanish splendor, stood tall and imposing in the doorway, flanked by three Spanish soldiers who carried the insignia of Generalissimo Francisco Franco's Spanish Guardia. Their faces were grim, their stance unyielding.

With a flourish, Felipe leaned forward slightly, "May I introduce myself to you, Herr Muller. I am Felipe Lan—"

With a pathetic wave of his hand, Muller dismissed Felipe. "I am well aware of who you are, Herr Lanzarote. I am also aware of why you are here."

Chapter Forty-Eight

The room and its occupants stilled for one long moment; no words, no movement, only sets of eyes that darted in all directions as they assessed the situation.

A cold tension permeated every cell of Juan's body as he quietly stepped into a corner behind Felipe. His eyes scanned the room and the faces of the Germans. The hairs on his neck prickled and his heart rate quickened, a sure sign of impending peril.

To his right, in the opposite corner, Blackeye stood with his hands behind his back. Juan watched his handsome profile for a long moment – why, he didn't know. Blackeye knew he was being watched and turned his head toward Juan and their eyes met. At once, Juan saw the fear in his face. Steadily, he held Blackeye's stare; there was something more. Blackeye turned his gaze to Heinrich Muller.

In three steps, Muller moved behind Garcia. His two agents positioned themselves on either side, slightly to the rear of their superior.

Felipe waited, the extradition documents in his hand. He turned slightly to his left where Juan stood with his arms by his side, his eyes never leaving Heinrich Muller's face. Felipe saw Blackeye scanning the room, taking in the two agents, Heinrich Muller and the troubled face of Garcia Quinones.

Outside the building, Luis stood at the ready next to the door, facing the four German soldiers, soldiers who continued to hold a tight grip on their weapons. The snap on Luis' holster was loose, his Browning's hammer cocked. Unbeknownst to the soldiers, Luis glimpsed the movement of Marcel and his compatriots skirting the woods behind them. The French again – they could not resist an opportunity to shoot a German.

Heinrich Muller raised his heels off the floor and took command of the room. His eyes turned to his right and fell upon Juan and lingered there. His stare penetrated the spy, crept upon every inch of his body and finally moved away, a smirk on his thin lips.

In that one instant, Juan realized things were not as they seemed. He looked at Garcia and saw the torment. Turning his head slightly, he saw Blackeye's chin move in a slight nod.

Behind Felipe, slightly hidden from the agent on his right, Juan moved forward a few inches, giving him a better view of the two agents.

"I am sad to tell you, Herr Lanzarote, that your prisoner has murdered one of our agents. It is impossible to release him in your custody." Muller again turned and looked at Juan.

Felipe spoke with authority, his courtroom voice deep and intimidating.

"Let the Spanish courts deal with this alleged murder, Herr Muller. The prisoner has to be dealt with in Spain for three murders he has already committed. Once he's tried in our courts, you may extradite him to Germany."

"How ridiculous. Let's just shoot him now. Why bother to go through the courts?" Muller laughed and raised his arms in question; then, rested one hand on his holstered pistol and slowly tapped his fingers.

Felipe stood firm.

"The Courts of Spain prefer to try Señor Quinones in Spain. Generalissimo Franco, were he here, would agree. We must respect his authority."

Muller smiled. "I agree. Take him back to Spain." The eyes of the German did not waver as he looked long and hard at Felipe, a contemptuous expression that revealed his distaste for Spaniards.

Bewildered, Felipe turned to Garcia. He flinched, suddenly understanding a shared sense of impending peril. He tried to appear casual.

"My appreciation to you, Herr Muller. Here are the extradition documents, properly signed and recorded."

Muller ignored him.

Instead, he walked around Garcia and, more or less, meandered across the room toward Juan. He stopped only a few feet away.

"Have we met?"

Juan took a moment to shift his position, moving an intimidating step closer.

"No, we have not."

"I am afraid you are mistaken, Juan Castillo. We have, indeed, met. Perhaps only through the Gestapo files at Prinz-Albrechtstrasse, but, trust me, I am quite familiar with you."

Nonchalantly, the Gestapo chief walked toward Blackeye. He laughed quietly under his breath.

"Do you really think I would travel from Berlin just to interrogate Garcia Quinones? How utterly stupid of you."

Instantly, Juan fell to one knee, pulling his pistol as he dropped. His first bullet hit the agent on his right, a shot between his Aryan blue eyes. His gun arm swung to his left, and the second agent crumbled to the floor, managing to fire only once from his black Luger.

In front of him, Felipe pulled his weapon and at the same time pushed Garcia to the floor.

Blackeye pulled his Sauer 38H and stood, flushed and panting, poised like a tiger waiting to spring.

Two meters from him, Muller stood watching the entire scene with a comic expression, as if he had just watched a Shakespearean play, only without a happy ending.

At the sound of gunshots from inside the outpost, Luis' large body dropped to the ground, his Browning out of its holster and firing its thirteen bullets at the rate of one every two seconds. Two soldiers twisted away as the high-powered 9mm bullets found their mark.

From the German Mercedes, the driver opened fire. Luis fired in his direction and caught him with the first shot.

Above him and to his left, the Frenchmen opened fire. Luis saw a German fall, the other turn his way and fire before he pitched forward onto the ground.

Luis felt the bullet enter his body. Searing pain knifing through his chest. He lost consciousness almost immediately, but not before his thoughts turned to Juan Castillo and their mission.

Chapter Forty-Nine

Inside, the smell of cordite hung in the air. The room's occupants looked at each other, guns drawn.

In the back of the room, two Gestapo agents lay dead, pistols still in their hands.

Garcia remained on the floor, Felipe stood over him like a guardian angel, his black cape draped across his back.

Muller remained stoic, arms crossed over his chest.

Juan rose from his crouch, gun pointed and ready to fire. His eyes swept by Garcia and Felipe before he pointedly turned his gaze to Muller and Blackeye. The German remained aloof as if he were at a tea party and boredom had set in.

Blackeye stood silently, avoiding eye contact – a rare thing for such a gregarious man. Juan knew him well.

He moved toward Muller, his steps cautious, all his senses screaming *beware*. Muller's eyes opened somewhat wider, anticipating.

At two meters, Juan stopped and opened his revolver for reloading, never taking his eyes off the German.

He spoke almost casually. "Put your gun away, Blackeye. You're too close to the German,"

Then, to Felipe. "Felipe, move a little closer this way."

To Garcia, he said, "Stand up, Garcia. Get a pistol from the dead German."

No one in the room noticed that, after loading his gun, Juan had pointed it not at Muller, but at Blackeye.

The master spy eased toward Muller almost casually, as if there was no war, no German troops only thirty kilometers away.

"Felipe, open the door and check on Luis."

Then, to Garcia. "Garcia, check your weapon. How many bullets does it have?"

"Blackeye, I said move away from the German." Juan's peripheral vision captured every detail of the room and recorded it; a skill he had honed to perfection.

Juan tasted the bile in his throat, felt the anger in his blood. He was going to kill the German. Not only that, he was going to enjoy it.

But, first, a little conversation.

"So, you think we've met, señor?" Juan addressed Muller almost pleasantly.

Muller, who had not spoken since the bullets first flew, lifted his chin. "Is this an interrogation?"

"Interrogation? What do you think?"

"I feel threatened."

"How have I threatened you, Herr Muller?"

Muller stumbled as he searched for words. "I am assuming it is your duty as a spy for the Allies to kill me. That is all."

Juan toyed with him. He had at his disposal, a Nazi, a Jew killer. Why kill him right away?

"A spy for the Allies? How do you know this?"

"Ha! You underestimate our abilities, Herr Castillo. You are well known. The Gestapo has been searching for you for years."

"So, you have found me. So what?"

Muller hesitated. He seemed to be at a loss for words. Muller stole a quick glance at Blackeye.

The door opened and Felipe stood, grim-faced. "Luis has been shot. Looks bad. The French have him."

Juan nodded. "Come inside, Felipe. The French will care for him well."

Felipe moved by Garcia, who held the German's Luger steady in his hand. Juan studied the German with an unusual intensity, causing the German to shift his position and clear his throat. Nervous, of course. His holster was empty.

"I am curious about something, Herr Muller." The Spaniard paused and seemed thoughtful. "It would please me greatly to know how you were able to determine my presence here today."

Arrogance spread across the German's face like an evil blush.

"The Gestapo is the most elite information-gathering organization in the world, Herr Castillo. You, of all people, should know this."

Juan's jaw tightened. He pushed his gun forward, only inches from Muller's heart.

"Answer my question," he said, with cold hatred.

There it was again – the German's almost imperceptible glance at Blackeye.

"I...I have my sources."

In the pause that followed, Juan heard the click of a Sauer 38. A semi-automatic. Made by Nazi Germany. In one orchestrated move, he stepped behind Muller and quietly placed the barrel of his gun into the German's neck. His eyes circled the room and landed on Blackeye.

"Is there something you would like to tell me?"

Blackeye, one of MI6's most valued spies, pushed his gun into the back of Garcia Quinones, pulling him into a corner. He peered from behind him and pointed his gun toward Felipe. "Move away, Felipe." Felipe complied, glancing at Juan in confusion.

Garcia felt the pressure of Blackeye's pistol in his back. The same fear that consumed him when the Gestapo pulled him from his bed now riveted his body, along with growing rage. He watched Juan's face and saw an unbelievable composure. Juan felt the bile of betrayal creep into his throat. *Traitor.* His mind ran rampant with visions of past MI6 missions, missions that had been inexplicably compromised, thwarted or ended with a dead agent.

He continued to stare at Blackeye while he pressed the gun harder into the German's neck.

A sardonic chuckle. "Trying to figure it out, my friend?" Blackeye's smile was cunning, like a knife whose blade gleamed with the anticipation of a kill.

"You underestimate me," replied Juan. "Your lack of confidence in my abilities will see you in a cemetery. "

Again, the laughter.

"You amuse me, Juan. You have always had grand illlusions regarding your skills. Now is no different."

Juan spoke harshly. "I have an idea—you kill Garcia, I'll kill Muller. Then, you and I kill each other. What do you think, Blackeye?"

Blackeye stared at Juan in confusion.

Juan noticed the perspiration running down the side of Heinrich Muller's face and it pleased him.

"I think we should consider my plan, instead." A note of anxiety crept into Blackeye's voice.

"And that is?"

"I guarantee Garcia's safe release. You guarantee Muller and me a safe return to Berlin. We'll leave here in the Mercedes. Call the French off and we'll keep the Germans from following you back to Spain."

"How generous of you."

"I don't want to kill an old friend."

"You confuse me. You were willing to turn me over to the Gestapo. I hardly think they would have let me live much longer than a few hours."

Blackeye shrugged. "It's called war, señor."

Juan turned toward Felipe. "Felipe, check with Marcel on Luis. See what the French say about Germans in the area."

Felipe nodded and headed for the entrance. Over his shoulder, he called, *"Espera para que yo le ayude a matarlos." Wait for me to help you kill them.*

Juan felt the German shift his weight. "This pistol has a hair trigger," he whispered. "I wouldn't move if I were you."

The German's body tensed.

"Here is what I will do for you, Blackeye. I will release Muller to return to Berlin. You release Garcia back to the Spanish government."

Blackeye hesitated. If Muller was released, he would have the Germans converge on the small outpost. The soldiers were not that far away and the French Resistance would be unable to withstand such an onslaught. They would flee in the mountains or die.

If he did not submit, Juan would kill the German and Blackeye's only hope. If Muller lived, his desire to capture the master spy would entice him to return for Blackeye, a double payoff. Two spies, one of them a double-agent.

Blackeye pushed his Sauer .38 harder into Garcia's back as he watched the pulsing of the large vein in his neck. Slow and steady, it seemed to be sending a message in a covert language, a code—*I am more than a pianist.* The steadiness of Garcia's heartbeat caused an uneasiness in him. Why should he be afraid of a pianist?

Juan pulled Muller to the entrance of the building and opened the door. "Felipe! Take the German. Put him in the Mercedes and let him go. Tell Marcel to give him safe passage back to Perpignan."

Confusion on his face, Felipe did as he was told. "Come, you bastard. Get in the car."

Juan watched from the doorway. The expression on Muller's face was smug, but he said nothing as he pressed the accelerator and the flags of the Third Reich lifted and began to flap in the breeze.

Felipe spoke. "The Germans are close by and headed this way. Marcel will be moving his men out as soon as they stabilize Luis."

Felipe's face was grim. "What is the plan? The German is gone – we have no leverage. What of Blackeye?"

Juan looked across the small meadow where fields of lavender shone in gaslight purple, then toward the mountains. The safety of Spain lay on the other side. If only they could get to the higher elevations where the Germans would be in unfamiliar territory.

"Tell Marcel to wait for us in the woods." From inside the outpost, Blackeye called out. "Come, Juan. Let's settle this."

Juan stared at his pistol, wondering where the next bullet would fall. He did not have Muller to shield him. Instead, he stood in front of Blackeye, an Allied spy turned Nazi. A double-agent. A man he had trusted. What had gone wrong? Before he killed him, he wanted to know.

Chapter Fifty

"Was it a woman, Blackeye?" Juan closed the door behind him. Blackeye watched Juan as he moved across the room. He pushed his pistol firmly into Garcia's back. Somehow, Juan knew.

"If you kill him, I will kill you," he said dispassionately. With the ghost of a smile, Juan cocked his head. "Who's the woman?"

"You're so clever, my friend. Always a woman, eh?" The handsome face broke into a grin, but his eyes were pensive.

"Tell me, Blackeye. Why not tell me why you betrayed your country? What happened to honor? Loyalty? Or, did they even exist in you?"

"Exist in me?" Blackeye raised his voice. "Those things are my life!"

"*Were* your life, Blackeye. *Were* your life. Now, those things are gone." He paused. "Who is she?"

A long silence lingered between the two men. "It doesn't matter who she is," Blackeye said. Then, "I swear to you, Juan, I have not given the Germans information on the Allied landing. They know nothing of the operation. They only wanted you."

Juan raised an eyebrow, contempt in his voice. "Still, you gave your country away for a woman?"

Blackeye hesitated and then slowly slid the pistol in Garcia's back toward his right side.

On the other side of the room, Juan steadied himself and fired. The bullet landed far to his right, obvious he did not intend to shoot Blackeye, nor Garcia by default.

At the same moment, Blackeye fired his gun and watched as Juan fell to one knee, blood seeping through his sleeve. Again, the smell of gunpowder drifted in the room.

"Did you think I would not kill you, Juan?" Blackeye pushed Garcia away and cocked his hammer. He walked forward a few paces before aiming his pistol at the head of Juan Castillo, His Majesty's Secret Service's most beloved spy.

"You have been foolish. You should have aimed at my forehead." His finger rested on the trigger, the barrel shaking.

Juan held his gaze, no emotion on his face. Had Blackeye been able to read his eyes, he would have seen the sweep of memories there, memories of their world escapades, of whiskey shared in dark hiding places, of narrow escapes through German lines.

Behind him, Blackeye heard the click of a pistol, a Luger. He knew the sound well.

Without turning around, he said, "Leave, Garcia. You are not in this war. Go back to Brasalia and herd your goats. Play a tune on your piano."

Garcia's mind was clear. He knew who he was – he herded goats in the great Pyrenees Mountains, played the piano until he wept and, on starry nights, watched the skies for signs from the gods. He knew he was a gentle man, tender and compassionate, who, above all else, was a lover of freedom.

He fired the pistol once, the bullet entering the back of Blackeye's head and exiting above his right eye, a clean small hole on the handsome face. Blackeye's body fell toward Juan, who reached out to catch it.

Juan held Blackeye like a baby and stared at the serene face. He seemed to be sleeping, the beginning of a perpetual smile at the corners of his mouth; a word forming, perhaps, of regret or sorrow. It was too late.

The outpost door opened slowly and Felipe's pistol entered the room before he did. He saw Garcia standing over Blackeye's body, pistol in hand, a stricken expression on his face.

Below him, on the floor, Juan pushed back the hair on Blackeye's forehead and whispered softly, barely audible. "If I could, I would bury you near the woman you loved."

"He is dead?"

Garcia nodded. Juan said, "Yes."

Felipe stood silently while he watched Juan lay Blackeye's head gently on the floor.

"Juan, the Germans are only minutes away. Let us go." The urgency in Felipe's voice was apparent yet Juan found he could not move. Within him, a sense of loss had paralyzed him.

Felipe walked to where Juan knelt above Blackeye's body and removed his cape and gently laid it over the body. He touched Juan on the shoulder. "Please. We must leave now."

Chapter Fifty-One

"We must hurry, Juan," yelled Marcel from atop a rock high in the foothills. "We do not want to have our testicles removed by German bullets, heh?"

Marcel waved frantically as he summoned the Spaniards, then turned and disappeared into the mountains, followed by the small party of French Resistance fighters, two of whom carried a make-shift stretcher with the wounded, semi-conscious body of Luis.

Juan watched the retreating Frenchmen as they lost themselves in the woods. Without them they would have a difficult time escaping the Germans. He opened his pistol and checked the bullets in his gun. Missing three bullets. He reloaded and yelled, "Felipe! Garcia! Take any of the German's weapons you think you can carry. Ammunition, too."

Blackeye's bullet had only grazed his arm. Intentionally? How could he know? Had it not been for the pianist, he would be dead.

He turned from the mountains and looked east toward the road that led to Perpignan. The Germans, like snarling, rabid dogs, would advance quickly and try to flush them from the mountains. The only advantage they had was their knowledge of the hills.

They lost themselves among the rocks and trees in a matter of minutes, using familiar escape routes that had been established at the beginning of the war. Marcel led them on an ascent through a streambed for several miles to escape the German's tracking dogs. Once out of the stream, they advanced to elevations of five thousand feet where tall spruce and mountain laurel provided excellent cover. The cold swept upon them as though it were the breath of demons.

There were twelve men in Marcel's detachment, two of them carrying Luis. Amazingly, one of the Resistance fighters was the son of a doctor who lived in Bergeonne. He knew how to stop the bleeding and even had medicines that would diminish the pain.

Around midnight, they had traveled approximately twenty-eight kilometers, keeping ahead of the Germans, though a spotter plane, at the insistence of Gestapo Muller, had flown over them an hour after their entry into the mountains. Marcel halted his men as they entered an area that was used as a temporary camp. For years, they had stored food, weapons and ammunition in a small cave-like crevice, a haven where they regrouped and rested after long surveillance missions.

The night air was cold, the sky clear, stars scattered like billions of tiny white-hot coals. Juan sat down at the base of a tree and leaned back. The camp was familiar; he had stayed for a few days after a three-day mission into Italy after Mussolini had declared war on France. He had watched as German and Italian troops marched toward Paris; eleven days later France surrendered to the Axis.

Around him, the Resistance fighters rested, two of them tending Luis. Garcia sat down nearby, exhausted. Juan looked into the pianist's face to determine his state of mind, noticing a weariness that was not only physical but also emotional.

"I see you are troubled, Señor Quinones."

After a long moment, Garcia met Juan's eyes. They lingered for a moment, then turned to stare at his boots. Juan could barely hear him when he spoke.

"I was thinking of my father."

"Your father?"

"Yes, my father. I wondered if he ever killed a man."

"If he did, would he have told you?"

"Probably. I am thinking he would not be able to kill a man; yet, I found it so easy. You know, just pull the trigger." He looked at Juan, hoping for understanding.

Juan nodded. He had killed many men, mostly those who had tried to kill him. Admittedly, he had also killed men who had sat in chairs chatting with their lovers, eating dinner, drinking wine. Necessary kills. To rid the world of evil men, those who began wars, who gassed Jews. An easy thing to do. Involuntarily, his trigger finger twitched. He wondered to himself regarding his depth of morality or lack of it. "You killed a man to save my life. I am forever grateful for that." Juan paused, his tired eyes revealing his humility. "Look at me, Garcia."

Garcia raised his eyes. "Yes, I killed a man."

"Your father would have done the same thing. Killed to save another man. I'm sure of it."

"Perhaps."

Gently, Juan reached over and touched Garcia's arm. "This is a time of war, señor. The world and its people will only survive if you and I do what is necessary to bring down tyranny. We are patriots. We will not sit by and watch while the Hitlers of the world destroy what is good."

Garcia lifted his head and looked into the night sky. He searched the constellations and found Orion, the great Hunter, then found Betelgeuse in Orion's left shoulder. The Hunter stalked Taurus and behind him, his faithful dog, Canis Major, chased Lepus, the Hare.

The gods. For an instant, he thought he saw a volley of stars shaped into a smile. A message? He stared long and hard, mesmerized by the clarity of the formation, perhaps the star smile was a blatant attempt by the gods to soothe him.

Slowly, a peace began to envelope him, a balm on his wounds, a softening of his grief. Inexplicably, he began to feel a strength he had not felt before, a liberation of his mind and heart into a man he knew his father would approve of – a man of convictions – a man who could play brilliant music, but who could also venture forth into the world and be the man the gods had intended, that his father intended; a man of courage.

He turned toward Juan and smiled.

"This spy thing. The Gestapo chief confirmed that Hitler gives credibility to the bogus information. He is sending a large concentration of troops to Pas de Calais."

"That is what Allied intelligence tells me."

"What next?"

"What next?" Juan laughed. "Your interest amuses me. Perhaps this game of espionage has trapped you like a spider's web."

He became serious. "I will have to return to England and brief MI6 regarding Blackeye, among other things. Once we cross these mountains and return to Barcelona, I will become a Spanish businessman and fly out on a transport of some kind. It gets complicated."

Barcelona. He would see Iliana before he fled to England. There were times he thought his love for her would cause him to end this game. But, not now. Too much at stake. He would spend a few days with her and dream of a life together, maybe even children. In his mind's eye, he saw her face. So real, he almost reached out and smoothed the lips that smiled at him.

"And you, señor? Your plans after you return to Brasalia? Jordana?"

"Ah, Jordana. I have deep feelings for her. I will have to soothe her mother though. If that is possible. Then I shall ask the señorita to marry me."

Garcia looked into the sky again. "When I return, I will visit the grave of Señora Albeniz. And, her sister." A sadness crept over him. Blanka had never tasted the delicious scallops she so desired. He saw her standing on the roadway, her orange skirt blowing in the mountain wind, a toothless smile, her eyes looking toward the blue Mediterranean.

The two men fell silent for a while.

Garcia shifted his body toward Juan and leaned closer, his words but a whisper. "I never knew I could be these things. Was it what the gods intended all along – a pianist turned patriot?"

"Fate," replied Juan.

Felipe walked across the camp and sat beside them.

"Luis is sleeping. Seems to be better."

"Good. We must get him home safely, without further injury. Without the French, we could not do this."

"True. Marcel tells me we'll be moving out in one hour and to get some rest. No fires despite the cold. Can't have smoke in the air with Germans tracking us."

"I've heard no dogs. Think we've lost them?"

"Could be."

Juan relaxed his body farther against the tree, but did not close his eyes. Instead, he searched the woods and saw a French sentry standing quietly in the dark shadows, rifle across his shoulder. He listened to the owls and was reminded of Luis when they worked missions together. Finally, he closed his eyes and dreamed of Iliana, her softness, her languid eyes.

Chapter Fifty-Two

The first German bullet hit the sentry, a solid hit that promised death. The sentry fell forward, a thud sounding like a sledgehammer hitting a tree stump. His rifle never fired.

The French rested with their rifles still in their grasp and quickly rolled over and took positions that allowed them to fire down the mountain. They had the high ground. If the Germans had waited, they would have caught them in a descent and slaughtered them.

Marcel positioned his men into a half circle approximately one hundred meters in diameter, leaving each man to cover eight or nine meters of ground. They waited.

From the ground below, Germans inched their way forward. Their leader, Lieutenant Wilhem Erndt, had chosen his best men, including two snipers and two machine-gunners. A meticulous man, he wiped his rifle where his sweat had covered the stock. When he finished, he reached for a flare.

Erndt had pushed his men hard when they left their camp, deciding to leave the dogs behind. Instead, he had Sergeant Lyudovik, a half-German, half-Ukranian, who could track as well as any hungry bear. He would scent and whiff until he smelled the very blood of those he pursued. He would find the French and, more importantly, the Allied spy.

Without the dogs, there was no chance their barking would alert them. Instead, Erndt's men followed Lyudovik. They planned to surprise the enemy, a favorable tactic. Muller had commented the French had no balls. Erndt knew differently.

He placed the flare into the flare pistol and aimed it high into an area almost one hundred fifty meters ahead of them. Despite the trees, the intensity of the light would allow them to determine what they were facing.

He fired the flare and watched as it soared above the trees and hang in the air with an umbrella of white light edged with radiant blue, like a comet that had suddenly frozen in space.

As the light lingered above them, Marcel and his men crouched deeper behind the trees and rocks, protecting themselves and their weapons from what they knew would follow.

From behind a large tree, Juan scanned the mountain and spotted two Germans crawling toward the camp. He stepped into full view and got off two quick shots from twenty meters away, each one finding their mark. The instant he ducked behind the tree, a large caliber bullet grazed the bark, sending splinters into the air. Sniper. Juan lowered himself to the ground and crawled backwards toward the large rock that protected Garcia.

"That was close." Garcia looked across from his hiding place to Felipe, who raised his eyebrows and pointed to another German running in the waning light of the flare, darting from tree to tree, only fifteen meters from the camp.

Marcel had seen him, too, and lifted his rifle, waiting for the German to move again. The German stepped from behind a tree and began to run. Marcel fired, missed and hit a tree. A second shot came from behind Marcel. The German soldier groaned as he fell hard in the brush.

From their right, a volley of machine gun fire spit across the camp, kicking up dirt, glancing off rocks and trees, until it had covered the full half circle of Marcel's fighters. Another volley from the left.

Marcel crawled toward Juan. "You and your friends must leave."

He pointed to a small opening between two large rocks. "Get to those two rocks and ease through the opening. From there, you'll be able to find cover enough to run up the mountain. We'll cover you."

Juan turned and saw the two rocks jutting out of the earth, only fifteen meters from where they crouched. "Leave? That's impossible, my friend. We will stay and fight."

A grenade sailed through the air and exploded above the French. A cry was heard from Juan's right and Marcel ran to his men.

Felipe called to Marcel, "Toss us some of your grenades."

At once, Marcel pulled three grenades from his sack and tossed them to Felipe who caught them one by one, passing them to Juan and Garcia. He smiled his courtroom smile, easy but mischievous. "Let us do some damage, my friends."

The three Spaniards inched backwards, to the two rocks with the narrow passage. They squeezed through the opening and circled around to a stand of thick trees fifty meters from the edge of the camp, farther down the mountain. The Germans were one hundred and fifty meters below. The grenades were a favorite of the French, fragmentation grenades used primarily as anti-tank grenades, providing an effective casualty radius of almost fifty meters.

"Branch out," Juan said, "but, stay lateral to me." He pointed to his left and then to his right. "Stay in sight of each other and move in unison."

Felipe and Garcia did as they were told, each holding a pistol, each with a grenade. They separated ten meters from Juan and began their movement down the mountain.

Above them, grenades from the French launched at regular intervals, exploding into thousands of deadly fragments that peppered the woods where the Germans hunkered down.

Marcel sent two of his men to his right, opposite Juan, who circled to his left. He instructed them to silence the machine gun where three Germans rotated its operation. Bursts of fire pierced the air in rapid succession, throwing up a veil of smoke.

On the left, Juan gained ground by crawling forward into the brush, Felipe and Garcia crawled parallel and kept their eyes on the gunfight. The Germans had advanced only a few meters, kept at bay by the firepower of Marcel and his men.

When they reached a stand of large trees, they took cover. Juan hesitated, calculating the distance between the Germans and where he stood. They could throw the grenades forty meters – twenty meters short of where the Germans fired a second machine gun. From his right, Juan motioned to Felipe to move forward in a crawl. To his left, he instructed Garcia to do the same. He crouched down and began to move closer to the Germans, closer to the deadly machine gun.

It took them ten minutes to reach their positions. They could almost smell the Germans.

Juan held up his fingers, one, two, three. On the count of three, Juan reached down and pulled the pin on his grenade, then lifted his arm in a powerful swing, the grenade soaring through the air forty meters in front of him. Felipe and Garcia followed and three simultaneous blasts rocked the ground. The shrapnel blasted out a radius of fifty meters – a radius in which they themselves hovered.

A moment of silence followed, as if the noise of the blast had stolen their ability to speak. Then, the guns on the left of the camp began to strafe the trees where the Spanish lay pushing their bodies into the earth. Endlessly, the bullets came, cracking the trees, thudding the earth and demolishing the bushes. There was no machine gun fire, the big gun had been destroyed when the grenades landed almost on top of it.

At last, the heavy firing on their position ceased and the sound of Germans moving forward became the only sound.

On the ground, behind a large tree, Juan lifted his head. His pistol was in his hand, his breathing rapid. Across from him, on his right, he saw Felipe. Felipe was looking at him, eyes wide, the whites visible in the darkness. On his left, Garcia had also stood and was reloading his pistol. He knew what was to come.

Firing resumed from the camp as Marcel and his men readied for the Germans. Marcel instructed two of his men to take Luis farther up the mountain. He made a quick count of his men; eleven alive, only two wounded, the sentry dead. The machine gun on his right had been destroyed along with the three Germans who manned it. Now, he concentrated on the Germans moving up the mountain. He estimated at least fifteen to twenty of them. He muttered to himself, "Come, you bastards. We have a bullet waiting for each of you." A shiver ran across his back as he checked his ammunition and patted the knife that lay in his boot.

Garcia saw the bullet strike Juan. As if he had been hit himself, he grimaced, dove to the ground and rolled to where the spy lay, blood seeping from his shoulder.

"You are hit. Let me see." Garcia lifted the Spanish Guardia jacket and saw the spread of blood on Juan's shirt. Juan's face contorted in pain.

"Ah, señor , we must stop this blood." Garcia pulled the shirt aside and saw the entry wound. A large caliber bullet had struck his left shoulder, splintering the bone and lifting his shoulder blade into a compound fracture.

Felipe crept up behind Garcia. "Let me see." His hands gently touched Juan's shoulder. He sighed heavily. "Let's get you out of here."

"No, no. I order you to leave. I can still fire my pistol. You must continue over the mountain to Barcelona. To Rosina. To Jordana."

Garcia stared at Juan in disbelief. "You cannot be serious, señor. We must stay and fight."

"Yes," said Felipe. "We will not leave you."

Juan raised up to a sitting position, gritting his teeth as pain shot through his shoulder. An angry growl escaped his lips. "I am in command of this mission. You must obey my orders."

Garcia shook his head back and forth. "I cannot obey your orders, señor."

Felipe stared at Juan. "It is impossible to leave you, my friend," he said.

Juan's eyes narrowed and his face became stone. "By the authority vested in me by His Majesty's Secret Service, I command you to follow my orders."

He raised his pistol slowly and leveled it at the two men. His face twisted in pain, yet he breathed calmly, holding the pistol steady.

Felipe looked at Garcia, a look of helpless resignation. "It is so. We are duty-bound to follow orders. We must leave."

"Leave? Ha! Do you think he would shoot us if we stayed?" Garcia looked from Felipe to Juan, defiant.

Felipe's shoulders slumped. He looked at Garcia.

"We are honor-bound to leave, señor."

Felipe's words were spoken with such humbleness that Garcia hesitated. "Go!" shouted Juan.

Garcia faltered. "But, we…"

"Go!" shouted Juan, again lifting the pistol and pointing it toward Garcia.

Bullets whizzed around them, striking the towering fir tree they hid behind with a resounding thud. Without a glance back, the two men sprinted up the mountain, taking cover behind rocks and trees. Beyond the camp, they ran until breathless, through a stream, past huge boulders that towered above them and behind them.

Farther away from the spymaster.

Garcia was in the lead, Felipe struggling to keep up. Suddenly, Garcia stopped and turned. "Give me your pistol," he shouted with surprising authority, his breath coming in spurts.

"My pistol?" Felipe was confused as he leaned over and tried to catch his breath.

"Yes. Now!" Garcia walked slowly toward Felipe.

"I don't understand."

"I need your pistol. I'm going back."

"Going back? Are you crazy?"

"Crazy? No, I'm simply not going to follow orders." Garcia raised his chin and shot a challenging stare at Felipe.

"Your courage is commendable. But, I hardly think you are doing the right thing. We must follow orders."

"Orders? Since when does a goat herder take orders? Or a pianist? I play the piano and herd my goats. No one orders me."

Felipe watched the face of the young Spaniard. He saw resolve, strength and a fervent desire to follow his heart.

Felipe smiled. "No one orders you?"

Garcia's eyes smiled. "Only the gods."

He looked up into the sky. There they were. The same stars, lined up in a row into the shape of a smile. He followed their alignment from one curve of the smile to the other.

Then, his eyes caught another group of stars nearby. Squinting, he followed the lines star by star. Stars in an almost humorous shape of a goat and, above and to the right, the outline of a grand piano.

He turned his eyes across the mountains, his heart pounding. Bach's *Toccata and Fugue* played loudly in his head, the notes echoing as though asking him a question. *Who are you?* Garcia turned toward the battle that raged below him and reloaded his pistol. *A patriot*, he replied.

EPILOGUE

London April 21, 1944 – *Juan Castillo was debriefed by MI6 in London after escaping the Germans in the Pyrenees Mountains of France. When he arrived at Whitehall, he was gaunt, weak with fatigue and not very amicable. A large bruise, the color of vineyard purple, ran the length of his cheek and across his brow. His wounded shoulder still carried the stiffness of a compound fracture. He brought with him a beautiful Spanish woman, a woman whose belly was swollen with child.*

Garcia Quinones was swept into hiding by MI6. Perhaps he was not yet aware that his life as a spy did not end in the mountains of France. It was rumored that distant sounds of a piano were heard coming from an old hotel in Paris in late 1944 where the Nazis continued their demonic rule. Some say the pianist turned patriot continued his new found status in His Majesty's Secret Service as its most willing spy.

The battle in the great Pyrenees Mountains ended with the French Resistance outfighting the Germans. Though outnumbered, their tenaciousness was unheralded, backing the Nazi soldiers into the side of the mountain and unleashing unstoppable firepower.

The graves of Senora Albeniz and her sister remain on the hillside above Brasalia, where nearby trees sway in the mountain breezes. From time to time, flowers appear on their graves, purple lilacs. Some claim to hear the eerie bray of a donkey calling throughout the small village, spooking Tomas as he pulls the weeds in Senora Lazarote's garden.

-Whitehall Files 44-4-21 Top Secret #009

Sue CHAMBLIN Frederick

Sue CHAMBLIN Frederick is known as a sweet Southern belle, a woman whose eyelashes are longer than her fingers, her lips as red as a Georgia sunset. Yet, behind the feminine facade of a Scarlett-like ingénue, lies an absolute and utterly calculating mind – a mind that harbors hints of genius – a genius she uses to write books that will leave you spellbound.

A warning! She's dangerous - only six degrees from a life filled with unimaginable adventures – journeys that will sweep her readers into a world of breath-taking intrigue. Put a Walther PPK pistol in her hand and she will kill you. Her German is so precise, she'd fool Hitler. Her amorous prowess? If you have a secret, she will find it – *one way or the other.*

The author was born in north Florida in the little town of Live Oak, where the nearby Suwannee River flows the color of warm caramel, in a three-room, tin-roofed house named "poor." Her Irish mother's and English father's voices can be heard even today as they float across the hot tobacco fields, *"Susie, child, you must stop telling all those wild stories."*

Sue and her husband live on twenty acres in the piney woods of Florida where she is compelled to write about far away places and people whose hearts require a voice. Their two daughters live their lives hiding from their mother, whose rampant imagination keeps their lives in constant turmoil with stories of apple-rotten characters and plots that cause the devel to smile.

VISIT THE AUTHOR AT: www.sueCHAMBLINfrederick.com

16250055R00159

Made in the USA
Lexington, KY
12 July 2012